D1256328

THE MAN
IN THE MIRROR

A NOVEL OF ESPIONAGE

by

FREDERICK AYER, JR.

HENRY REGNERY COMPANY
CHICAGO

All characters in this novel, including those
assigned official positions, are purely fictitious.

CHAPTER I

THERE IS VERY little to laugh at in Moscow—and in the Aparat espionage nothing at all.

Chief Clerk Dimitrov was himself not amused. It was the end of a long damp day, a miserable twelve-hour day. The big basement room was cold, and his old wounds ached. His new shoes hurt. They were poorly made and too tight, and if he eased them off, the chill of the concrete floor struck through his soles and into the metal repair work of his shin bones.

He reached for the half-filled tea glass before him on the desk. It, too, had chilled and the surface was unpleasantly sticky with sugar. Unconsciously, Dimitrov licked his fingers and wiped them along the leg of his trousers. He lit a cigarette and leaned back, his eyes raised unseeing to the ceiling. He had always hated this room. But this was where his job took him, would probably always take him. That was that.

The room lay three stories beneath a dreary stone building on Gorki Street in Moscow. It was crowded with heavy steel filing cabinets, metal-topped desks and silent men. Various pieces of technical equipment stood on benches along one wall; photo-copiers, enlargers, comparison microscopes, a tape recorder and two massive punch-card sorting machines. This far underground all ventilation was supplied by blowers which provided only the deadness of recirculated air. The room was heavily guarded at all times. Also, as Dimitrov knew, it harbored hidden microphones so that those upstairs could overhear at will any idle, or not so idle, chatter. Thus, the men working there chose to do so in silence, here in the

1

file and record section of a very special branch of the Soviet Secret Intelligence Services.

Dimitrov flicked the ashes from the black Georgian tobacco, picked up once more a file he had already studied. Somberly at first, and then smiling tightly, he scanned the first page. So be it! He tossed the file back on to the desk where it landed with a loose slapping sound. Damn! They wouldn't believe it upstairs; they wouldn't even like it. This made no difference since they would have no choice. They had asked him, and he had merely asked the machine.

The machine had engorged thousands of cards, cards listing the most qualified English-speaking agents of the Aparat as well as men who were believed, for quite compelling reasons, to be potentially useful in such a role. Dimitrov had pressed the correct keys, set the tiny spindles spelling out a list of requirements which some of the code-punched cards must surely fit.

He leaned forward and ground out his cigarette, ran his eyes down the list of specifications again and quickly checked off each with a pencil:

Age 50 to 54; height 1.85 meters; weight 82 kilos; hair iron-gray and fairly thick; eyes greenish,

he noted failure on this point and read on

aquiline features, erect posture; complexion light to pink, must speak French and perfect English—Boston or Oxford accent preferred; dramatic and all-around athletic experience if possible; well read in politics and history.

Bachelor, orphan without living brothers or sisters most desirable.

No doubt about it. They had been most specific upstairs. What did they expect anyway, an exact count of the hairs remaining on the head and identical fillings in the teeth?

No IBM machine can really think, not even a giant Russian replica of one. Certainly it is not capable of irony.

No matter, the machine had whirred and clicked, finally ejecting an even dozen cards; these and no more.

Each card carried a master-file number, and each corre-

2

sponding file had been drawn for the one essential preliminary study, that of the subject's photograph. This was not Dimitrov's job. It was handled by two men, a portrait photographer and a plastic surgeon. For comparison they used two 15 x 25 centimeter black and white glossy prints of a middle-aged man whose clothing seemed to mark him as a North American.

Dimitrov knew in a general way that the two men had looked for the closest possible facial resemblance, particularly in head shape, structure of cheek and jaw bones and spacing of the eyes. These were permanent; they could not be altered. Modern surgery, he was aware, could, however, change the shape of ears and nose, even the details of lips and eyelids. He had seen the faces of several comrades rebuilt from almost nothing after terrible disfigurement by the wounds of war. Two of them had seemed stiff and lifeless, but two others faithfully mirrored his memories of their original features.

He picked up the cards on the desk and tapped their edges together against his thumbnail. Those two geniuses had finally selected three cards from the twelve handed them by Dimitrov and left the room. The top card read:

Walter Matthews—USA, professional cell NYC, writer— *Stars and Stripes,* columnist *New York Standard.* Educated: Harvard, London School of Economics. Narcotics user.

Then a final item:

Tried to turn informer. Now incurably insane.

The second card bore an even terser entry.

Joyce Barham Willson: British Nuclear Scientist. Shot, Moscow, 1962.

Shot, thought Dimitrov. Quickly and so mercifully dead.

He knew why these cancelled cards had been retained. If only the men of the MGB were aware that a man was dead, many useful things could be done in his name. Papers such as a passport or an identification card could be very valuable.

He had stapled the third card to a fairly thick file which he picked up and thumbed open to the summary:

3

Karl Friedrich von Tetlow—ex-Colonel of Waffen SS. Formerly of 23rd Light Armored Regt. Wounded— assigned to Killer Kommando—wanted for atrocities, including genocide. Believed to have escaped with wealth and now living in the Argentine.

There was much more. He did not want to read it. They were welcome to the man, the men upstairs. They could have the swine if he was what they wanted. After all, he was the only one left, and when there remains but one, there can be no choosing. Dimitrov had seen too many such Germans in his time. He would prefer to use von Tetlow for a bullet through the brain or, even better, the lower belly. However, he had learned long ago to suppress emotion or even curiosity. So, they could have this bastard for whatever purpose they had in mind; they could have the man—if they could find him.

The Russian Chief picked up the two photographs, the German and the American, and studied them one last time. Damn! It was extraordinary how alike they were—almost twins. Except for one thing. This von Tetlow looked as if he never smiled.

Some think the style of the *American National Weekly* amusing. Marjorie Weston Storrow of Back Bay Boston and Washington's Georgetown thought no such thing about the terse article on her husband.

Marjorie was seated in the library of a handsome brick house on N Street, N.W., an exclusive and expensive section of the city. The room was pleasant, tastefully furnished. In its center stood a very good refectory table, and on the street side between the windows a handsome square desk, both pieces polished mahogany. The desk chair was straight-backed, the others upholstered in maroon leather, studded with brass nail-heads. This was also true of the sofa. Two walls were devoted to books. Unlike those in many libraries, these books had all been read. That is, Roger Storrow had read them.

Marjorie was comfortable, and her feet were warm. She had removed her shoes to stretch her toes toward the hardwood flames crackling happily to themselves behind the hand-wrought fire irons. Although barefoot, she was otherwise correctly dressed: tailored skirt, a gray cashmere sweater over her blouse, and against the wool the warm luster of her daytime pearls. Her still auburn hair was newly set, but skilfully and softly.

She reached for the scotch and soda on the table beside her. It was still cold and bubbles still trickled slowly toward the surface. She had always loved this room, since she had first seen it in Roger's single days.

Yes, she was warm and comfortable and secure. But she was annoyed. Why couldn't those reporters leave Roger alone?

She was secretly proud, and, more secretly, truly fond of this man. They had not been married too many years, and furthermore she was his first wife. Marjorie had been married before, and little of what she had experienced had urged her to repeat the experiment. Yet she had done so, and to an only son and perennial bachelor at that.

Many of their friends thought it strange that these two had come together. But it was not, not really. Marjorie admired the man. In certain ways he was much as she remembered her father. Furthermore, she was childless and still wanted children, and she knew the time for their easy delivery was drawing to a close.

Roger, for his part, had played the field, a pursuit today bereft of much of its flavor. With his parents dead, he had grown lonely. Every day the house seemed more empty and more bleak. Here was a handsome and desirable woman, although she did appear a trifle cold. Roger was certain that this would change; he was sure he could change it.

He had, therefore, just a little pompously, asked for her hand and had been accepted. Not at all pompously he had asked for much more. She had wanted to, really she had, but somehow she had not been able to give so freely. Now she even felt that it might have been partly her fault.

Marjorie sighed deeply, flipped open the magazine again and looked at the photograph. This was a good man, certainly a brave man. Still, his bare knees did look a little bony and foolish below the white walking shorts. His iron-gray hair and somewhat craggy countenance seemed too mature for the

5

jaunty golf cap—or perhaps it was that the golf cap was too juvenile for the rest. His grin might be too self-satisfied but, she had to admit, the posture was erect, the shoulders square and the belly flat. The forearms, the hands gripping the shaft of the driver, were tanned and powerful.

"His score no secret," read the caption. Then came the lead in boldface. "Where the Bodies are Buried."

Cabinets may come, Cabinets may go; the man who knows a nation's secrets goes on for ever.

Certain to be retained as Special Presidential Assistant for Security Matters (for which read super-clerk to the Super-Secret National Security Council) is North Shore Socialite, Roger Lowell Storrow. This green-eyed Harvard and Oxford ex-athlete yesterday smiled his smuggest smile after a round at Chevy Chase, one of his many exclusive clubs. Queried, replied Storrow, "Played very well today, my boy, as a matter of fact shot 73— keeps me fit don't you see—mens sana, and all that." Further asked if he expected to be kept on in this first year of a new administration his answer was typically arrogant, "I can imagine no possible reason why not."

Storrow, never a popular figure to the Capitol press corps, seems off on another typical season in the major leagues. There he will ponder national problems with only the President, perhaps the Secretaries of State and Defense—and, of course, with the Chief of the CIA. 'Twas not always thus. Note his abortive attempt to purchase a seat in Congress. Remember also with a shudder his first, and also last, appearance on the legitimate (sic) stage. Influenced by the bank balance of a tycoon father, the Schubert management once reluctantly agreed . . .

"Oh, damn! Why can't they leave him alone?" This was gritted out, not sighed, as Marjorie Storrow slung the slick pages into the open fireplace. The cover curled back, burst puffily into flames. "Well, at least they won't bother him while he crawls around his stupid old Mexican ruins—at least not for a month."

She ran her hands down over still firm hips. "And for my

6

sins, I will have to look at every damned one of his colored slides when he comes home."

She glanced at the mantel clock—a heavy brass ship's model, a favorite of Roger's, won in some long past ocean race. She still felt it was inappropriate to the rest of the decor. Half-past six—five bloody bells!—she had even learned how to tell ship's time. So now was the hour to start dressing for that ghastly reception. If only Roger were here. It was not much fun going alone. Even his most terse and vitriolic comments would be welcome now.

Well, if she really had to go, could not avoid facing all those *nouveau riche* influence-seekers, at least she would go in style. It would be the blue satin, bare shoulders, evening pearls only, no diamonds except a ring and the new and unnecessary girdle. It was her best Beacon Hill war-dress for the battle of Foggy Bottom.

Marjorie reluctantly climbed the stairs, headed down the hall to her room, past the empty one she had vainly hoped would serve as the nursery. She would have to hurry a little, since she had to don her armor unaided. It was her Ella's time off, Ella who had been her personal maid and confidante for so long. Ella's invaluable help would be missing.

Her pearls were missing also, and her diamonds, every one of them.

The gold charm bracelets, a number of charms, assorted rings and brooches, these still cluttered the velvet-lined jewel case. But not a single item of real value remained.

A calm then a somewhat frantic search of the house accomplished nothing. Obviously she would have to report the loss. Of course, everything was insured, but she did not want the money, she just wanted her jewelry. So it must first be the police, right away. Roger would be furious, the publicity and so forth, but she could not help that. Besides, Roger was thousands of miles away by now, on his way to some stinking jungle. What he didn't know would not hurt him. Right now she would not worry about Roger.

But then she did worry about the time and decided to postpone calling the police until morning. As it was, she would be more than fashionably late. That would never do. She moved over to her window and looked down into the street. Good! The car stood ready. So also, she assumed, did faithful James Chapman. Really, the Jamaicans were so much more reliable than most of the rather hopeless help one could get in Washington these days.

The faithful James, his true name George William Gordon Chapman, was not with the car at all. He was in a phone booth one block up the street.

"Yes, sah—there was no trouble at all—no, she did not call the police—not yet. Yes, they're where I said I would put them. Yes, that is right, sah—must go now or she'll be late for the party. Yes, sah, I'm sure what will happen, quite sure."

George William Gordon Chapman, named after the slave leader of the bloody and terrible rebellion of 1865, had been trained to be sure. Jamaica, his birthplace, had always been a land of violence or deceptive calm, brutal repression or revolution. There, outward subservience masked inner arrogance and racial hatred of all white men. For these reasons, and many others, it had long been a center of Communist strength in the islands of the Caribbean.

James was almost white, almost but not quite, and this made a big difference. The fact had, in his boyhood, ostracized him socially from the British owners and rulers of his native country. It had not, however, kept him from becoming well-educated, mostly through his own efforts. But this education had never served as a passport to social acceptability or, even in the beginning, to a seat at a soda fountain in the capital of the "free" world. His bitterness had grown, and the Communist party had much use for intelligent and bitter men.

He had served his apprenticeship, first as an assistant steward on a Caribbean cruise boat, then as a neophyte member of a waterfront party cell. Later Chapman had graduated to seaborne courier, then to waiter in a popular yet expensive Washington restaurant where three-martini luncheons loosened tongues. After serving a stint as a well-tipped Capitol Hill cab driver, he finally graduated to unaffiliated job-seeker. The jobs he looked for and obtained were always as a valet, chauffeur, handy man and bartender to Washington's elite.

8

It is interesting that otherwise alert citizens seldom notice household servants, waiters, taxi-drivers or hotel maids. They scarcely ever recognize one seen even twice before. The great exceptions to the rule are barbers and bartenders. Even with these exceptions, however, the rule is useful. It is extremely useful to any well-financed espionage Aparat.

This is so not only because people fail to notice servants, but more because they hardly ever suspect them of crimes more serious than laziness or insolence. It is a matter of official record that at one time the trusted houseman of two succeeding air attachés in Athens was the second ranking member of the Communist espionage organization there during the Greek Civil War. He was finally arrested in his master's absence while entertaining in that colonel's house two of the most wanted Communists in Greece. James Chapman had always been much more discreet than this, and therefore had been more fortunate.

He was a highly qualified servant, quiet-moving, big and strong, exceedingly polite. He could afford to be select in his acceptance of employment. You could count on the fingers of one hand the household jobs he had held. You could not count on the hairs of a cat the government secrets to which his few employers had been privy.

James knew his job, no doubt of it. Everyone said he knew how to keep his place. What scarcely anyone knew was how very well he served his real masters. During his years in Washington, he had done nothing to alert the FBI, and his police record, at least in the United States, was spotless.

Ella Washington was most unfortunate. She had not been trained to be sure of things, or as a youngster to be anything at all. One of eleven children, the daughter of a sluttish mother and an unknown father, she had been in some kind of trouble almost since the day she had been able to talk. As a child she had learned to steal because there was not enough food in the house to still the hungry cries of the little ones. Later she had badly cut up a neighbor's twenty-one-year-old son to protect herself from rape.

In less than two years she had, so to speak, become a ward of the city for believing a promise of marriage too soon. All

9

this was before she had reached sixteen. One thing she had accomplished, however; she had managed somehow to keep her child. Marjorie Storrow, at that time Marjorie Weston, had helped. Since then Ella had been guilty of no crimes, unless they were complete loyalty to Marjorie and a sad lack of book-learning or ability to express herself. She would no more have stolen from the household, toting privileges excepted, than she would have murdered in their beds the only real family she had known.

Roger Storrow would have understood this. Marjorie really did, or would have, had she given the matter thought.

She returned from the reception, however, seethingly angry. How could anyone have behaved so abominably as that ghastly wife of the new Secretary? Even her very correct Roger would have told her off. Yes, Marjorie came home in a rage and, in truth, just a little drunk. Nevertheless, as always before retiring, she gulped the iced orange juice poured from the silver thermos jug on the bedside table. She did not know that James Chapman had made a careful addition to the juice as his last duty of the day.

As a result she awoke late, still vaguely angry and very worried about something she could not quite remember. She suffered from a serious hangover. This was not the hangover of the aching head or the butterfly stomach. It was the one where unreal things threaten, where there is certainty that someone behind is about to lay a hand on one's shoulder, and yet a convulsive turn to look finds no one there. This was the morning after, when thunder might have been soothing but the yapping of a puppy could set the nerves to screaming outrage.

When the police arrived Marjorie was far from gracious. Even hardened Sergeant Holloway of the robbery detail was happy to end the formalities and proceed to the actual investigation. This man had learned his trade by harsh experience, and experience had taught him that more than nine times in ten the most obvious would prove to be the correct solution. He went straight to that point and found what he sought—the missing jewelry sewn rather inexpertly inside Ella Washington's mattress.

Nevertheless Sergeant Holloway had certain qualms. He was impressed by the immaculate condition of Ella's small

10

half-house. His father's heart went out to the beguiling twelve-year-old daughter, cleanly starched in dress and glossily pigtailed. And something happened which was rare in his experience. When he asked permission to search, Ella looked up at him open faced and wide eyed, "Why, of course, Mr. Policeman, but whatever in the wide world for?"

The girl's later, almost hysterical, denials carried some ring of truth. Still, interrogation brought out that she was not only deeply in debt to a local loan shark, but also that she had no intelligible ideas as to how the jewelry had reached its hiding place.

Marjorie Storrow was no help to her at all. She stood holding one hand on her aching head, "Oh, for God's sake, Sergeant. It's all so obvious isn't it—no, I can't explain it. No, I won't swear out a complaint right now. You have your evidence, have you not? All I care is that you keep it out of the papers. I'll even see to it that Rog—I mean Mr. Storrow, does something about a reward when he gets back."

Well, recovered diamonds were recovered diamonds. A quick solution to such a case looked well on the record, and a reward sounded promising. Of course, one was not supposed to accept. Still, there were ways. So Ella Washington was taken to jail. God knows she had been loyal, but past loyalty was not enough. She would have to be replaced by someone new and unknown. Right now there was no one left in the employ of the Storrow household except the well-trained James.

Shortly the big Jamaican received congratulations, and his new orders. They were plain enough: "Continue to make very careful study of Mrs. Storrow. Note everything, especially the times she normally goes out, both day and evening. When and where does she go for walks? Where does she usually park the car when she drives home herself? Does she regularly take the dog for an airing at night? When and where? Did she have any visitors? Does she expect any later in the week? Is she drinking more or less than usual? I don't have to spell out the rest. We insist that you make no mistakes, that you be absolutely sure."

George William Gordon Chapman did exactly as he was told.

Marjorie Storrow did much as she had always done on the

11

many occasions when Roger was away. She played bridge. She enjoyed the dubious company of a small dog on her walks and drives, just as many women who are childless and lonely. And just as some of them, she drank a little too much.

Admittedly she had been lacking in judgment, faith or understanding in this case of Ella Washington. Perhaps she had been selfish and thoughtless, and therefore cruel. She should have known better. She knew this now and realized she would, as a result of her failure to believe in Ella, be even lonelier.

She was a woman who was kind to her husband, in her own way affectionate to him. She was socially and personally ornamental. She was an excellent hostess. She was loved by her husband; she loved him in return, but could seldom bring herself actively or outwardly to show it. She knew that it was his cross that he must take so much on faith. Actually, she was no worse, possibly even a little better, than most wives in Capitol society.

CHAPTER II

KARL FRIEDRICH VON TETLOW was born to be a gentleman. He had become an officer. He had grown up strong, and developed into a fine athlete. He had native intelligence, refined and polished by a superior education. He had been, in fact, a young man of great promise. In the end, however, he became a criminal, a mass murderer, a relentless, almost mechanical destroyer of those he was told were his enemies. He had often refused to think more deeply than that he had followed orders. He had killed and killed again. Worse, toward the last he had killed only the defenseless. He should have been hanged. But he had lived long enough to run, like a tough handful of others, he had escaped.

In a way he had escaped. He had not been arrested—never jailed, accused or tried. But he could not flee from memory. He could not forget.

No, even when wanting to he could not forget his beautiful—that was the right word—his beautiful father, Colonel of Hussars Otto Friedrich von Tetlow. Karl had been only a boy at the time, but sometimes he could still hear the trumpet call to colors, the music of the march to war; its drum beats had echoed deep in his square little chest, and the cadenced tramp of troops marching for the fatherland. He could still see Papa: slim, elegant, tense as tempered steel, a falcon poised to swoop upon and destroy his enemies. Papa had worn his uniform as a tiger its skin, his helmet like a lion's crest. Everyone spoke of manhood, of courage, of glory. Yes, he had been but a boy, but he could still remember his mother and how she had kissed Papa at the last good-bye,

13

then handed him his saber and stood back sadly as he buckled it on. She had not said a word. There was nothing to say.

Papa had stood silent for a moment, then pivoted on his heels and, never looking back, strode to the door, to his regiment and to battle.

The papas of some of his friends never returned. But his had, twice, three times, each time increased in rank, each time wearing new medals. And always he seemed to bring with him the sound of bugles, the flutter of flags—each time, that is, until the last.

The last time was not a thing to remember. Yet it, too, was a thing impossible to forget. The day had been gray and cold; the house was cold also, since somehow there was no longer enough coal for the grates. He had been told that Papa was coming home again, but he could not understand the nervous, distraught manner of his mother. Nor had he understood why she had tried to keep him from rushing to the door at the sound of the approaching carriage.

Then he had seen, not all at once, but in pieces of gradual recognition, first the emaciated figure, angrily yet feebly brushing aside the corporal seeking to help him step down from the carriage, then the cane with which Papa tapped ahead of himself along the pavement. The cane was in his left hand, not his right—then he saw there was no right hand, not even a right arm. The empty sleeve was pinned across the breast of the tunic, and the uniform no longer fitted like the striped skin of a tiger, but hung floppily like the rags of some old beggar. Now he was close enough for Karl to see his face: a white empty face, disfigured by a terrible red scar diagonally across the forehead to the bridge of the nose. And the eyes—my God, those eyes! They stared straight ahead, unseeing. His papa was blind.

Later—how many times later?—his father would sit before the even emptier fireplace, holding the cane swordlike in his only hand, and would declaim, "It is finished. We are done for. It is all over. We have been betrayed."

In the beginning his mother would remonstrate, refusing, against all evidence, to believe that invincible Germany was in the death-throes of defeat. But Papa always said, "No, we

14

are done for. The filthy Jews have sold the Americans into war. Soon there will be millions of them at our throats. And worse. Oh, the damned treasonable swine! The Jews are selling us out at home, too. You will see," a vicious stab with the cane. "You will see. They are lining their pockets with the gold we paid for in blood. Soon they will have everything. We will have nothing. You will see."

Karl and his mother had in fact seen. Soon came the terrible, shameful day of surrender. And not long after, they indeed had nothing—no fire in the grate, scarcely any light in the wrought-iron sconces, almost nothing on the table. Soon the von Tetlow silverware was sold for too little food. The two great hunting dogs were mercifully shot before they starved or became killers in the neighborhood. Even Karl's small piebald pony, Wilhelm, was butchered for stew meat.

And every day he heard repeated the refrain: "The Communists—the filthy thieving Jews—the Communist Jews!"

Then one day someone had brought the news of revolution, of agitators marching with red banners in the streets of Hamburg. Papa had risen from his chair, trembling in rage, cane brandished above his head. His lips tried to form the beginning of a terrible oath. Only an agonized groan emerged. The cane clattered to the floor. The one hand clutched briefly at his tunic's breast where the iron cross still hung, clutched at his stricken heart, the heart which had stopped by the time he crumpled to the floor.

There had come worse times: times when his mother had had to fill a market basket with paper currency merely to buy a few beans or beets or potatoes; times of chattering cold and sickness; times when his mother was so weak she was forced to remain in bed for most of each day. Then came the terrible night she died, quietly and without complaint, as Karl, older now but not much bigger, clung in stunned despair to her stiffening fingers. After that he must have been terribly ill because he remembered nothing until he awoke in another month in another bed. He was in the house of his Uncle Konrad in Munich, Uncle Konrad who had but one child of his own, now to have two.

Eventually better times had come. Uncle Konrad, who was

15

in some way allied to the Krupp family, made money. There was plenty to eat. There was enough money for Karl and his cousin Hans' education, first at home and later in England. Karl worshipped Uncle Konrad and believed everything the man preached. It was always the same sermon: Be strong. Only strength counts. Democracy is rule by ignorant fools. We must have one mighty leader. And always: Revenge! Revenge for your father! Revenge for your mother! Revenge for the Fatherland! Revenge now or tomorrow against the Jews who murdered them all: your father, your mother, your country—the Jews, the Communists, the Jews!

The rest had followed as the night the day, the terrible darkening night of Nazi history. And Karl had been part of this history. He had helped lead it until the day on the Russian front when he saw his regiment ground to mincemeat under an inundating torrent of enemy artillery, saw his fellow officers drop around him to freeze solid in the position of their fall, felt his sanity gradually leave him under the merciless, endless concussion of exploding shells.

He had spent quite some time in a hospital, then in a recuperation center and had finally been assigned to a special kommando organization for the purpose of "solving the racial problem." He had condoned mass murder, he had ordered mass murder, he had participated in mass murder. Scarcely ever had he felt a twinge of conscience. He was following the orders of his leader, and he was taking revenge.

Toward the last, however, he noted a terrible phenomenon. Day by dreadful day the number of concentration camp murders increased. The number of doomed inmates increased even faster. As the German armies lost their thousands and retreated on all fronts, Germans to the rear destroyed more thousands of their fellow-men. It was as though the Nazi system, now out of control, was eating itself up with the cancer cells of its own dissolution—like the mythical snake which in terror devours itself alive.

Finally his task had sickened him. Even today he could not be sure whether this had been because of a returning sense of humanity, of decency, or merely because everything he did had become so terribly useless. He had known then

16

that Germany was again losing a war and, unless she lost quickly, this time it would be to an enemy more terrible than the last. The real reason would never matter. The fact was that Col. Karl Friedrich von Tetlow joined the July, 1944 conspiracy to assassinate Adolf Hitler, the leader he had sworn to follow to the grave.

He should have been executed as a traitor then, when Hitler survived the bomb attempt. He should have been executed later as a murderer, a war criminal, a designer of atrocities against humanity. The escape route had been long and perilous, painful and hard, but he had survived.

Tonight it was better to forget it all, and much better to be glad that he was now Señor Heinrich Schmidt y Mendoza of Buenos Aires, that he had more than tripled the small fortune in Nazi diamonds with which he had escaped, and that now, years later, he was returning to Europe, returning luxury class on a beautiful new ocean liner.

He examined himself in the stateroom mirror. He had grown quite used to his new appearance over the recent years. The hair, once blond and close-cropped in Prussian style, was now wavy and iron-gray. The upper lip, then scrupulously clean-shaven, was now adorned with a neatly trimmed moustache. The eyes, still cold blue with perfect vision, were disfigured by the heavy rims and ear-pieces of those eyeglasses that are featured by screen directors everywhere, and seemingly by all lawyers in Paris and Madrid. He had also gained weight. No one would recognize him now, he was quite sure of that. Even his voice had changed a little. He no longer spoke in the crisp peremptory tone of the Prussian Junker. He now used the more leisurely tongue of the German merchant who must deal each day with Latin American businessmen, and his Spanish was nearly flawless.

He was looking forward to this evening. There would be a small cocktail party in the captain's cabin. It would be very select since the captain had a practiced eye for the beautiful and the available among his lady passengers, and a practiced smile and handclasp for the affluent or influential who might bring important business to the line. Heinrich Schmidt y

17

Mendoza smiled to himself to think that he had been included among the latter. The smile grew softer as he thought about the beautiful Contessa.

He had first seen her the night before in his favorite ship's bar, the small one on the upper deck. Antonio, the line's most voluble barman, had been showing her his most profitable card and coin tricks. Since she was leaning forward attentively, von Tetlow's first sight of her had been from the back. First of all he noted the loving fit of her high-necked white dress, curving in from the graceful shoulders to the narrow waist, then caressingly outward over the rounded hips. Her feet were hooked around the metal legs of the bar-stool, so he could see that her legs were long and well-shaped. His eyes moving up again caught the blue-black highlights of her heavy hair.

And so it had begun for him once more, gently and slowly. He hoped, in fact he believed, that it had begun for her also.

He had studied her carefully that night at dinner—after a generous tip, the *maître d'hôtel* had effected a suitable change in seating arrangements. Her face was beautiful, somewhat exotic. Some Spanish or Near Eastern blood? Was she really Italian? He could not be sure, but what did it matter? Her eyes were deep and questing, her mouth was a trifle large, but it appeared warm and eager. Her body was not top-heavy with the lushness of what some of his friends called the mammary age. Nor did she suffer from the skeletal look of so many fashion models. No, he thought, she was softly slender and moved with a sinuousness, somewhat like a cat. He felt that this was a genuinely sensual woman.

Over champagne, they talked of everything and of nothing until very late. She suddenly pressed a hand tightly against her forehead, her brown painfully contracted.

He reached for her other hand, "What is it, my dear?"

"Only a sudden, terrible headache—I have them at times, almost a migraine. I must sleep now."

"Shall I accompany you to your cabin?"

The Contessa rose quickly. "No, *caro*. It is not necessary." A sudden warm smile, "But tomorrow I shall be better, much better. We will have a *rendezvous?* Of course, only if you wish it."

18

He too had risen. "More now than anything."

He had meant what he said. Captain Barolli would have keen competition, and surely he could not make love to each of his charming guests. Von Tetlow felt he had established a valid prior claim. He carefully adjusted the white carnation in his lapel, tugged at the edge of his dinner jacket. There would be champagne and music, and the moon. He had already lived too many lonely nights. This one would not be lonely; it would be one to remember.

The Contessa was even more beautiful to him, her scent more seductive. He again felt an invitation in each glance and gesture of each slight touch of hand or shoulder. The little floor was much too crowded, both by the plodding resignation of the old and the desperate athletics of the young. Despite their hips, elbows and shoulders, however, von Tetlow felt alone with his Maria.

Then there came a crashing end to the music, the last clinging moments together, the too conscious drawing apart. He looked down into her half-closed eyes. Slowly their lids lifted. She did not seem to look into his face, but to something far beyond. And he could not understand why that look first seemed so very cold.

A rapid drum-roll now brought the far too jovial master of ceremonies to the microphone.

"*Signore, signori,* ladies and gentlemen, we announce now the dance of the balloons."

Von Tetlow took the Contessa firmly by the elbow. "Oh, my God, not that idiot again. Games for middle-aged children I cannot bear. Let us go where it is quieter."

She pressed his hand between her elbow and body. "Yes, *carissimo,* let us go."

It was a very short walk to Maria's cabin. At the door she slipped the key into his hand. "Open it for me, please. I am foolish, I am afraid to go in alone in the darkness."

He wondered vaguely what man had opened the door on other nights—or if anyone had. There was something too easy about all this, something planned and deliberate in the moves. His mind held back a little. His body, however, followed the orders of his earlier thoughts; his hand went forward, inserted the key, turned it, pushed open the cabin door.

Only the dressing table lights were lit. The bed, the rest of the comfortable cabin, was in semi-darkness. Still, he could see the dull gleam of a German silver wine cooler, the wet glistening of the broken ice and the dark sheen of the bottle. He looked speculatively at Maria, whose eyes were raised to his as her grip on his hand slowly increased.

He did not hear the bathroom door open behind him.

A strong arm wrapped itself suddenly around his neck. A hard hand roughly covered his mouth. At the same time other hands forced his arms cruelly together behind his back. In seconds, with only the slightest struggle, he was bound, gagged with tape and forced into a chair. Someone turned on all the cabin lights. Across from him seated on the foot of the bed was a stocky, olive-complexioned man, holding across one knee a short silencer-equipped Mauser automatic. At his left stood a heavier, taller man, lifting with persuasive pressure on the rope which tied von Tetlow's wrists together. "One little move, just one, and I will tear your arms from the shoulders."

He did not move. He looked at the Contessa leaning against the dressing-table. She was holding a thin sheaf of photographs and papers. Her eyes were hooded and cold. Hers was no longer the face of Rome; it was more ancient, more barbaric. Not Venus, he thought wryly, more, much more a Judith, even a Medusa. He shifted slightly to ease the discomfort of his arms. Whatever this was all about, whoever she was, he had been partly right. She was no Italian contessa.

"These," she indicated the two men, "are Jacob and Otto. You need not know more than that. You should, however, know who I am." She paused to strip away one long glove, held her left arm so that he could see the puckered skin at the bend of the elbow. She had become inhuman. "That is the number your people tattooed there. God knows why, since I was branded in any case for the slaughter house, for the gas chamber."

He tried to look puzzled, to show a lack of understanding by a shake of his head and an upward movement of the eyebrows.

The woman did not pause. "But I lived, I existed for a

20

while, since men found me beautiful. How I despised them. They made me hate this body even when it was alive and beautiful." A downward sweep of the hands, "Then they tired of it and mutilated it. Now I am dead inside." She tapped the sheaf of papers. "Even so, it is impolite not to introduce myself. I am Hilda Meyer of the Israeli Irgun, and I have here the warrant for your arrest."

Again he tried to register incomprehension.

"Do not shake your head at me, Colonel von Tetlow."

Her head came forward like a snake's. She spat in his face. "Perhaps I should say 'excuse me.' Sometimes I lack manners, Colonel. But I am not a lady, not even a woman. I remember what you people did to me. How would you like it, von Tetlow, if our men had taken your sister, stripped her naked and forced her . . ."

Pacing back and forth within the narrow cabin, Hilda Meyer, her words burning like acid, detailed things which sickened her prisoner. Numbly he shook his head because he could not close his ears.

"I wanted to kill you slowly. Others voted to shoot you like a rabid dog. But naturally we are all too civilized now. So you will have a trial, you will have a lawyer and, von Tetlow, a sentence. Now," she reached to grasp the edge of the tape across his mouth, "we will let you speak and tell the truth, but quietly—oh, so quietly—otherwise you will never speak again." With a wrench she tore away the tape, hair and shreds of skin clinging to its surface.

Flinching from pain, he fought to collect his composure, decide how to carry conviction. He thought it best to show bafflement and outrage, an undertone of fear. Use of the Spanish tongue. This seemed the only possible approach.

"But this is absurd. You have made an incredibly great mistake. As you well know, I am Señor Schmidt y Mendoza. My government will hear of this. What right have you . . ."

The harsh voice cut him off. "Your government, you have no government. It died in flames long ago. At least be man enough to tell the truth about who you are."

"But I tell you . . ."

"You are telling me nothing." In a quick motion she

21

snatched the heavy glasses from his face, flicked a finger at the dark moustache. "Even older, fatter, once this is gone, our photo is your younger twin. You did not have a twin, did you, von Tetlow?" She turned to the heavier of the two men. "Otto, untie his wrists. Jacob, see that he stays quiet."

She busied herself for a moment with some equipment at the dressing-table as Otto unknotted the tight ropes at his wrists. Then, standing before him, she ordered, "Hold out your right hand. Place your fingers here." She held a flat plate smeared with heavy ink. Involuntarily his hand shrank away, then returned. What was the use? If he refused it would be easy to take the prints by force. He pressed the tips of his fingers, his thumb to the plate.

"And now the other."

Complying, he wondered if this was just a sham. Did they really have his prints? How could they have got . . .

The Meyer woman answered for him, "Set your mind at ease. We do not bluff. You Germans were so efficient, so meticulous, making copies of everything. So were we in searching their files. And you, of course, were an important man."

He knew she told the truth. He knew now that she was utterly ruthless, and that there were ways to make any man talk. So he would talk his own way.

Suddenly he leaned forward, grasping the arms of the chair. Jacob's pistol jabbed in his direction, but he did not settle back. This time he spoke in German, the words clipped, metallic, brutal, "Very well, you Jewish swine. Of course, I am von Tetlow. I see I should have had more of you killed."

Hilda Meyer smiled grimly. "Ah, that's better, much better. We like frankness. We admire the truth . . . Otto."

"Yes?"

"Make sure that our distinguished guest remains quiet for a moment. Jacob, you may leave now. As you go, hang the 'Do Not Disturb' sign on the door for the steward. He is a nosey, romantic Italian and surely knows I am entertaining a man."

Hilda Meyer went into the bathroom for a moment and returned wearing a silken robe. His eyes swung automatically to the white-clad figure. For an instant she looked once more

22

like a woman. Then he remembered and shudderingly looked away, but not before he had seen that Hilda Meyer held the glass barrel of a hypodermic in her hand.

"The right arm please. Otto, roll back that sleeve. You wanted to spend the night here with me, von Tetlow, and so you shall. We go ashore at Cannes tomorrow, the three of us. You will enjoy revisiting Cannes." The needle drove into his arm. The glass plunger pressed home. "And now, pleasant dreams."

Too early in the morning, drugged and staggering, he went ashore on the arm of a beautiful woman, at times assisted by a quiet dark man who seemed to be his servant. From time to time the latter handed him a flask from which he defenselessly drank.

The French officials were only half awake, and were also cynically amused. How could a rich tourist let himself be so drunk in the company of a lovely and affectionate woman? He was not worth their attention. So they did not note that the trio wandered away from the customs area and drove off in a quiet, ordinary little car.

No alarm was raised when the ship sailed without Señor Schmidt y Mendoza and his friends. Even a nosey, romantic Italian cabin steward has his discretion. Further, the Contessa had been so beautiful and had tipped him well. Captain Barolli was a most tolerant man. Doubtless these foolish people would send to Genoa for their trunks. As for the French officials, why should he bother them? If he did, they would bother him, and the captain simply detested bother.

CHAPTER III

FINALLY AWAKING TO some awareness of his surroundings, von Tetlow found himself on an iron cot in a small, bare room. Except for a slop bucket, a water pitcher and a glass on a table, there were no other furnishings. The one window was high in the wall and barred by an iron grille.

The light was dim. Probably this room was tucked in under the eaves. He had no idea of the time but suffered from a throbbing headache and a desperate thirst. He looked again at the water jug. Suppose it too is drugged? But what possible difference could that make now? Ignoring the glass he drank deeply from the pitcher. It was only then he noted that he was naked, and that all his clothing had been taken away.

He tried to think clearly about his position. It was certainly not enviable. He had been a fool, he supposed, but twenty years of freedom had convinced him his escape was complete. He was in the hands of a powerful and efficient organization. That much was clear. His fate was far from being so. That damned Meyer woman had talked of a trial and a sentence. He wondered about that. They had already produced one showpiece with Eichmann, and it had not been a major hit. Why try another? And besides, the woman wanted personal vengeance. Or, here was a new thought, was this kidnapping for ransom of some kind, the threats merely part of a softening-up process? He was relatively wealthy—quite wealthy, in fact. It was possible that . . .

Almost noiselessly the door opened. It was the burly Otto carrying a tray of food. He placed it on the floor. "Even

24

swine must eat. So you eat. Later Fraulein Meyer will talk with you. I will come." The door swung closed.

Forty-eight hours and no meals later Otto returned, forty-eight hours which had not brightened von Tetlow's reflections. Still naked, he was escorted downstairs and along a wide hall of what appeared to be a wealthy villa, and into a large office or study. Seated to one side of the desk was Hilda Meyer, now severe in a tailored suit. Behind the desk sat a man he had not seen before—a man with pale, unhealthy skin, a high forehead and a wide, flat nose, wearing steel-rimmed glasses. His pudgy hands toyed with a paper knife. The glasses glinted up at him in the light of a goose-neck desk lamp. "Ah, von Tetlow, so good to see you well. Stand, please, do not sit down."

What the devil? he wondered. But he stood. That face was certainly in no way Semitic, and the accent not German, or German Jewish—no, not German at all. Who could the man be?

The Meyer woman had risen. She carried a flat-sided riding crop in her hand. Slowly she walked around him; slowly, and in silence. Automatically his head swivelled to follow her. Only then did she speak. "Stand still, you scum. Stand completely still."

Twice, three times she circled him. "What a lovely example of manhood, von Tetlow—but such wrinkles in the flesh. What a fat, soft belly! Why, I don't think you are even worth killing."

Suddenly there was a report, sharp as a pistol shot, as she smashed the leather crop down against the desk top. He stared convulsively. Another slap of the whip. "And so nervous, too. Stand still, I said."

Von Tetlow stood still for further inspection. Naked and cold as he was, sweat had started out all over his body. He suddenly remembered that this was the technique used so successfully by the British Secret Service during the last war to break a prisoner-suspect. The thought gave him no comfort.

At last the man behind the desk spoke softly. "That will do for now. Otto, take him back to his cell."

A day later the process was repeated but with one

variation—after a few minutes von Tetlow was invited to sit down, was even offered a cigarette.

The pale man was again toying with the paper knife. "Look here, von Tetlow," he said, pointing with the knife to one side of the desk, to a coiled hangman's noose. "That is one choice. And here is a pen and paper, that is the second. Ah, I see you need not ask. I see you recognize the rest of the old British method—death or cooperation."

The man leaned back in his chair.

"As usual, Fraulein Meyer has been most efficient, has even acted with restraint. She hates Nazis, you know, really hates them. I do not hate anyone; I simply do my job. You do not know me. It is time you did, time we stopped this foolish charade." He pointed the paper knife at himself. "My name does not matter. Here in France it is Emile Davidoff. In Moscow it is otherwise."

Moscow? Someone was insane, thought von Tetlow.

"In Moscow, I am of the MGB. I come directly to the point. I am empowered, von Tetlow, to make you this offer. You may call it a free choice. Would you like to hear it?"

He could only nod.

"Very well. One, we turn you over, complete with documentation, to the Israeli. That is the noose. The Israeli will hang you. Two, you work for us, an important job, risky, of course, but most rewarding. That is the pen. You sign the document I have prepared."

He shook his head, "I see, but why the Jewish masquerade?"

"Oh, come, von Tetlow, think a little. You are a German, once Colonel of the Schutzstaffel, once of the Killer Kommando, once of the Third Division on our front. You might have been stubborn in admitting who you were to the MGB. You might have made trouble, noise even. We also wished to give you time to think, to undergo, shall we say, a little moral suasion. We are," he rammed the knife's point into the desk top, "capable of much more, but we prefer volunteers. Do you wish to volunteer?"

"I cannot see that I have any choice."

"Of course not, but it will not be so bad. First we take a train to Moscow," he opened the desk drawer, "with a

26

beautiful new Soviet passport for you. We are even going first class. In Moscow you will study very hard, intensively. Then with another new set of papers you will fly to the 'New World,' where you will study even more arduously. Shall I continue?"

Again von Tetlow merely nodded.

"Next, if you pass all tests—if not you will, of course, no longer care about that or anything else—you will go to the United States, which as you know is run by rich Jews. You personally will live richly and perform for us, and for yourself, a most valuable service. It should be very interesting—very interesting indeed.

"And there is something else, von Tetlow. You German officers want to be on the winning side again. We know you. We know that is what you want. I assure you that you shall be on the winning side. That is a certainty."

Von Tetlow slowly signed the document which had been prepared for him.

In Moscow he studied and he worked; he concentrated harder, much harder than at Oxford or during his early days in the military. He read books and papers. He recited aloud. He watched films and listened to recordings, all dealing with the United States. He studied dress, speech, manners, clothing, style of walking, makes of cars. Much of this he already knew from his years in the Argentine and from his observation of Yankee tourists.

Newest of all was his study of one man, one of whom he had only vaguely heard, perhaps from some vignette in *Time* or *Newsweek*. First were several photographs, two taken within the last month or so. "You note," Davidoff had told him, "the hair is different in cut. The face, the whole body, a bit more lean. The hair we can arrange; the moustache goes. The thinness you must manage yourself, especially the belly."

This was the first inkling of the role that he was being forced to play. That he would be palmed off somewhere for some reason as an educated North American he already knew. That he was expected to pass as some specific person shocked him. It was impossible.

"But, my God, this impersonation business was passé with

27

Oppenheim. Surely you can't expect anyone to get away with it today!"

The pale, sickly man wearing glasses answered, "You are sadly misinformed. We have gotten away with it several times, as the Americans say. You are learning, and we will get away with it again."

"I don't quite believe you."

"Oh, think, von Tetlow. Use your memory. Think of recent history. Why, in the First World War one of your people killed the Russian liaison officer to the Royal fleet, then impersonated him and managed to poison Lord Kitchener. In the last war, for a matter of weeks, as a decoy a common English soldier played the roll on various fronts of their famous General Montgomery, and no one even suspected. There are many such examples—only we do not boast about ours.

"We can teach you to walk alike, dress alike, even to use his style in a memorandum or report. We have quite a few samples, especially from the wastebasket in his home. They are very careful in government offices. They burn twenty-times-used carbon paper. But they still think a man's home is his castle."

"But what about his voice? And who exactly is this man?" queried von Tetlow.

"You need not know until we are reasonably sure you qualify. This way is much safer for everybody. As for the voice, you have both studied at Oxford. You have both a clipped, precise manner of speaking. I can tell you this much, in his position he must listen much more than speak. Of course, we have certain recordings, campaign speeches and the like. Also, we have quite a few from microphones in this man's 'castle.' You will study these by day, and at night you will not sleep often out of range of that voice—in seriousness, in anger and in laughter."

And night after night, ultra low-pitched but still audible, the man's sentences ran ceaselessly into his ears through a tiny hearing aid. Time after time he was wakened and ordered, "Now repeat back the last sentences you recall." Later his own recorded words were compared with the original, and he would repeat and repeat until detectable differences were reduced to the minimum possible.

It was clear to von Tetlow that the man he must ape was a government servant, most likely highly placed. This became surer when he was given an album of photos to study. Each bore a name, a nickname if any, family status, home address, etc. On these he was quizzed, as in a basic course in fine arts with its monotonous black and white prints of masterpieces. In the end he could call out for each whether the face was to be addressed Mr. Secretary, Mr. Jones, George, or "Stinky." All, or nearly all, of them were federal employees or appointees in Washington.

Next he studied maps of that city, concentrating on the northwest section and the richer suburbs of Virginia and Maryland. Again he studied photos of street scenes, exteriors and interiors of buildings, major route junctions. On these likewise he was repeatedly questioned.

A street corner shot would be flashed on the screen and the order, "Now tell me your exact route on foot from here to the East entrance of Old State." Or a double pair of gray concrete columns. "What Club? Where are the phone booths? You might be paged for a call. On what floor is the men's bar?" Or a view down the fairway of a sun-drenched course. "What hole is that? What club would you normally use for the second shot?" A sudden pause, "You do play golf, don't you?"

"No, never in my life."

"My God, then we must teach you."

But even his best instructors could not do this. Golf is frowned on in Russia. It is held to be non-productive. Clips of tournament action from *Sports Illustrated* were little help. This point brought on a worried conference, but caused only a determination that something must be done. Karl Friedrich von Tetlow, amateur actor, professional equestrian, swordsman, linguist and murderer, would never master a fluid swing from the tee in time, or an explosion shot from sand. He did, however, feel that putting was not entirely beyond his capacities.

Over a number of weary days he was attended by an

29

oculist who fitted him with contact lenses and taught him to insert and endure them. He asked his instructor why.

"Think, von Tetlow. Or rather, think, Roger. From now on you must learn to answer automatically to Roger."

He thought, "The color of the eyes perhaps."

"Brilliant. Roger's are greenish, yours bright blue, we do not have the exact shade of green, but we will make many different shades, and one will be correct. Also, you will have several pairs. Since it is your life you will be protecting, what other ways do you think your mask could be removed?"

"Scars, perhaps?"

The man ticked off an item on the paper in front of him.

"We have looked into that. You are both disgustingly healthy specimens. You have no noticeable scars. I am not sure about him. When we find out more, we can always duplicate any—on your skin, that is."

"How will you find out any more?"

"That is no concern of mine or yours. What else would worry you?"

"False teeth, fillings, extractions—things of this sort."

"True, but our dentists are really artists today. What else?"

Von Tetlow held out his hands, palms upward, and smiled tightly. "Well, naturally, there are fingerprints."

"Yes, that's a major danger. In the position you are to assume, we doubt they will be asked for again. If you arouse enough suspicion that this becomes necessary, you, of course, are dead, by your own hand. Or so it will be made to seem."

The sickly-skinned man raised an admonitory hand. "Don't say anything. Just a moment ago you smiled—almost. . . . Please do so again."

"Why should I? What is there to smile about?"

"Your hope for life, perhaps—perhaps nothing. But I order you to smile. Think of food, or women, or killing me. Think of anything, but smile."

"I'll think of killing you." Von Tetlow's lips drew rigidly—laterally away from his teeth.

Davidoff studied him for a moment and looked again to a photograph in his hand. "Just as I thought. Even with something pleasant in mind you cannot really smile. Roger Sto—I mean this kind and foolish American, he thinks things, even

30

people, are humorous. And he really looks amused. You, von Tetlow, will require a delicate bit of surgery about that mouth. Also, there must always be someone nearby to remind you from time to time to smile at life."

"May I ask how you plan to keep such close 'control' over me?"

"Of course, I can tell you in part." The man took a photograph from a folder, a full face one of a handsome, almost white, mulatto—Carib? Jamaican? He was not sure.

"This man, James Chapman, is your, or Roger's that is, houseboy—I mean manservant. He will be your tutor in many things. After all, he has closely observed his master for four years. He may serve as a contact for a courier. He is to act as your chauffeur also. He is a well-trained man. He will keep his eye on you; he does not make mistakes."

"Then it seems I am to have a happy home. By the way, am I married? Do I have children?"

"You are married. You have no children."

"Well, Oppenheim's man was safe because his wife—or do I mean the wife of the other?—had become insane, did not at first recognize him. What am I supposed to do?"

"That is no concern of mine. Others will handle it later. But you have started an idea. Any woman can become insane or very ill."

"Or even dead?"

Weeks later, Marjorie Storrow was, as usual, taking her Pekingese for its walk before bedtime. Nanky Poo always had his walk except when there was snow. Then he used a sandbox like a well-trained kitten. Roger would actually have preferred a well-trained kitten; at least it would not have yapped petulantly at him. He had said this twice, then learned the value of silence.

Majorie wondered vaguely what Roger was doing. She had had but one phone call from him, three days ago from Mexico City. He had made appropriate remarks, but had not sounded as if he missed home very much or regretted having to miss the Andersons' big party. He had sounded as though he had other matters on his mind. Well, so what if he did? She still missed him, and she wished she had told him so.

31

Well, no curing that now. Nanky Poo needed airing, so Marjorie was airing Nanky Poo. It was quite late, and she was not completely sober. All of Georgetown, save for a few fairies in an all-night restaurant, had gone to bed, or at least were not on the streets.

Still, one had to be careful of cars. Nanky Poo had to be picked up when crossing the street. She did so, and cooing affectionately to the little beast, wholly forgot to look either way as she stepped off the curb.

The car, driven rapidly and with skill, neither slowed down nor swerved after the mushy impact. It was a big, quiet car. Georgetown, used to sports car exhausts, resents them late at night. House owners sometimes even call the police. The car proceeded directly to a small wrecking concern on the outskirts of Baltimore. There the engine was removed and loaded on to a lugger, to be dropped the next morning far out at sea. The rest was cut apart or dismantled and was finally pressed very flat by a highly legitimate hydraulic press and carted away to the smelter.

Shortly afterward, the driver felt sick. There was something about looking through a great gout of fresh arterial blood quivering down a windshield. In fact, he felt so sick that he took a double dose of the heroin which had been given him in partial pay, to ease the monkey from his back. He assumed the drug had been cut by the seventy-five per cent customary in the trade. He died shortly without regaining consciousness. The police were not amused, but at least were satisfied as to the cause of death.

There had been no joy in the affair for anyone. Even the well-trained James was sad. He had not, until the end, really understood the reason he had been ordered to report on Marjorie Storrow's movements. He had been fond of the woman; she had always treated him well. Until now, abetting murder had been beyond the range of his crimes. If he had known, however, it would have made no difference. James had always followed party orders. He always would.

CHAPTER IV

ROGER LOWELL STORROW had looked forward to this trip to Mexico. He had wanted to go since taking classes at Harvard under the brilliant and eccentric Dr. Hooton. Archaeology fascinated him, especially that of the Mayans and Incas of the New World.

He had been to Mexico City several years ago with his wife and two other couples. They might as well have gone anywhere else. They played golf at a breath-catchingly absurd altitude, swam in water as warm as a tepid bath, and on at least two occasions the allegedly continental cuisine brought on a truly formidable dysentery, known locally as "Montezuma's revenge." They had taken a trip, via two roadside tourist traps, to the Temple of the Sun, where three bus loads of people photographed each other against stone carvings of Quetzalcoatl.

In partial compensation there had been the bullfights, which Roger had genuinely enjoyed. In her way, so had Marjorie. Open-mouthed and showing more than a glimmer of sexual awareness, she had vocally admired both bull and matador, the latter slim and graceful in his "suit of lights." Roger had shown great restraint, and had not told Marjorie that El Magnifico stood only five three in his white silk stockings and was the most notorious homosexual in the city.

This time things would be different. Starting from Merida he would have nearly four weeks to explore the most recently discovered ruins of the vanished Mayan cities. He would take as guide and companion for most of the trip Dr. Felix Rafael Nunez, a former classmate and one of Mexico's leading

33

archaeologists. Nunez had a flare for finding ancient ugly idols and beautiful young women. It promised to be a most enjoyable month. In fact, he was enjoying himself already.

Taking a firm constitutional stand, Roger had defied the FAA regulation prohibiting consumption aloft of any alcohol not furnished by the airline. United States Airlines provided or would sell only two pre-bottled martinis, obviously concocted by some misanthrope in a New Jersey laboratory. Roger had brought his own, in adequate quantity and mixed to his taste. The meal had been no more than fair, the wine less than average. Next time he would travel on a more civilized carrier.

No matter, at the moment he was relaxed. For twenty-six beautiful days he would be free from Washington pontificators and from the far worse, fuzzy-minded professors transmuted by some evil alchemy of politics into shallow replicas of statesmen. God preserve us, he thought, from the highly educated fool. Splendid! Absolutely splendid! For the time being he was rid of their unformed faces, too-precise voices and half-baked ideas. He was drowsy and would not even think of them. He would sleep, and no one, at least no one who mattered to him, would care if he snored.

He awakened to the nasal voice of a stewardess and the smell of coffee. The coffee was disappointing, but at least it was hot and the stewardess was pretty. The plane was just turning on the first leg of the landing pattern prior to descent into Mexico City's airport. This is one of the most beautiful approaches in the world; to one side two towering snow-capped mountains, directly below the pearl-strands of street lamps, and above the earliest evening stars. At this altitude both sets of brightness were wholly free of smog and cloud. The air, he knew, would be thin to breathe but dry and clean and cool.

A few minutes after landing, all immigration and customs formalities were over. He suspected this unwonted speed had something to do with the presence of Dr. Nunez, whose broadly-beaming face he had quickly spotted beyond the barrier. He was delighted to see his Mexican friend again. And Nunez was effusive in his greetings, embracing him in

34

the Latin manner, then thumping him heartily between the shoulder blades.

"*Hola,* you puritan gringo—burner of witches and drinker of tea. How do you like my English. It is excellent, no? How is your health? Also excellent, I can tell. And your government which works so hard trying to save us from being Mexicans? How is Marjorie, that ice-goddess you have married? Oh, excuse me, *amigo,* sometimes my tongue . . ."

Roger laid a hand on Nunez' shoulder. "That's quite all right, Felix, old boy, quite all right. But my God, man, slow down. I'll go to the hotel, shower and shave, and all that. Then we'll have a long drink—only then will I try to answer ten thousand questions—and, as you say, not in Spanish."

"No, Roger, you will not go to your hotel. In fact, I have cancelled it. I am still a bachelor. So we will go to my apartment. Do not argue. It is a most beautiful apartment. And you are my guest. So come."

It was a very handsome apartment, high above the lamps of Avenida de la Reforma. They drank long, cool drinks made with rum, and talked of many things. Then they left for an out-of-doors restaurant at the edge of the city and under the stars, to meet the ladies. Nunez had said they were friends of his—old friends, but not too old. Roger would see.

"But, Felix, my boy, who are these girls? I know they aren't your sisters, and I hope they aren't tarts."

Nunez lifted both hands from the wheel. At the speed he was driving, this was quite a sporting gesture. "My poor Roger, what a disastrous idea. Surely it is that you have been again in the north too long. Tarts, you said. So now I am insulted."

"So be insulted, but for God's sake steer this car."

"But it is such a lovely little car that it will steer itself. However, I do as you wish."

He steadied the wheel, pressed even more heavily on the accelerator. "Listen, such a splendid manly exhaust! Now I tell you about the ladies. One, Dolores, is so very nearly a real blonde. She is—how do you say?—a very particular friend of mine, and you need not concern yourself with her. Naturally you are permitted to look, but not to touch."

"And the other?"

"The other is Evita Martinez. She is truly blonde. She had a French mother. Very beautiful."

"Felix, a question."

"I listen."

"Do we pay these girls and all that?"

"Such a question, Roger. With Dolores that is my business personally. For you, I tell you only Evita is of good family, is now a widow. She has been an actress and is a well-known model for photographs. Her husband was not such a beautiful driver as I—such a sad accident. And Evita must keep her apartment and pay also for a little girl away in school."

"Thank you. That clears everything up."

"You are much welcome, Roger. I was so certain that it would."

Somehow Roger had expected a taller, more ample girl. He was not sure what had put the idea in his head. Maybe it was the word "model." Evita, however, stood barely an inch over five feet and had the beautifully economical body of a diver or an acrobat. She stood very straight and moved with controlled grace. She must dance beautifully, he thought. When they were introduced, her slightly wide-set eyes looked up frankly and appraisingly, and her generous mouth broke into a smile of pleasure. Her hand was warm and firm.

"*Encantado,* Señor Storrow. With pleasure I could kill this horrible Felix. He said to me that you were an old man."

"Thank you, but he almost told the truth. I'm not very young."

She looked at him again, directly. "You are young inside. I know this." It was stated not as an opinion but as an obvious fact. Roger was pleased.

Seated at a small table beside a dolphin fountain, she lifted her glass to him. "*A votre santé.* Now we will talk in French. It will be easier for you than Spanish."

"How do you know I speak it?"

"Simply because I know. I could tell, just as I could tell you were embarrassed to meet me, and that you are married."

"I am married. But I am not embarrassed. Not now. Not at all."

She placed a hand lightly on his arm and leaned toward

him. "That, Roger, and now you are Roger, that also I know."

Nunez laughed, banged his glass on the table. "Roger, *por favor,* some politeness, please! I said you must not touch my Dolores, but at least you can speak to her, look at her and talk to me, your rich and gracious host. You two are not alone."

"Oh, go to hell, Felix. What's the matter, old boy? Don't you understand pure Parisian French?"

"Of purity I would not know. But I do understand, and more than you think." He beckoned to a waiter. "And now we eat. We eat roasted little quails and we drink some white wine from Chile." He placed a hand over his heart. "Even so great a patriot as *el ilustríssimo* Doctor Fleix Rafael Nunez cannot tell a lie about the white wine of his own country. It is disastrous."

The food was delicious, the Riesling just right, and the company excellent. It had been a long time since Roger had enjoyed himself so easily. Evita was a skilled conversationalist and had an eager and inquiring mind.

Later, with the arrival of a small but enthusiastic orchestra, he found that she danced even more gracefully than he had thought. Yet he felt a little stiff and awkward trying to follow the unfamiliar rhythms of the Latin music. Evita laughed up at him, "You must relax, Roger. You do not relax very well. You think too much about the problems of politics, bombs and Russians."

"Part of my job, you know."

"Not now, not tonight. Your job is to dance with me. Here, I will show you."

"Not until I have a new drink. I will have a nice, large scotch."

"No, I will not permit it."

"Why the devil not?"

She smiled seriously, "Because whiskey is bad for a man. Rum, however, is excellent. I want you to be a man, Roger."

"Now you do almost embarrass me."

Evita took his hand, led him toward their table. "No, Roger, I do not think I do, because I have discovered something else about you. I know also that you are kind and strong, but that sometimes you are very lonely. I do not want you to be lonely."

He awoke once during the night, or so near dawn that the deepest darkness had begun to leave the sky. He stretched happily. Evita snuggled against him, rested a warm hand on his chest, "So you are awake, my Roger?"

He silently covered her hand with his own.

"Roger?"

"Yes, little one."

"I know something else."

"Yes, Evita?"

"That it is a bad thing for man and woman to sleep apart."

He picked up her hand, kissed the palm. "And I, too, know something."

"Yes?"

"I know that you have given me back something I thought I had lost."

She kept her hand against his mouth. "Hush, please. It was never lost. It was always there, I know."

Later, Roger was seated with a towel knotted around his waist. He idly stirred the thick black coffee. Evita smiled across at him. "You know, you look much better without clothes."

"How so?"

"Because in that suit and vest you looked like a gray-haired banker. Gray-haired bankers are fat, and fat gray-haired bankers are not attractive and are no good in bed."

"That's the damnedest non sequitur I ever heard."

She pretended to scowl. "It is not. It's quite logical, because I said it."

"I won't argue, little one. You look lovely with or without clothes. My uncle was a very wise man."

"What has your uncle to do with it?"

"He always told me, 'Roger, you should never go to bed with a girl with whom you would not enjoy having morning coffee.'"

Evita reached for his hand. "He was a wise man, Roger, even if he was a Yankee from Boston and probably a banker."

"He was both. Sometimes you almost scare me."

"I'm glad. But must you leave for Yucatan today? I want myself to show you this city."

"I'm afraid Nunez has already made plans. It might upset him."

"I'll bet you ten million pesos. Call him. The phone is over there."

He looked up the number and dialed it. Evita had come to stand close to him. "Hold out the receiver so I can hear—so that you cannot cheat."

"Hello, Felix. This is Roger. I called to find out . . ."

There was sudden laughter from Nunez. Then, "Everything is arranged. I have cancelled the plane. I have a car for you and tickets to the bulls."

"How in the hell did you know what . . ."

"A puritan burner of witches would never understand. *Adios, amigo, buena suerte.*"

A small hand was held palm up before him. "Ten million pesos, please."

He took the hand, pulled Evita hard against him, tilted up her chin, "Just try to collect."

She pressed her mouth to his. Against it, she said, "I think perhaps some way I will."

He drew back just a little, "You smell of you and you taste of coffee. What a beautiful way to begin this day."

Taking a picnic lunch with them, they drove to Oaxaca. There they sat happily in the sun chewing fried chicken legs and drinking wine in the company of ancient Mayan gods. Two large bus loads of tourists came and went and did not bother them at all. They ignored them completely.

After eating, Roger admitted that he was sleepy. "But it's quite a damned long way back to the city and a bed."

Evita leaned back against a tall stone step, stretched out her legs. "Here, Roger, put your head in my lap and sleep for a little while."

"Do you mind? I mean, won't you be uncomfortable and all that? Marjorie would—" he interrupted himself.

She laughed. "Please, my Roger. I know you too well. You were about to tell me that your wife would think it undignified for you to stretch out by an old temple with your head in her lap."

"Afraid you're right. I still think you're some kind of witch."

"Not a witch, just a woman. Now stop talking. Put your head here and I will keep the gnats away while you sleep."

He slept until it was time to drive back into the city. They arrived at the Plaza de Toros barely in time for the opening trumpets of the corrida. They were fortunate. Joselito Huerta fought that afternoon and drew two very good bulls. The second one he killed beautifully, going straight in over the wicked pointed horns to drop the animal instantly at his feet. The din of the crowd was tremendous as Joselito stalked in a walk of arrogance toward the President's box. His black hair was still unruffled but a red stain smeared the satin cloth of his right thigh.

"Where did all that blood come from, Evita? I certainly didn't see him gored."

She leaned forward intently. "No, Roger, he was not gored. That blood came from the side of the bull the last time Joselito turned him."

"Too damned close. Now I'll try to win back my ten million pesos or its equivalent kiss. I'll bet you he gets both ears and the tail."

"You will die a pauper because that is another foolish bet."

"How so?"

"You have not seen many fights. I have seen hundreds. He was not that excellent."

Evita was wrong, and Roger behaved in a most Bohemian way. He leaned over and soundly kissed her. Those in the seats directly behind them applauded. Roger turned and bowed acknowledgement to them.

Evita laughed delightedly. "I think you should spend more time here in my city. It is very good for you."

The next matador was not at all lucky. He was a *novillero,* a novice, too clumsy and too brave. One of the flashing horns caught him at the juncture of thigh and trunk, tossed him in the air. The youngster landed heavily, lay still for a few seconds, and finally lurched painfully to his feet. He stood, holding his bowels together with his hand, staring in numb horror as blood poured out between his fingers, rapidly dyeing his stockings with its crimson and forming a little puddle in the sand around his feet. Suddenly he crumpled to his knees, pitched sideways, thighs drawn convulsively against his chest.

Evita reached over and took Roger's hand. "I'm sorry, *caro*. No matter how often I see this I cannot grow accustomed. It still makes me a little sick."

"Then let's go. I don't find it very pleasant either. Even if the poor bastard lives, I doubt he'll ever sire any children."

"Have you children, Roger?"

"No, little one."

"That is sad. A man ought to have children. I am sure I could still give you children."

He ruffled her blonde hair affectionately. "Well, you'd best not try."

Slowly she turned and looked at him with a half smile. "You know, I do not think I would mind. Somehow I have become most fond of you, married or not, and in such a very short time."

They were passing under the cool shade of the stands. Roger walked in silence for a moment, then said, "Do you know, the same thing is true for me."

"Then I will see you again?"

"Now wait a minute. We still have this evening and tonight."

"That is very little time, and you have not answered me."

"I haven't answered because I cannot tell."

The next morning she brought him coffee and with it a small square card. On it was written 333678.

He took it, looked up at her. "It is an easy number. I will not forget it."

"You will remember only if you want to. Should you ever need me, you will call. I think you will need me."

"Why do you say that?"

"You said yourself I am prophetess, or maybe a witch."

"So I did. I know I'm going to miss you. Would you like to take a trip to the jungles?"

"You know I cannot do that. Now hurry, or you will be

41

late to the airfield. I will not go there with you since I do not like long good-byes."

At the door she kissed him warmly. "Take good care of yourself, my Roger. *Adios y buena suerte; que Dios te guarda.*"

"And may He keep you, too."

He turned to go. "And, Roger . . ."

"Yes, little one?"

"Wipe off that lipstick."

"No, I'm going to keep it on. Very good for Nunez. Good-bye again—and may God keep you also."

CHAPTER V

NUNEZ DROVE HIM to the airport to catch the plane for Merida. "I will be there with you myself, Roger, in about five days, and then we will truly travel. Right now, however, we will sit and have a reviving drink."

"Splendid, but my plane leaves in fifteen minutes."

"Do not believe it. Hardly ever does this particular plane depart on the hour. The pilot, he has a very demanding *señorita* near Oaxaca. He will leave when she permits him, no sooner. And you, you must get ready in Merida so you only leave at this time, no?"

"Yes, Felix, or is the correct answer 'no'? Why do you splendid Spaniards make a question of a statement?"

"Because, Roger, we have existed a much longer time than you. We know that all assertions bear certain doubts, and that true knowledge is contained within questions."

Roger laughed. "That will be quite enough. A slight hangover, even fleshly memories, these I can accept in the morning. Philosophy, never."

"But this is not philosophy, Roger. It is just words, and you always loved words."

"Not now." The garbled multilingua of the PA system interrupted them. "Thank God, they're announcing my plane. Now I can be alone with my thoughts instead of yours." He extended his hand. "Good-bye, Felix. See you next week."

"*Hasta la vista,* Roger. *Vaya con Dios.* I will meet you very soon."

Three days later Felix received a wire from Merida saying that Roger was feeling poorly and that they would have to postpone their trip until later. Two days after that he was summoned by a sub-Cabinet officer and was told that the government was prepared modestly to finance an expedition to the interior of Baja California if the eminent Doctor himself would lead it. This was an offer that no archaeologist could afford to turn down.

That the government was interested was not true. That the government really would from its own funds finance the expedition was a lie. Monies, however, were made available from the Soviet Embassy to a local party functionary, then in the form of payment from an export-import house via the sub-Cabinet officer who kept for himself the regularly permissible percentage. It was useful to have such an official on the payroll. If he cheated or threatened to become dangerous, he could always be denounced for accepting bribes.

And, fortunately or not, most scientists seldom seek the true source of their financing. Felix Nunez was no exception. When, later on, he received a telephone call from Roger Storrow in Merida, he asked after his health and expressed deep regret at being unable to join him. He even suggested another friend of his as a guide. He then wished Roger good fortune and happy hunting among the ruins.

The telegram from Merida to Felix Nunez had in its own way told the truth. Roger Storrow was indeed feeling poorly. Physically he was in excellent shape. His room was spacious and well furnished, the bed broad and comfortable. The bath even boasted a supply of hot water. All of his meals had been excellent, and he had not wanted for any form of drink he desired. He really had nothing to complain about except that he had been forcibly abducted, was a closely guarded prisoner and had been told he was being held for ransom.

It had been managed with frightening simplicity and efficiency. At the airport a smiling young man in a chauffeur's cap had come up to him, bowed, "You are the Señor Storrow, no?"

He had been unable to resist. "I am the Señor Storrow, *si*."

"Bueno, I am José of the Hotel Central. I drive you." He beckoned imperiously to a ragged porter. *"Hola, Pepe, las bagajes aquí—pronto."* The bags stowed, Roger sank gratefully into the limousine seat and José started for the Hotel Central.

Roger was a stranger to the area, therefore he did not know exactly where they drove. It became rapidly clear, however, that it was not in the direction of a city hotel. In fact, they drove away from Merida at race-track speed. He quietly asked the driver to slow down. José answered, *"Si, si, señor,"* but slightly increased his pace. What in hell was going on? Whatever it was, Roger's immediate reaction was that it was nothing pleasant. "Damn it, José, stop this idiocy! Drive me to the hotel."

"Como, señor? No comprendo nada."

Roger then tried the door locks, the window handles. They were immovable. José turned his head slightly and grinned. This really made no difference since it would have been fatal for him to attempt to leap from the car. Maybe he had to do with a madman. No, his instincts told him otherwise. Perhaps he could somehow overpower José, take over the wheel. He leaned forward, automatically clenching and unclenching his hands. The Mexican seemed to read his mind, moved his hand to a button near the left door. A heavy glass plate smoothly closed off the driver's seat from the rest of the car. Roger did not have to look to be sure that there was no similar button within his reach.

Well, that, until he arrived wherever in hell they were racing to, was that. With fingers remarkably steady under the circumstances he lit a cigarette, then braced his body to ease his discomfort in the careening car.

It took, he noted, about twenty-five minutes to reach a hacienda whose entrance was guarded by a heavy iron gate set in high and solid adobe walls. José signalled with his horn twice, then twice again, and the gate swung open. At the end of a rutted driveway the car jolted to a stop. Immediately, down from the front steps came a tall, moustachioed, broad-shouldered figure in ranchero's costume, complete to the flat, broad-brimmed hat. He even wore a long-barrelled revolver slung low in a holster at his hip. The big man opened the rear

45

door of the limousine. "Ah, good evening, Señor Storrow. I hope that the trip to Merida has not been too uncomfortable. Please be welcome."

The best Roger would muster was an icy, "Not at all, my good man."

"Ah, but I am not your good man. I am Don Henrique de Cordobal y Guzman, and I am the owner," a proud sweep of his sombrero, "of this hacienda. Come inside, please, where I may offer you refreshments. I have cancelled your rooms at the Central, a most uncomfortable place, hot and with flies. I have also, in your name, asked that your baggage be sent here. Soon you will be at ease."

"Indeed?"

"Yes. Indeed." A negligent gesture of the right hand toward the butt of the pistol. "Now, please, you will come inside. Kindly to go first."

Inside he led Roger across a cool, stone patio, down a long, well-lighted hall and up a flight of mahogany stairs to a comfortable study. He was invited to sit and offered his choice of tequila, rum, scotch and soda, coffee or tea. Going deliberately against his wishes, he asked for tea, "China tea, if you have such a thing here."

"But, of course," and the tea was quickly brought by smiling José.

Sipping it he sat in complete and, he hoped, dignified, as well as outraged silence. But damned if he would act either outraged or fearful. Let Don Henrique de Cordobal y Guzman make the first move.

"You wonder why I have had you brought here," Don Henrique said. Roger looked up briefly and then returned to a study of his teacup. "I am not surprised. It is so simple, however. I was once rich; and am now so poor. You, of course, are rich and you will be poorer, but not so much that it will cause excessive pain. I have adopted a fine old Yankee institution. I have had you kidnapped. Why, *por Dios,* kidnapped? A word I never did understand. You will pay me some dollars, then you return to your home."

"Idiotic, my good man. Kidnapping is a fine way, even in Mexico, to get yourself hanged high."

"But no. You do not really know who I am. I said I was

46

Don Henrique de Cordobal y Guzman, true. But in this country that is more than a name. Here I am very well known, very well recognized indeed. The Jefe de la Guardia Civil of the province, he is my brother-in-law. He has married my most beautiful sister."

"How nice for your sister." Roger put down his teacup, pointed his cigarette at his host. "But as you may not know, I also am not without influence, although without beautiful sisters. This influence goes even to the President of my country. You, Don Henrique whoever the hell, are playing with worse than dynamite. When they hear that I am missing . . ."

"Ah, but why should they hear? No. Do not interrupt. Who will tell? Not you, because you will not have the chance. You will merely write a check on the Riggs National Bank and another on the—such a quaint name—Old Colony Trust Company of Boston, to the Institucion Archaelogica de Cordobal y Guzman, along with a note to the Boston Museo that you have purchased certain antiquities of immense interest and great value. Oh, not too great, not exaggerated, merely to a total of $50,000. I am, as is clear, a very reasonable man."

"And if I refuse—as I shall!"

"But why refuse? It would be so foolish. Of course, you will wish to write to your señora about this purchase and also some letters which we can mail for you from time to time about your explorations."

"I'll be damned if I will."

The Don's amiability had gone. Leaning forward in his chair, he stared directly into Roger's eyes. Each syllable dropped into place with the same deadly emphasis. "In this you are wrong, Señor Storrow. You will be damned, yes damned, if you do not. Stronger men than you have refused to sign letters but have finally begged on their knees to be permitted."

Roger rose rapidly to his feet, levelled a finger at Don Henrique. "Listen, threats sound empty from someone in your position. They know at home where I am going. They know I am going to meet my friend, Dr. Nunez. He expects me in four days. When I fail to appear . . ."

47

"Please," the Mexican's hand was raised in admonition. "Please, Señor Storrow, do not excite yourself. Sit down."

Roger remained standing.

"So be it. Please yourself. You spoke of your friend, Dr. Nunez. Permit me," pushing back from the desk to reach into a lower drawer, "here is a message already sent to Dr. Nunez in your name from the Hotel Central. Read it, please. He will be concerned that you were feeling poorly perhaps because of strange food, and that you must postpone his joining you for a while. You will not need to worry about him, I assure you, not now, and not later."

"But, dammit," Roger stopped short. Better, he felt, right now to talk less and listen more, with as much dignity as possible. And this was quite a lot. He lowered himself again into the chair. "And so, Don Henrique? Anyone can invent a message."

Surprisingly, the man smiled. "So, Señor Storrow, I have much to do, and I am certain you desire to wash yourself and to rest. Please to follow me. I will show you to your room."

There seemed to be no reasonable choice. Roger followed.

"And should there be anything you wish, anything, naturally, except to leave my home, you need only ring. José will bring it. We have much to talk of later."

That had been five days ago. During the period of his— what was the polite word? house arrest?—Roger had enjoyed several well-prepared meals with Don Henrique, the others alone in his own room, and always served by a smiling José. He and his host had spoken of nearly every subject under the sun: art and politics, sports and women, or both, religion, history. Whatever type of criminal he might be, the Don was a knowledgeable man. But he did exhibit most surprisingly mercurial moods. As a result some of the talks were pleasant, some angry. A ransom demand had been made, on two occasions, with no result and then, for some reason, had been dropped. Occasionally the two had played chess, sometimes the two-handed gambler's game of piquet. The Don had said, "This gin rummy is for little babies, not adult players."

On the fifth day Don Henrique walked in and announced: "Señor Storrow, this man here is my most personal physician,

48

the Professor Doctor Don Matera y Lopez. And this other, I assure you, is the most estimable dentist of the province, the Doctor Sanchez. They will attend you."

"Delighted, of course, gentlemen, but, dammit all, there's nothing at all wrong with me or with my teeth. So I do not need to be attended."

"Most probably, but then," again the moustache-bordered smile, "one wishes to be certain. Occasionally our food, our climate, does not agree with everyone. I would never have you to feel that here you had not received every care."

Roger shrugged. He was still not sure whether Don Henrique was really a serious kidnapper, a genial madman or a dangerous psychopath. Whatever the case, the examinations by Doctors Lopez and Sanchez were incredibly thorough, including blood tests, the use of portable X-ray equipment and careful photography of the teeth from the front, from below and from above. They finally bowed, almost in unison, announcing that their North American visitor was in a most splendid condition, save that the heart must avoid too great exertion, strain or anger. They withdrew, leaving Roger Storrow of Boston and Washington, D.C., more baffled, if possible, than ever.

In the room next to Storrow's, von Tetlow was not baffled, but was nearing mental exhaustion. It is extremely hard work and requires intense concentration to study someone else's every waking moment by X-ray mirror, binoculars and microphone. It is baffling and enervating to look into a face so hauntingly like one's own and yet somehow distorted—not so much because of the occasional grin as because the right side was where the left should be. No man can see his face as others do, only as it looks back at him reversed by a mirror. It calls for memorizing endless details in order to absorb another's knowledge of and reactions to a great variety of subjects, and to be quizzed repeatedly on the same. It is deadly monotonous spending hours repeating fragments of conversation to a tape recorder, then intensely comparing the results with the sounds played from another tape. It is nearly soul-destroying to contemplate that one can do nothing else for some three long weeks more. And it was galling that he must obey the smallest order of a tall, powerful, moustachioed man whose name he had never been told and concerning whom he could discover nothing beyond than that he was called the Don.

The more von Tetlow thought about it, the less he liked it and the dimmer gleamed his hope for success.

He now knew that the official he was to impersonate prepared the agenda for and sat in on the deliberations of the National Security Council of the United States. He was privy to the most closely guarded plans and secrets of his country. He had been the confidant of Presidents and Cabinet officers, as well as of the previous Directors of the CIA. At least three members of the present Cabinet had seen and talked with the real Roger Storrow several times before. Now he was to penetrate this group of Prussians in Back Bay clothing and report back through cut-out agents to the Kremlin. It would require great luck to succeed; it demanded and would demand an almost inhuman intensity of effort.

It really had not cheered him at all when his mentor, the Don, reminded him, "Of course you can succeed. Do you not recall that the North American spy Benedict Arnold once impersonated with success George Washington's very brother?"

CHAPTER VI

MUCH MORE OCCUPIED von Tetlow. He spent hour after hour copying samples of Roger Storrow's writing, particularly the signatures on packages of cancelled checks retrieved from the wastebasket of his study in Georgetown. He now considered himself perfect in the reproduction of the heavy, upright lettering, but he continued to practice because he knew that he would soon be put to the test. Storrow's manner of walking, stance, carriage of head and gestures he practiced in front of a large looking-glass, and later in front of a camera in order to compare his performance with that of Storrow's. Strangely, the most difficult thing of all was to keep his hand from straying to stroke the mainstay of his first disguise, a moustache which was no longer there.

It was tedious. The detailed and protracted medical and dental attentions were worse. First there had been the creation of a short, puckered scar low on the right side of his abdomen, then a longer crescent-shaped one inside the left knee to indicate earlier removal of the internal lateral cartilage. There followed endless hours in a dentist's chair, pain only partially numbed by novocaine, while muscular fingers blocked his mouth, suction tubes gurgled and high-speed drills assaulted tender nerves. But, after all, splinting and capping seven teeth, reproducing and cementing in a dozen inlays of gold or amalgam, plus the extraction of three perfectly sound molars to replace them with an exact fitting bridge, took time even if, as Don Henrique had said, Dr. Sanchez was the most estimable dentist of the province.

Before the dental torture, however, von Tetlow had been

51

called on by the Don. "Now, my friend, comes your first real test. We go to the Hotel Central where you will receive a call for the Señor Storrow from this Dr. Nunez of Mexico City. It will be at two o'clock, the time when the operator was informed the señor would have returned. You will tell him your health is much improved. The rest you must improvise as you proceed. Then we will see."

"We will see what?"

"If any suspicion is aroused. The tone of Dr. Nunez' voice, his questions, and other things. Naturally I will monitor this conversation, but I think there is no cause for worry."

"And why not?"

"Because you will have a valuable ally in this charade in the telephone system of this great democracy. There are times on the wires that I could not recognize the voice of my own brother—not with certainty."

However, the connection was perfect, the voices clear and distinct. "Hello, Roger, it is I, Felix, who speaks."

"How are you, old boy?"

"More important is how goes it with you—with your health?"

"Fine. Much better."

"You do not sound entirely well—a little too much, how do you say, restrained. Is there a woman with you?"

This was easier. "No, I am sorry to say. At least not at this hour of the day, not this time."

"Good then—I have both sad and magnificent news."

"I hope, no one . . ."

"Oh, no. All is well with my family, but I cannot, I so deeply regret, join you on our explorations."

He knew the right line. "And just why in hell not?"

"Because—and do not become irritated—I have received an offer I cannot afford to refuse."

And so it had gone, easily enough until the very last. "Roger, you can find another guide as good. Old Fernando Guzman, I have his number here. I will call him to get in touch with you at the hotel."

What should he say now? "But, Felix, this is all unnecessary. I will phone him directly."

"No, he has a new position now, and I doubt he will

remember you after so long. Are you still there, Roger? Do you not like this idea?"

Von Tetlow thought involuntarily of the listening Don, passed the back of his hand across a sweating forehead, coughed lightly. "Of course, I was just lighting a cigarette." That reference to "old" Fernando, that helped! "No, I'm sure he'll remember me, or at least my name. Don't trouble yourself, please. Just give me the damned number."

"As you wish; 443756 is the number—at the Institucion Historica de Merida. Give him my regards."

"That I will."

"Then *adios*, Roger. *Buena suerte.*"

"Good-bye, Felix. Good hunting."

A few minutes later a satisfied teacher was saying, "My congratulations, Roger. You are becoming, perhaps, an actor of ability. We shall wait to see."

A little grimly, "Thank you, and I am glad it is finished, but what if Nunez does call this old friend, Guzman?"

"And if he does, what would you do, Roger—I am pleased you have learned your new name so well."

"Let me think. What would be in character? Believe I'd tell him that since Felix Nunez cannot come along, to hell with it. I have changed my plans and will just take a less difficult, more public tour, perhaps do a little hunting and fishing."

Don Henrique was smiling a little. "Bravo! Entirely correct since I think the same. Perhaps you will go far. If so you will live longer."

Von Tetlow also smiled. "You, señor, are correct. I will do my very best to go, as you say, far. What do we do next?"

"Not we, you. Soon you will help Señor Storrow to finance at least part of this costly experiment."

"Just how do we do this? He seems a very stubborn man."

"Oh, this will be done without his knowledge. The time has come for you to use your new-found art—forgery."

Von Tetlow lit a kitchen match by drawing his thumbnail across the tip, put it to his cigar. "This damned habit of Storrow's! Three times I have burned the devil out of myself with phosphorus beneath the nail. So, I'm to forge a check. Isn't that too much of a risk at the moment?"

"A risk you will have to take many times later on—that is, if you succeed now."

"I suppose so. To whom do I make out this check, and for how much?"

"You make out no check. You do just as I told Señor Storrow he was to do. You write to his bank, to the trust officer with whom we know he usually deals, telling him you have found some very remarkable ancient jade ornaments which you are buying. You request the bank to make out a certified check to the Institucion Archaeologica de Cordobal y Guzman. This is because the Institucion is not willing to accept a personal check against valuable jades, or that they prefer a certified check as a readily negotiable instrument for some international dealings they plan. Yes, that is the better idea. And," Don Henrique smiled thinly, "it is so close to the truth, is it not? And I so admire the truth."

"But if we get the money this way, why all the masquerade of making Storrow think he is being held for ransom?"

"Oh, that was simply the first idea we had. Also, it was to give you the opportunity of studying Señor Storrow's reactions under pressure and in anger. He reacted, one must admit, with magnificence. Did you not think so? And now to work."

It was a very careful letter. Roger Storrow would have nearly believed it was his own. Confronted with the signature in court he would have had great difficulty denying its authenticity. He could claim he did not recall having signed any such letter, even deny having done so. Perhaps, a handwriting expert could have backed up his claim. And perhaps not.

Roger was in no position to make claims or enter denials. He was, in fact, under heavy dosage of scopolamine and answering questions concerning details of his work, his habits, also the personalities and quirks of character of his Washington associates. He himself would have been amazed to hear how lowly he held the judgment and courage of some of these associates. Roger Storrow was a New Englander, a very careful man by upbringing. Years of official Washington had added to his value of the closed mouth. But now he was helpless, and von Tetlow listened hour upon weary hour.

In Washington, Mary Margaret Kelly entered the office in the old State Department Building on 17th Street where she had worked for the past eleven years. She did this daily, even though her employer was on vacation. She was a loyal and conscientious worker and wanted to be sure that all important papers, memos and messages be sorted out properly and summarized against the day of Roger Storrow's return. Mary Margaret was not quite young and not quite pretty, an exception to the rule in many Washington bureaus. She was, however, well-dressed, extremely intelligent and efficient, also a glaring exception in a Civil Service where promotion depends on seniority, and where tenure, short of provable criminal guilt, seems to be for ever.

She knew her employer's idiosyncrasies, likes and dislikes, habits, dress, speech and sentence structure certainly better than anyone else including that stuck-up society clothes-horse, Marjorie Storrow. As a matter of fact, Miss Kelly could and often did write letters or memoranda for Roger's signature in many routine matters. Roger often signed them without a reading since he was aware that Mary Margaret knew how he would have phrased them himself. She was, as many near-perfect secretaries are, more than a little in love with her employer—a condition she would no sooner admit than walk naked down Pennsylvania Avenue.

This morning she was late, distraught, even outwardly trembling a little. Inwardly she was almost shaking apart with the memory of fear and the heat of righteous anger. She could scarcely credit what had happened to her, happened in the darkest, coldest hour of the night in her own second floor apartment on 21st Street.

She knew she had locked the door. She always did. It was as automatic as placing the three heaped spoonsful of coffee in her percolator in readiness for the morning, brushing her teeth or turning off the lights. For four years now, since her mother's death, she had always lived alone—well, almost always—and she knew how to take care of herself in this city. Certainly she had locked the door, then lain down in bed to read Henry Miller—disgusting man! I mean really! At a little past eleven she had composed herself for sleep, sleep which came rapidly.

There had been no noise. She was sure of that. No one had turned on a light. Still, there had been light. At first bright red through her eyelids on into her brain, as when a dream is ending but consciousness has not quite begun. Finally her eyes opened to the glare of what must have been a powerful flashlight aimed directly at her face. From behind the light came a low pitched, monotonous voice. "Don't move, lady. Don't make a single move and you'll be all right."

She had opened her mouth to scream. All she could produce was a dry, gagging sound.

"Quiet, lady! Look here! "Here" was the other hand, held just beneath the flashlight. In it shone the cold steel of a straight razor. "Now hold very still. Don't move an inch."

The razor hand snaked toward her paralyzed throat, then swept away again stripping the bed clothes from her body. Now the light was turned away from her to shine up into a flatly staring, distorted face—nose mashed out to the cheek bones, ears almost invisible against the skull, eyebrows and upper lids drawn horridly away from the eyes. Exactly the effect, had she thought of it, achieved by children on Hallowe'en with nylon stockings drawn over their heads.

Slowly the light moved down over a naked chest, down to the beltline and then to the open zipper, and the man monstrously exposed. The figure moved closer. With the feel of what was both fire and ice, the flat of the razor blade was laid against her throat, the hem of her nightgown was slowly lifted. She fainted.

In seconds, or many minutes, she had no idea which, consciousness returned. Her pulse drummed with sickening force and rapidity. Blindly she lunged for the bedside lamp, knocking over clock and water glass, groped agonizingly for the switch, found it and at last flicked it on and stared wildly about. Thank God! She was alone in the room. Vaguely she noted that the bed clothes had been replaced over her body. The only alien presence was the very faint odor of something resembling insect repellent. She gathered her courage, reached for the phone.

Commendably soon a tired but experienced policeman leaned back against her desk, repeating his routine questions for the second time. His colleague had finished examination of the door, checked the knob for prints and was now examining the bathroom windows.

"How tall was he, Miss Kelly? I mean about how tall?"

"I can't say, but he looked huge."

"What color was his skin?"

"I couldn't tell. I know it sounds stupid, but I really couldn't."

The policeman sighed wearily. Damn women anyhow. "How do you mean you couldn't tell, Miss Kelly?"

"Just what I said. It was a horrid, sick color, not like real skin at all." Her hand was held out pleadingly, her voice rising in pitch. "What do you expect anyway, with that horrible mashed-up nose like a leper in the movies and the eyes pulled crooked . . ."

The officer interrupted gently. "O.K., miss, O.K. Now I think I understand. I believe you, see."

Mary Margaret still had the spirit to say, "You're much too kind."

Patrolman Clafflin ignored this. "Now I have another question. Was there anything unusual about his voice: accent, use of words, anything?"

"No, except for a sort of deep rumble, resonance, whatever you call it."

"And you say he exposed himself?"

She merely nodded dumbly, the shock still showing in her eyes.

"Did he touch you at all, anywhere?"

She shook her head, although she could still feel the cold steel at her throat.

"And you've checked your belongings?" Nothing has been stolen or disturbed?"

"I don't think so. I mean I'm not sure. But I don't care," her voice edged toward hysteria. "I don't care at all, but do something. Just don't stand there and talk and ask silly questions."

"Please, miss, take it easy. We're doing all we can. The dogs will be here soon." Turning to the other policeman, "Anything at all, Mike?"

"No, boss, not a mark anywhere on the door or lock, except the usual key scratches. No marks on the windows either, not a damned thing."

"Now, Miss Kelly. Mary Margaret Kelly, is that right? Forty-seven, single, no relatives here in Washington, occupation, secretary in the Executive Offices. Anything like this ever happen before?"

"No, thank God."

"Well, I'd advise having a chain bolt on your door, so it can't happen again. Are you sure you can't help us any more on that face you said you saw?"

"Said I saw? My God, I did see it. All flat and stary and horrible."

She heard a car drive up rapidly and come to a stop before the house. The street door was unlatched. She could make out voices.

The officer in charge seemed glad to drop his questioning. "Good, the dogs are here now. We'll see what they can pick up."

The dogs tried. They sniffed around where directed, but the faint, flat chemical odor which met their sensitive noses was of no interest to them. If there were any other scent, human or animal, it had now vanished or was effectively masked. Taken to the stairway, they sniffed once or twice, then turned disillusioned eyes on their master.

Later, in the patrol car, the younger officer hazarded a guess. "Some of these older dames are a little crazy, boss, don't you think? Did you see the whisky bottle, and that stuff she was reading? Father Donovan says the publisher should be thrown in jail. What do you think?"

"I don't know, Mike. Let's wait till we check the prints. I just don't know what to think."

Obviously the clods hadn't believed a word she said. Mary Margaret pulled open the lower drawer of her office desk, took out a bottle and a small glass. With trembling hands she poured out a good, stiff slug of whiskey. "To hell with both of you, you miserable flatfeet. You can go back to tagging parked cars and arresting apple stealers."

In point of fact this was a little unfair. Since the doorknob and other polished surfaces showed no recent prints except Mary Margaret's own, it must be admitted that the Washington police had done all that could reasonably be expected under the circumstances.

Half way down the pile of correspondence in the "in" basket, Miss Kelly found an envelope addressed to her in an unfamiliar squarish script. Puzzled, she slit it open, withdrew and unfolded the single sheet of paper, flattened it out on the blotter. "Miss Kelly, I have been studying you for some time, you drying-up old bitch. I tell you what you need and some night I'm going to come and do it. What you need . . ." What followed would have made Henry Miller blush. It was detailed, and pathologically obscene.

Mary Margaret's face flushed deeply. Convulsively, she tore the paper in shreds, dropped it as something unclean in the wastebasket. After a moment's reflecting, she took out the pieces and blindly tore them into smaller pieces. Twenty minutes later she thought better of it and called for one of the security guards. To him she said, "I guess the postal authorities had better see this after all. I don't want to look at it again. But you'd better. Here are the pieces in this cellophane envelope. Take them out of here and put them together for yourself. You'll see the lowest, dirtiest thing in your life."

Painstakingly the man sorted out the ragged little squares of paper, fitted them together with scotch tape. The damned stuff kept sticking to the desk-top or to itself. At last, he had the whole page assembled, read it and shook his head. By God, sometimes women were hard to understand.

He took the letter with him. "I did like you said, Miss Kelly, but I can't for the life of me see what you're so all-fired-up about."

In outrage she almost shouted, "You can't, can't you?"

"No, I can't. Look at this for yourself."

Mary Margaret did so in total disbelief. The paper bore nothing more than a short handwritten note inviting Roger Storrow to a golf dinner at the Congressional Country Club. Frantically she reached toward the wastebasket, then stopped herself. It was no use. She knew the receptacle had been empty and that she had torn up only one piece of paper. She felt she must be going out of her mind.

She really couldn't be blamed. Appearing and disappearing inks have been tools of espionage as well as mystification for many centuries. Mary Margaret Kelly did not know this. Even if she had, she would not have thought of it, not in her present state.

These incidents marked only the beginning. There were no more night-time intruders after the installation of the bolt and chain. But there were other harassments designed to murder sleep and set the nerves on edge. After a while it becomes nearly impossible to ignore a telephone ringing in the night. It is hard to say which is worse, to hear an obscene invitation, a muttered horrid threat, or to hear simply nothing at all except some heavy breathing. It is not—detective fiction to the contrary—a simple thing for a private citizen to trace a call, and useless if that call originated at a pay phone.

It is very unpleasant to sense, in fact to be sure, that one is being followed on the streets, especially at night. And yet, why complain to the police if there has been no physical violence or even jostling? What good does it do to report threats or filthy suggestions whispered, if no one else heard them and their speaker cannot be identified?

As a matter of fact, anyone who makes enough unverified complaints to the police or any other security agency, including the FBI, is eventually listed in a special section of the card index file. This is impolitely, but generally accurately, called the "Nut File."

That is what happened to Mary Margaret Kelly. In a short time she had lost most of her credibility with the police and a considerable portion of her nerve. Not all. She came of tough Irish stock who no longer heard the wail of banshees or sought to placate the little people. But tough Irish stock traditionally takes to the bottle in times of black trouble, and she was no exception. Likewise too many doctors who prescribe before they really look hand out tranquilizers like lollipops to children. The resulting dreadful depressions, for which some people then take benzedrine or some other stimulant, can result in a condition where a patient will doubt his own sanity. And so will others. Add to this the normal tensions of the lonely spinster at menopause, and it is easy to see that what James Chapman had done in the beginning was quite enough to achieve his purpose at the end.

In short, the dedicated and observant Miss Kelly would not have noticed if her employer's eyes had suddenly changed color. And if she had ever reported to anyone that he did not seem to be acting his usual self, anyone would have merely shaken his head and said, "Certainly, my dear, and I think you ought to take a nice long quiet vacation somewhere. Now run along. I'm busy."

No one would now believe any of her allegations of shady doings. Maybe she herself would never again entirely credit the evidence of her own senses. In a way, she was lucky. If things had not worked out as they did, she might have been murdered. Or maybe not: the party apparatus did not balk at assassination, but it disliked, with becomingly shy reticence, causing the publicity of suspicion to be directed at itself. Two violent deaths so close to one so close himself to the throne might have alerted even the most liberal sections of the press, and conceivably some influential senators who still did not quite believe that the Communist Aparat existed in these United States.

Meanwhile in Mexico, von Tetlow had just learned that he would have one final advantage in his masquerade.

"Here is a telegram for you, Roger, a most sad telegram. Your wife, Marjorie, has been killed, only last night by— how do you explain it?—by a hit-and-run driver. There will be a funeral the day after tomorrow."

Bafflement, then understanding and anger, kept him silent for a moment. Finally he managed, "What do you mean, my wife? Not once . . . not ever has this been so much as . . ."

Don Henrique shrugged deprecatingly, raised his hands lightly, palms up. "Of course not. Were there a wife you could not go. We would not need you. You would be worthless, even such a great actor as you."

"But what in God's name—I mean how . . ."

"How? Most simply. Since the wife no longer exists, now you can go."

61

"Not what I mean. How did you know?"

Again the shrug. "An accident, my esteemed Roger Storrow. An accident. We are experts with accidents."

CHAPTER VII

VON TETLOW SHUDDERED inwardly. He was hard and ruthless. Certainly he had been a murderer. Still, his victims had been to him faceless statistics in a war for survival, or at least he had lied so to himself. And it had been a long time ago. Here, however, a harmless, hapless woman had been coldly wiped out, in peacetime, to make way for a spy—for himself.

Don Henrique was still talking. "You ask why we never described this wife to you. It would have been of no value. We could not have sent you to another's wife."

"Very well. The poor woman is dead. I suppose I must go to the funeral."

"You cannot go. There would be too many strangers for you at one time. You could not remember them all, no matter how well you have studied our photography."

Von Tetlow shook his head. "But I will be expected. What excuse could there be? How can I not go?"

Don Henrique smiled slightly. "Now I ask that you think a little. You remember, of course, that you cannot play golf. This is so?"

"What the devil has golf to do with it?"

"Oh, very much indeed. We must not expose you to this foolish game. So we kill two crows with one arrow."

"I still do not understand."

A gesture from the powerful hand. "Ah, but you will. You have already sent another telegram saying you fell, a most bad fall, while climbing some ruins. You have been to the surgery. You are in the hospital and must not yet be removed." Don Henrique stroked his moustache. "This, we

63

think, is a most clever thing. Although your letter and the signing were perfectly accepted, we wish to escape any more such risk as possible. If you cannot write for a little, this suffices. Is it not so?"

The German thought for a moment, glared angrily at the man. "Yes, of course. But I'll be damned if I like this. I refuse to be butchered by some peon of a Mexican surgeon."

"But you cannot refuse, not while you are my guest. And you are my guest for so long as it pleases me. They say you are a man of courage, von Tetlow, I mean Roger, and this will not cause as much pain as a dangerous fall. In fact, we will be most skillful. I do not believe you will be too much crippled. It is only unfortunate I did not think of this before. We will do it at the same time as the other surgery."

"Haven't you done enough, tearing out teeth, drilling holes in those left and gouging scars into me? What in God's name are you talking about, this other surgery?"

"Something which may save your life. Tell me this with honesty. How many long hours have you now studied Storrow? Do you truly believe that you are his twin?"

Von Tetlow thought for a few moments. "With the contact lenses, now that my eyes no longer pour tears, and with my hair bleached a little more, I would say almost exactly."

Don Henrique pointed a finger at him. "I, on the other hand, have been studying both of you, oh so carefully, and I say you are not his twin. First," and he touched von Tetlow lightly below his nose, "your upper lip is a bit longer. This gives you a gloomy look. Second, Storrow thinks some things are most amusing, and when he smiles the corners of his mouth turn up. You, however, remain the stern Prussian. When you try to smile, your lips draw back only to the side. It is more as if you were planning to bite than to laugh. Go to the mirror over there and see for yourself. Think of something amusing."

"Dammit, there's nothing amusing to think about."

"Perhaps not. But with very delicate surgery we can change you so that you can some day smile with the Storrow smile. And that is not all."

"In the devil's name, is there more?"

"Another thing good for you. For at least four weeks you

64

will have to wear a dressing all the way across your upper lip and to the sides—a wonderful help to the masquerade—then, even after the dressings are gone, there might be a small scar. This too, happened, of course, when you fell down the side of that ancient pile of stones."

In the attic of the hacienda an operating room had been efficiently improvised. Von Tetlow lay on a sheet-draped wooden table placed so as to catch the bright sunshine from the skylight overhead. His face was not covered by an ether mask since that would have blocked access by the plastic surgeon. Instead the mixture of gases was being fed into his lungs through a thin tube taped into his nostril and pulled upward. The upper half of his body was bare, and two gowned and masked figures leaned over him. Don Henrique stood watching, a few feet away. Dr. Don Matera y Lopez was talking, holding a threaded suture needle in a delicate needle-holder.

"I think that will accomplish the wished-for result. I have cut out a tiny piece from the risorius muscles here," as he touched a spot above one corner of the mouth, "and here." He touched another, "And I have sutured the ends together. I have also cut into the upper lip and made a small contraction there. I am quite certain that when this man tries to smile it will give the proper effect. Now I shall close the wounds carefully. It should leave only a tiny hair-line scar. I think . . ."

Don Henrique interrupted, "No, Doctor, the corner incisions, yes, but do not close the wound across the lip."

"But of course I will close it. Otherwise it will leave an ugly scar, almost a disfigurement."

"Excellent! That is just what I thought. So when the bandages are all removed, and it can be seen that the mouth does not exactly resemble that of our model, then there is a good reason. He split his lip when he fell from the ruin."

"But, Don Henrique, I should . . ."

"You should do as I tell you. Just put on the dressing and attend to the hand and the arm. Do you hear?"

"I hear and will follow your orders, señor, of course, but I hate to do this to the hand."

"So would I hate to, but get on with it."

After dressing the incisions, Matera's assistant bent down, picked up a wooden block and placed it beside the patient on the table, then covered it with a folded towel.

"He must have a bad bruise on one side only. Now turn the patient on his face."

This finished, the man's right arm was pulled out at right angles to his trunk and the padded block slipped under it just about the elbow. Turning to his assistant, the surgeon ordered, "Now hold it tightly, exactly so." Next he picked up a heavy mallet, the surface of which had been coarsely roughened, raised it high, aimed carefully, and smashed it against the extended arm between block and shoulder. There came simultaneously a sickening mushy sound and a dull crack as the neck of the humerus shattered.

Don Henrique shuddered but managed to say, "And now the hand."

This time the block was moved toward the table edge and von Tetlow's hand held firmly so that the wood's edge was just under the second knuckle joints of the fingers. Again the mallet smashed down, to a sharp cracking sound as of many splintering twigs, as bones and tendons gave way. Now the fingers bent hideously back at right angles to the hand.

Don Henrique's face was white and shiny with sweat. "You have earned your pay very well. I think I shall step outdoors for a little air." He turned to go, then stopped to say, "Yes, and one more thing. Do not mend those fingers too well. We do not want our patient to have to forge any checks for a long, long time. I am so pleased that I thought of that. It is for his own good, but I doubt he will be appreciative."

Twelve hours later, von Tetlow was suffering the nausea and misery that generally follow ether. His right hand and upper arm and chest were heavily bandaged. His whole right side throbbed with exquisite pain. Well, one thing was sure, he would not have to prove whether he could properly swing a golf club, or anything else, and it would be months before he could even try to write. He reached up with his good hand, touched his face. Here, too, was dressing running from cheekbone to cheekbone across his upper lip. He found it hard to move his mouth. Forced to admit that his new masters were very thorough, he was almost glad that the Don had not told him everything the surgeon had planned to do.

Four days later he said good-bye to Don Henrique. Jovially, the Don slapped him on his good shoulder. *"Adios, amigo. Vaya con Dios.* Certainly we will be hearing from you many times. I trust it does not become necessary that you hear from us. That would be bad. Oh, very bad."

Von Tetlow had asked several times how he was to communicate but had been told, "You will learn this only after you have arrived and are considered to be—how do you say?—in security."

The flight north had been smooth and uneventful and had provided time for careful thought, and thought was essential. Von Tetlow managed to force himself into a calm, analytical state of mind in order carefully to review his position. He was embarked on a mission of high-level espionage, one which had and still seemed fantastically improbable. Within a few hours he would walk into Storrow's house and assume the acquaintanceships, the routines and the work of another man, and he was to do so without raising so much as a flicker of suspicion. He was to listen to, even participate in, the most secret deliberations of the top rulers of another country and report on them to the Soviet espionage apparatus, and do so undetected in a jittery, ultra-security-conscious milieu. The odds against him were suicidal.

Was there a way out? Why should he go along with this dangerous charade? Suppose he went to the authorities, to the FBI? Suppose he told them the whole incredible story? Would they believe him? Was there any way he could prove the truthfulness of his account? Of course there was. He could let them take his fingerprints, to compare with those of the true Roger Storrow. He could remove his contact lenses. He could not, however, really tell them where Storrow was held prisoner, since he himself knew only that it was in some house within twenty miles of Merida in Mexico. Further, he, unlike Storrow, had never learned his host's name.

But having told the authorities, then what? Who was he but a man without a country, or identity of any kind, except the spurious one he had assumed. Could he answer, when asked, "Who are you then," with "I don't really know" or "I won't tell you." He could do the former, of course, but to what useful end? None, he feared, except to keep himself alive—and most probably in prison. If he were not jailed, and were permitted to live somewhere in relative freedom, he had no doubt that the agents of the Aparat would quickly run him to earth.

There was another possibility. Perhaps the FBI would want him to go along with the scheme as if nothing had happened; that is, act as a double agent and report also to them. Yes, possible, but not likely. Would or could the FBI use a man of unproven identity? He could see little reason for his fingerprints to have been transmitted to Washington by any military authorities or by the Israeli. If they had, he would, of course, be finished. This would likewise be true if he decided to admit his actual identity. Even the weak and tolerant Americans, even to penetrate or to save themselves from a top level Russian spy ring, would not use him. They would not in their own country, at least, use former Colonel of the SS Karl Friedrich von Tetlow, a wanted war criminal and murderer. Yes, if they found out who he was, he would be finished.

He shifted uncomfortably in his seat. His hand and shoulder ached horribly. Damn those people anyhow! But suppose the American authorities were actually willing to use an unknown man as a double agent? Obviously they couldn't, the government could not permit him freely to transmit reports of its top secret deliberations and plans. The best that could be allowed would be a much watered-down version of the most important discussions. This would eventually, in fact probably quite soon, result in suspicion by the Aparat. Suspicion would quickly become certainty, then he would either be exposed as von Tetlow or summarily executed as a traitor to the Aparat. He rather thought the second alternative the more probable.

No, there was only one thing to do. At least he had one possible advantage, he thought. What he had to do would not be done from convictions or loyalties. His emotions would not be involved. His aim would be the most basic in the world: avoid suspicion, carry out the job and stay alive. He did not want to die.

He rang for the stewardess, to order a cold martini—one American institution of which he heartily approved. He watched her appreciatively as she leaned across the empty aisle seat to adjust his tray. "Would you like your lunch right away, Mr. Storrow, or later?"

"Later, my dear. I'll want another of these first. Can't fly on one wing, you know." He wondered if he sounded as affected in speech as he felt. No, probably not, and anyway the stiffness of his facial muscles somewhat blurred his accent. Of course, Roger Storrow might have sounded affected when he talked that way, but the manner had been wholly natural to that man. By God, it had come to seem so with him.

The stewardess returned with a fresh drink, her eyes sympathetic. Glancing at the black mourning band on his sleeve, she began, "I'm sorry about . . ." then thought better of it and studied instead the sling, the heavy bandages. "We're having steak, Mr. Storrow. Would you like me to cut up your meat for you?"

His left hand, moving to touch his moustache, met only adhesive tape. Quickly halting the futile gesture, he smiled ruefully. "Yes, my dear. You'd best do that. And afterward, bring me a pillow, and then tuck me in so that I can sleep a bit. It would be nice to have you tuck me in any time."

With stern crispness, "Yes, sir, Mr. Storrow. I've got to tend to the other passengers now. . . ." To herself she said, Some of these old men, especially the VIPs, who do they think they're impersonating anyway? Really!

It was a strange sensation setting foot in a country studied so intensively but never seen before. Even his intense preparation did not make him feel at home in the rush, the pressure, the loud, harsh-sounding voices. His tension was heightened by the fact that he was the first escorted off the plane and that several reporters were present. However, he kept in character. This time it was easy. He had reasons for disliking reporters. He brushed rudely by the newsmen, snapping, "Nothing now, dammit, nothing at all. Except, it's indecent even to ask. You're just vultures."

One turned to his colleague, "Stuck-up bastard hasn't changed a bit."

"Yes, but after all his wife died, you know. Hit-and-run. Can't blame him if he's broken up."

"Sure, but he could still be a little human just once. One thing's for sure, vacation did him no good."

"Busted his shoulder all to hell, I hear."

"Too bad it wasn't his neck."

"You, my friend, are a man without charity, so you will escort me to a bar for a drink. Perhaps we'll invent a nice interview for his stuck-up excellency."

At immigration and through customs von Tetlow kept his left hand clenched in his pocket. He was afraid it would tremble. Here was the first test. Had anything gone wrong? Would any suspicion be aroused? Would he really get away with it?

With great politeness and deference he was whisked through the formalities. After all, his luggage, his clothes, his passport, his vaccination certificate, his very name, belonged to an important Washington personage.

Waiting for him was a tall mulatto, immaculate in chauffeur's uniform. "Welcome home, Mr. Storrow, sah. Your car is directly in front of the entrance. I shall take care of the porters. Do you require any help, sah?"

"Thanks, no. I'll manage." This, obviously, was the very well-trained James, officially George William Gordon Chapman of Jamaica, houseman, butler and chauffeur; unofficially, Jim Chapman of the Communist Aparat, USA.

CHAPTER VIII

SOMEWHERE IN MEXICO Roger Storrow was far from happy. Some hours ago he had almost shaken off his drug-induced daze. His head still ached, however, and his mouth was desperately dry. His hands were cold and damp with sweat. Bright light hurt his eyes, and it hurt him to think. It was superhumanly difficult to maintain a coherent train of thought. Coherent! Good Lord, he wasn't even able to reconstruct with any accuracy what had happened yesterday, much less the day before.

It was obvious that he had been heavily dosed with narcotics. He remembered, awakening, as through the fog, a dreamlike sequence of questions. What in hell had they been asking him about? Some of the questions came back: his reading habits, his choice of restaurants and of foods, the idiosyncrasies of his friends and associates. Not, dammit, that he really had many close friends. A man in his position had to walk too much alone, keep himself aloof. It was Marjorie who had the friends—as well as quite a few enemies: poor Marjorie, at times she had quite an acid tongue.

Poor Marjorie: my God, now it came back! He had been kidnapped and held by that big moustachioed bastard. Ransom had been asked. Had he paid it? He could not remember. How long ago had that been? He must find out. What day was it today? He had no idea. He looked about his room; neither newspaper nor calendar, nothing of any help. He slipped on the silk dressing-gown draped over the footboard of the bed, knotted its cord, and went to the door. It

71

was locked again, dammit. Angrily he stabbed at the bell-push.

Footsteps sounded almost at once, and there was the sound of a key in the lock. A man stood courteously in the entrance. Well, at least he knew who this was. It was José.

"You have rung, *señor?*"

"No, I fired a cannon. Oh, never mind. José, I have a taste in my mouth like dry horse-dung. I want much cold water, *pronto.*"

"*Si, señor.*"

"And, José, I want a newspaper."

"I am distressed, *señor.* We do not have a newspaper."

"Why in hell not?"

"Because, *señor,* I cannot read. Only Don Henrique brings a paper, and he is away."

"When does he come back?"

"He did not say, *señor.*"

"Oh, all right. What day is it, José?"

"This I know. It is Thursday."

"Good. Thursday the what, José?"

"Thursday the twenty-third, *señor.*"

"Thank you. Now run and get the water. And after that, please, some beer and something to eat."

José bowed slightly and left, locking the door behind him.

Roger jammed his hands into the dressing-gown pockets, and stared thoughtfully at his toes. The twenty-third—twenty-third of March, it had to be. But when had all this started? Dammit, he just couldn't remember. When had he landed in his damnable country? When had he been trapped into this half-life of hallucination? There was—he struggled with the idea for a moment—yes, of course, there was an easy way to find out; look at his plane ticket. It must still be in the pocket of his suit jacket. Which one had he worn? He flung open the door of the room's largest closet, tugged at the cord of the overhead light. His hand went out to the lapel of his brown tweed jacket on its hanger, turned it back. Suddenly he grasped the whole garment, carried it over to the window. What in hell, he wondered. It looked like his coat, same material, same color, same cut, but it wasn't his; he was sure.

72

He gave his other suits and jackets the same scrutiny. None were his; and none contained a tailor's label. Baffled, he turned to the dresser, jerked open its drawers. Shirts and ties were harder to differentiate, but he felt sure that none of these belonged to him. Nor was the briefcase on the desk his. It was identical in appearance, but the leather was a little too new, the gilt R.L.S. too free of scratches.

"Curiouser and curiouser," he muttered. "Now I wonder if I stare into a looking-glass who I am going to see; myself or the Mad Hatter?"

Again the turning key, and the stocky Mexican sidled in carrying a tray and set it down. "Here it is, *señor,* as you ordered."

"Here it is be damned. José, where are my clothes, my briefcase?"

A puzzled smile, a slight shrug. "But where would you, *señor?* Here in this room, where they have been always."

"No they're not. Look at this, and this. You know bloody well these are not mine. Now, where are they? Quick, or I'll . . ." Although still weak, he managed to stride forward purposefully.

José had not seemed to move. He still smiled, but in his right hand glittered a murderously pointed knife. *"Por favor, señor,* do not become excited—do not cause yourself to be harmed."

Roger recognized the intelligence of this suggestion.

"Señor," José continued, "you are not yourself. These are clearly your belongings. This is not a house of thieves. Now I must go. *Adios, señor."*

"More like Kafka than Carroll," muttered Roger, continuing his search of the room. "Not a house of thieves, by God, no—just kidnappers, knife experts, dope users and, yes, thieves, too. Passport gone, wallet but not cash missing, traveller's checks gone, vaccination certificate gone. And grandfather's old turnip watch and chain. What in pluperfect hell would they want with that? Lord, I'm tired. I've got things to do, but I just can't think. Better go back to sleep a little while. Think about them later. Can't do anything now anyway, not till that S.O.B. comes back."

Don Henrique did not return for two days. Roger had more than ample time to think. There was little to do except walk back and forth in the locked-in garden, attempt to read some heavy Spanish philosophical dissertations, eat, sleep and wonder.

Roger's was a logical mind, and the illogical irritated him. What was not logical was wrong, and everything was wrong about this setup.

He finally remembered that he had made no arrangements to raise ransom money, that after the first few days there had not even been any further demand for it. There had been the druggings and interminable questionings under their influence. As well as he could recall, these had no bearing on a kidnapping or a ransom demand. What about the business of the clothes and passport? He remembered a few questions on secret matters within his own sphere of knowledge, but only a few. It really had not been, although it might yet become, a brain-washing for some foreign espionage ring, Soviet most likely. No one else would have that much interest, or take the risk of abducting him. He did not think, even now, that they could get away with it much longer.

March 25. He was already two days later than his scheduled return. Washington soon would become worried and then all sorts of Mexican hell would break loose. They certainly couldn't keep him hidden for ever. Of course, if the official heat became too great, his body could later be regretfully discovered festering near some jungle-infested Mayan city's ruins. It was an unpleasant thought.

He stopped his pacing, scratched a thumbnail across a match to light a long thin cigar and sat down on a stone bench. Good, these cigars were still his own: no imitation or substitution here.

Now he would start all over again and reason this thing through step by step. There had to be an explanation that would make sense, some purpose or plan behind what was happening to him. There was an explanation, there had to be.

Dimly he realized that there was a conceivable solution which could fit most of the known facts. But it was too fantastic to be seriously considered, not now, at any rate.

His meditation was interrupted by José bringing him

74

several letters. "Excuse me, *señor*, but I have obtained your mail from the Hotel Central. They might begin to question again where you were, to where it must be sent. I have no instructions from Don Henrique otherwise, so I give it to you."

"You're too kind. Now get out of my sight."

"*Si, señor. Muchas gracias, señor.*"

Roger slit open the envelopes, studied the letters. One was a chatty note from his friend Nunez, mostly about his projected expedition to Baja California. There were two personal letters forwarded to him from his office by the efficient Miss Kelly. There was none, he noted a little surprised, from Marjorie. She was usually a regular correspondent. Oh, well, that was when she was away visiting. He had never managed to get away for very long alone, at least not until now.

Here was one from the Old Colony Trust—some advertisement or announcement, no doubt. He started to tear it up, then paused. No, Kelly would not have bothered mailing a circular to him in Merida. Might be something important. He took out the letter and read: "This is to advise you that in accordance with your instructions of the fourteenth, we have this day mailed to the Institucion Archaelogica de Cordobal y Guzman our certified check for the sum of $25,000."

Impossible! He knew, beyond a shadow of a doubt now, that he had written no such letter. Drugged or not, he knew it and that was that. If not, then who could have done this and got away with it? The letter was signed by Stanley Adams, whom he knew and who knew his signature well. Forgery, most expert forgery, had been required in this instance.

His clothes, his wallet and passport, the detailed medical and dental examination—now this forgery. Almost automatically his logical mind slipped the last piece of the puzzle into place. It fitted perfectly. "By the beard of the prophet, that's what they're trying to do, all right. But it's impossible. Just plain cold roast impossible. And the bastards are financing this experiment with my money." He flipped his cigar butt toward some bushes. "Now I don't think they even need me alive."

"Talking with yourself, Señor Storrow?" Roger swung

75

around abruptly. Damn, for a big man Don Henrique could move softly. "It is very bad so to talk to yourself. But you are wrong. We do indeed need you alive."

"Glad to hear it. But whatever for?"

"Because just now some more questions arrive to which we must have answers."

"I'll answer no more questions, not one."

"Ah, but you will. Just as you have before."

Roger strode over to stand close to the man, facing him directly. "Listen, Don whoever the hell you are, this is stupid! Your man, who wears my best tweed suit, will be unmasked the minute he sets foot in Washington. You're insane even to think of it. He'll never get away with it, not in a million years!"

The big man idly stroked the left side of his moustache, then smiled. "My congratulations to your government for having chosen so brilliant a man. So, you have discovered what we are doing and do not believe we will succeed. I think that you are wrong. We have gambled some of your very nice money that you are wrong, and that I am right."

CHAPTER IX

VERY HAPPY AT seeing her employer return to Washington, Mary Margaret was almost tearful in her sympathy with his tragic personal loss. She fussed and fretted over his injuries and was overly attentive. *I do wish she would stop looking at me like a sick cow,* von Tetlow thought more than once. *I'm certainly glad Storrow wasn't having an affair with this one. To step into such shoes would be more than I could bear.*

He soon found that the masses of paper, repetitive paragraphs, cumbersome sentences and weasel words he was forced to read and digest were, likewise, almost more than he could bear. The documents were crammed with fine Washington Officialese, such as finalize, implement, program, allocate. All governments were alike in this love of verbiage, he imagined. But this one seemed to be more so. It was fortunate for him that he had closely studied Storrow under questioning about the minutiae of the routine of his office.

How many hours had he spent in all, he wondered, studying that Bostonian through one-way mirrors? A simple but useful device, the one-way mirror, both in espionage and counterespionage. He remembered reading about the Duquesne spy ring which the FBI had had under surveillance in New York. For weeks they had been trying to identify a woman operative of that ring. Then one day she had walked right up to the van in which Bureau agents were concealed, and used the mirror in its side to touch up her lipstick. The agents had been able to obtain a close-up photograph.

These mirrors had other uses, blackmail for instance. And there was the famous Paris story of the man magnificently

77

entertained, and for free, in a luxurious brothel. Nights later at the same address the entertainment had been as excellent, but the bill presented to him by the madam was enormous. The explanation had been, "But, monsieur, tonight you were not on television."

He thought now about the three days he had spent in Washington before he had first visited his office in the magnificent ugliness of Old State. It was a beautiful city, with large, cleanly designed government buildings, shiningly white monuments and memorials, broad avenues radiating from the Capitol, seemingly symmetrical streets gridironing the area. He remembered the basic plan was that of Pierre l'Enfant, who had done the same for Paris. The idea was that barricades and cannons could be placed at the outward termini of the avenues to defend against attack from any direction. If retreat should become necessary the result would be an ever more powerful concentration of defenses as the enemy neared the hub of the wheel. This scheme had seemed most desirable, especially after the British burned Washington. Today it created only chaos.

Synchronization of traffic lights was nearly impossible, and even where possible was not in effect. One block at a time was good progress, during rush hours half a block. Some streets were one way at certain times of day, reversed at others, and both ways in between. Certain streets and avenues proceeded uninterrupted for a commendable number of blocks, then vanished behind some obstruction, a bank, a park—even the White House—to reappear some distance later heading in a different direction.

There were also the traffic rotaries. One in particular combined the worst features of them all, Dupont Circle. Here even a pedestrian had to negotiate no less than six control lights in order to advance one hundred yards. Never did any light read "walk" at the same time as the one preceding it. Sometimes, as on Connecticut Avenue, the authorities arranged for the green light and "don't walk," the red light and "walk" to coincide. All in all, with the advent of high-powered automobiles and sleek air-conditioned buses, the rate of flow of traffic, as officially timed, had fallen to half the rate customary in the days of horse-drawn vehicles.

And von Tetlow quickly discovered that with the advent of telecommunications, IBM machines, electric typewriters, computers and motorized messengers, the rate of flow of effective governmental operations had slowed to a much smaller percentage than that obtained in the days of mounted messengers and quill pens. The reasons were much the same.

He had concluded that there was nothing to fear from the routine of his office—or from Mary Margaret Kelly, at least not yet.

The details of bureaucratic red tape he took in his stride. It was quite another matter contemplating his first meeting with the National Security Council (which, as almost everything else in Washington, was referred to only by its initials). Here would sit the President and/or Vice-President of the nation, the Secretaries of State and of Defense, the Attorney-General, the Directors of the CIA and FBI and probably the chiefs of the Departments of Interior and Labor. Certain other high officials would be present only when specifically invited, and, normally, it would be his decision as to when this should be.

He was, as Roger Storrow, in charge of arranging and putting forth the agenda for each meeting and of deciding who outside the cabinet should be asked to attend. No mean task, that, although over the years certain procedures had become automatic. With this new group now in power things might very well change. As Storrow, he knew only three or four: the President and the Secretary of State slightly, the Director of the CIA quite well, and, of course, the Director of the FBI. Likewise he was acquainted with Charlie Joyce, a permanent fixture for internal security matters and a graduate of the FBI.

The thought of the presence of these last two was unpleasant. They were in the tradition of the security policeman everywhere, whether Guardia Civil, Sureté Nationale or Gestapo; they would trust no one and be suspicious of everything. From diplomats, and especially from purely political appointees, he felt he had nothing or very little to fear. To them, civilian or military permanent government personnel, however high their rank, were simply part of the decor, pieces of interchangeable furniture. Newly created VIPs were

79

sensitive mostly to the kudos of their new roles and to the effect they themselves were producing on others.

At least he would not have to walk in on this august group after it had already assembled. It was his duty to be there first with all relevant documents. With his arm in a sling, he would not have to shake hands. Newly and tragically bereaved, he would be expected to speak less than usual, to participate less in any social chatter or even official discussions.

He looked at the clock on his desk, 8:47; then in automatic distrust at his wristwatch. There was no disagreement. Nor was there any more time for delay. He swallowed twice, moistened his lips with his tongue, pushed away from his desk. "The Hand of Time moves, Kelly old girl, so I'm off to the wars." His words sounded forced, undoubtedly they were. Mary Margaret Kelly, however, did not notice this, at least not consciously, and not then. She gazed after him a little anxiously as he walked away not quite in balance. It must be damned awkward, she thought, to have one arm strapped tight to one's side.

As always, the meeting was held in the White House. The council room was much like the boardroom office of any large corporation, and lay between the offices of the President himself and that of the number one presidential assistant. All participants sat at a long rectangular table. Each had his designated place. That occupied by Roger Storrow was near the center of the side to the President's right, close by that of the Vice-President. The chair directly next to the Chief Executive, at his right hand, was for the Secretary of State. Von Tetlow had no trouble remembering this as he neatly stacked the various papers on the table top.

The first council member to enter was recognized by von Tetlow, but he was not too well known by Roger Storrow. This was the Vice-President. They exchanged greetings briefly. Next came the Secretary of State, who spoke a few words of sympathy. Then one by one the others, including Charlie Joyce, whose contribution was a quick smile and a pat on von Tetlow's good arm. Last of the group to enter was the Director of the FBI. The two men merely nodded to each other. The German knew that the Director had never liked the man he called "that Back Bay Brahmin, Sir Roger Storrow."

80

Von Tetlow now felt a little more relaxed, although there was still a sense of being on stage in an unreal world. Here around this table were those faces, those personalities, he had studied so hard and so long in detailed intelligence studies and from Roger Storrow's mind. He found it difficult not to stare at any of the noted figures. He felt that they must, they had to be, staring at him; but they were not. They were chattering with each other or studying the papers before them.

Then, as if on cue, at exactly one minute to nine the rear door, closed until now, swung open. Everyone rose to their feet as the President of the United States strode briskly into the room. Then came a terrifying moment. Immediately after his "Good morning, gentlemen," the Chief Executive walked straight to von Tetlow, rested a hand lightly on his good shoulder and looked directly, sympathetically into his face. How hard it was then to return the gaze. "I'm sorry, Roger. So is Elaine. We'll have you to dinner soon, just the few of us," then a sigh, "if those bastards ever give us a chance to relax."

My God, he thought, that will be the real ordeal. That is asking too much from me, far too soon. Then he remembered what he had been told. The President, like many others in high places, or low, often issued general invitations, letting them die on the vine. His efficient wife, Elaine, and his appointment secretary saw to this. So von Tetlow answered his thanks, and if his voice sounded a little strained, it was not surprising—not with that plaster across his face, and after all that he had been through.

The session itself lasted over two hours and was followed for most of them by an unappetizing lunch in the White House Mess—the subject of many poor jokes. Still, it was surprising how insipid the food, how unimaginative the menu. Von Tetlow wondered if this was to pacify the political opposition, which he knew often screamed about extravagance. Austerity and frugality were popular only when practiced by others.

The hours after lunch seemed interminable, even with their mass of paperwork, condolence letters to be answered, personal phone calls ranging from sympathy to importunity.

Two of these had made him nervous. Despite his incredibly thorough briefing he had, under the day's frightening stress, forgotten whether these two men were to be addressed formally or by nicknames.

He had been called on his first error. "My God, Roger, since when have you become so stuffy? 'Mr. Secretary,' indeed! When you know damned well I'm only a high level consultant. You know that's the part played by the castrated tomcat."

Quickly he apologized, not too quickly, he hoped. "Sorry, old boy. I was a long way off. So much has happened . . ." and he let the sentence die off. His caller had understood that a bereaved man may be somewhat distrait.

On the second call he had avoided the issue of the first name and had been friendly and informal. After that he instructed his secretary, "From now on today, unless it's the President, not a damned call. Much too busy." Covertly he studied Miss Kelly. She was looking at him in understanding sympathy.

"Of course, Mr. Storrow. I don't blame you a little bit. I'll growl at them for you."

So far, so good. Evidently he had acted in character.

Returned at last to his house in Georgetown, he gratefully accepted a large drink from James Chapman. Then he carefully studied the miniature recorder the Jamaican had left upon his desk ."Very nice camouflage if I may say so, sah."

It was indeed. In size, shape and finish it was an exact replica, even to the words engraved, of a silver cigarette case Roger Lowell Storrow had won in a medal play tournament at Chevy Chase. It was also a triumph of workmanship and electronic sensitivity. It could pick up and record low-pitched conversations up to fifty feet away. But now he learned from James that for a while it would be worthless for its intended purpose. "But the man said you'd best not use it, sah, not at all till you are sure there's no counter-bugs in the room."

"What the devil are counter-bugs?"

"Devices, sah, to tell whether some recorder they don't want is operating."

"How do they work?"

82

"Maybe someone will tell you, sah. All I know is they do. Maybe you'll ask. It's not an unreasonable question for you."

"Right now it is, most unreasonable."

A verbatim transcript of the National Security Council meeting was out, at least for a while. Well, there had been an awful lot of important words, some idle conversation. Most of it would only confuse the Kremlin, even if they wanted it. Of course, the actual voices of the participants, rather than just a summary, would be a guarantee of the genuineness of the material. Too bad. For the time being his own report would have to do. At least it would use up less of the hair-thin wire of his recorder.

He might as well get to work while the morning's discussions were fresh in his mind. He pushed the concealed button on the case, held the silver surface to his ear. Only a small humming whirr was noticeable. He had to force himself into dictation. He had always felt an idiot doing this when no one else was present. "March 27, nine a.m., the following were present. . ."

Von Tetlow had a fine, analytical brain. He was possessed of an excellent memory. Still, this morning he had been under such pressure, he had not been too successful as a human tape recorder. Perhaps he should have made notes first. But notes, even with James Chapman to clean up after him, were dangerous. Notes could even be fatal.

He turned off the machine, sat back to think. There had been guarded reference to a new super-high-altitude reconnaissance vehicle, much better than the U-2. The Director of the CIA had hushed this. "That we can pass over for the moment. It will be taken up at a different session."

The Attorney-General had objected, "But, Arthur, if it's something like that—I mean, we all have the right . . ."

The CIA man stopped him, "No one, Ted, has any right. Just some of us *must* know."

The President had spoken, "Arthur is right. That's that. Let's go on."

Yes, that was a most interesting item for Moscow. He would dictate the whole conversation as accurately as possible. He pressed the button once more, talked for about three minutes, then changed to the subject of developing plans to influence the new African nations. These he summarized briefly.

They called to mind that there had been quite a lengthy discussion of segregation matters and some of the proposed steps to improve the situation. Almost all present felt that some progress had already been made, that things were much better, but that the back of the problem was not yet broken. He discarded these details. Obviously Moscow would not be interested. There was no new propaganda material here. He contented himself with saying simply that the President and the Attorney-General were concerned about some new civil rights legislation.

Then had come discussion of the military budgets, but nothing of importance that had not already appeared in the press. No, that was not quite true. There was something. It had become clear to him that the Secretary of Defense did not like the Chairman of the Joint Chiefs, and that the converse was also true. "You're just a typical, narrow-minded West Pointer. You can't see the over-all picture." "Damn the over-all picture. You civilians," almost as if it were a dirty word, "won't be seeing any picture at all, won't even have time to crawl into your plush shelter, unless we get the anti-missile gadget going—and damned quick."

Yes, there was something of interest here. A sharp propaganda wedge could be driven into this breach. Its effect would be felt all over the country.

Ten minutes later he was finished. He opened the case, severed the wire and removed the tiny spool. Slipping it into a sateened jeweller's box, he locked the box in his desk. It could wait until tomorrow, when James could tell him where and how to mail it. Right now he needed the Jamaican for other reasons. He wanted to enjoy a hot bath and a nap, and in his crippled state James was required in his role of valet. Another drink was then called for, then a respectable dinner at—where was that good restaurant? La Parisienne. He felt that, even though recently widowed, Roger Lowell Storrow would have been entitled to a decent meal after the White House Mess.

La Parisienne had a reputation as the finest restaurant in

Washington, or for that matter as one of the finest anywhere. Von Tetlow remembered his enforced Moscow and Mexican studies in this field. Strangely, the capital of the so-called free world merely tolerates a really first-class eating place, just as it does a legitimate theater, an opera and a symphony orchestra. Scarcely anyone who actually resides in the District is interested, and even if interested cannot afford such places. Members of the various diplomatic missions can appreciate but can rarely afford. What is more, they can dine more sumptuously and at much cheaper rates at someone else's home. Those who could afford and might appreciate it and who live in Maryland and Virginia rarely make the evening trip into the city. In sum, this is not a big city, it is a big provincial town, a majority of whose residents are Negroes.

So far these observations had seemed almost entirely justified. How Storrow had endured the city for so long he could not imagine, unless it was because of the interesting people he met, the sense of urgency and movement. This, he supposed, would have appealed greatly to the late Marjorie Storrow.

It was a chill, gusty evening, but not an unpleasant one, and it was a reasonable walk to the restaurant. He enjoyed going there on foot along the bumpy brick sidewalks of Georgetown between its trees and squat buildings. None higher than a few stories were permitted. He strode along, able to see through the bare branches the small futile clouds driven by the wind across the bright surface of a partial moon, the still dim newness of the early stars.

He was not disappointed in the restaurant. The decor was pleasing—good murals, some of them by the proprietor himself—the lighting neither glaring nor dim. He was greeted with obviously real pleasure and respect by Paul, the *maître d'hôtel,* who led him to what must have been Storrow's regular table and deftly removed the second cover. He turned to the waiter beside him, *"Un martini tres sec pour Monsieur Storrow, et tout de suite."*

It was delicious, icy cold and crystal clear. Much the best drink of the day, this one just before dinner, he thought. It was such a good martini that he ordered a second, then steak with pepper sauce, an endive salad and a Beaujolais '59. Thank heaven that Roger Storrow was a man of good taste and good appetite. But it was somehow humiliating to have another carve his meat for him. By the time he had asked for black coffee and brandy, he felt much happier. He even glowed a little inwardly.

To tell the truth, von Tetlow was a trifle drunk—a thing he rarely allowed himself and which he certainly should not have permitted now. He looked about the place, at the other diners in chatting groups or attentive couples. There was a damned fine-looking woman over there, reddish blonde, nice white shoulders rising from black satin. He felt he should know who she was. Anyway, he was certain she was much too good for the swarthy man who must be her escort. He probably was as rich as Croesus and responsible for the diamond bracelet on her right wrist. Some needed to have money, whereas he. . . . Oh, blast it anyhow. This was going to be a long, dull business, as well as dangerous. And it was going to be a very lonely one, especially at night. He signalled to Paul to bring him another brandy.

Gazing pensively toward the bar-end of the room, he recognized that something expected was no longer missing. The blonde in black had risen to greet four new arrivals. Obviously this was Monique. Once cashier, now official hostess, she was virtually manager and the major attraction of the place. He remembered some of what he had been told. "She has more real friends than almost anyone else in Washington. Most of the wives like her. They have no cause for jealousy since she is entirely faithful to one man at a time."

He studied her carefully as she escorted the quartet to a table. Hers was a lovely figure, and there was allure in her walk. Having seated the late arrivals, she turned in his direction, red-blonde hair upswept and shining, lips breaking into a welcoming smile. She slipped into the chair beside his. "Welcome home, Monsieur Storrow. How good to see you." She placed a warm hand on his arm. "And I am so desolate for you. But best we do not talk of these things." Her eyes met his in sympathy, "And you are badly wounded. They did not tell me of this."

"Hello, Monique. I am glad to see you too. Yes, I was stupidly clumsy in Mexico. I'll recover. How lovely you look. Will you have a drink with me?"

86

"No, Monsieur Storrow, not with you. You will have a drink with me. You have been away too long." She snapped her fingers, *"René, ici, deux verres."*

Perhaps it was this added glass, perhaps it was perfume, body or smile, perhaps it was only long absence from woman. Perhaps it was all three; but certainly it was not intelligence. Whatever it was, von Tetlow grasped her arm too hard, leaned toward her too purposefully, let too much desire flavor his speech. "Please come back to my place after closing, Monique, and I'll give you a beautiful brandy."

Monique drew away, "But, Monsieur Storrow, you know my friend would not permit this. I am surprised at you."

Suddenly, almost soberly, he recognized that the withdrawal was real, the surprise genuine. Actually the girl was shocked. He was Roger Lowell Storrow of Boston, and a widower for only a few weeks. There was a cold weakness in the pit of his stomach as he realized he had made more than a trifling social mistake.

More than once Monique glanced at him as he paid his bill and was helped into his coat. She thought, *"Mon Dieu,* but this is strange. He does not seem at all to be himself."

CHAPTER X

HE HAD MADE up his mind. However fantastic the scheme for his impersonation, it really existed. Roger knew now that Don Henrique was deadly serious. The efficiency of those who had planned and executed his abduction was impressive. And he was aware that during the weeks since that event they had studied him minutely. The examination by the doctor and dentist told him they must have duplicated his dental work and his scars. They were in possession of his clothes, luggage, wallet, passport and pocket watch. But why all this? What impelled the man? What compulsion, or what unknown pressures had driven the Mexican to such extremes, to take so wild a gamble?

What did they have in mind anyway? A murder in Washington, a theft of secret documents, the scandal of a single great security leak? It seemed clear that it could only be one act, a hit-and-run affair of some sort. The impersonator obviously could not get away with it for more than a few hours. He would immediately give himself away to at least two people, the very first time they saw him. Even at a distance Marjorie would recognize the fraud. Even if she was a poor correspondent, she was not . . .

Horror struck him. Marjorie! It was too long since he had heard from her. He had written her only a few letters, those carefully edited by Don Henrique. This had begun as soon as the kidnapping for ransom charade had been dropped. She should have answered at least one. What could have happened? There was no way in which this impersonator could possibly escape detection if once he were seen by Marjorie.

Then they must—No! They couldn't have gone that far. They wouldn't have dared.

Coldly, furiously, he analyzed that idea. Yes, they would dare. An organization which, at a public airport in a free country, could cold-bloodedly kidnap a special assistant to the President of the United States would dare almost anything. But Marjorie, poor dear lonely Marjorie. Somehow he must find out. He had to. He started toward the door, to ring the bell, had already raised his hand. No. If he found out what he feared, he would try to kill Don Henrique with his bare hands. But that would be useless. Even if he could kill the man, he would then never find a way to escape from this prison, might, in fact, very well end up dead himself. He must swallow his desperate anger. He must think. He turned from the door, dropped heavily into a chair, bowed his head in his hands. For just a little while he wept.

Neither grief, nor violence, nor fear, however, was a luxury he could afford. He had one important job to do, escape. It was important now. He needed, however, quite a long time to think. Long thought always brought him to the same line of reasoning. Unarmed and locked in, he must find the human key to open the hacienda doors. He must therefore find and attack a basic weakness of one man's nature. Obviously the place to begin was with one of his jailers, the one who seemed the least strong. He rose from his chair. This time there was no hesitation. He rang for José.

Courteous, smiling as always, the short, powerful man bowed his entrance, "The *señor* desires?"

"Come in, José. The señor is thirsty and needs a drink. The señor is bored and wishes to talk. Bring me first a very cold beer—and, of course, one for yourself."

"As you wish, *señor,* at once."

He returned in less than two minutes with the beer and glasses. Prisoner and jailer toasted each other. "*Salud y pesetas y amor*—health, money and love and life long enough to enjoy them.

"The *señor* said he wished to talk with me."

"I did indeed." Roger offered him one of his cigarettes, which the man eagerly accepted. "José, are you of the Church?"

A nod of the glistening dark head, "But of course."

"Then listen carefully. I, too, am of the Church, where we worship the same God. This God says that the family is a good thing in his eyes. He ordains that a man stay with his wife and family and protect them. He says that it is a sin for a man to leave them. Is it not the same with your God?"

"Precisely so, *señor*."

"Then if a man forces another to leave his wife, to go away from her and leave her unprotected and alone, this man then is causing a sin in the eyes of God. Do you follow me?"

"With ease, *señor*." A quick, mirthless grin. "You argue that in helping keep you locked up in this hacienda I, José Mateos, commit a sin. This is so. But," with a shrug of dismissal, "I am afraid there are already many sins to my name. For these the priests promise me I will have much suffering in the next world. *Señor,* I am a poor man, a worthless one, yet Don Henrique pays me to obey. If I do not, then there will be nothing to eat for me or the little ones. He would tell the police about me and I would go to prison, a bad thing, *señor*. Or perhaps he would have me killed."

"Listen some more, José. You have heard that I am a rich man, correct?"

"This I have heard."

"Well, then, I can make you rich also. I can give you here five hundred North American dollars since that is all I have with me. Then you help me leave here. You will have helped me go back to my family. This is a good deed and cancels a sin. Once free I can pay you more. Then you can feed your little ones. Also, you can give to the Church. Then, I am sure, your priest will reduce your promised suffering. This is how it works, no?"

José gently rubbed his hands together. *"Si, señor,* you are correct. I am a poor man as I have said, but this is a most dangerous thing. Don Henrique can be most dangerous, most cruel. I would dare nothing unless he was far distant from here on some business. A question, *señor*."

"Yes?"

"How do I know that once escaped you will pay to me more? How do I know you will not go to the *policia?*"

"You don't know, José. If I give you the five hundred

dollars now, how do I know you will not just keep it and do nothing; or worse, keep it and tell Don Henrique that I tried to bribe you, his loyal servant?"

"You offend my honor, *señor*. If I take your money, I swear on the grave of my mother I will help you. My lips will be sewed closed."

Roger resisted the impulse to doubt aloud that José knew who was his true mother, never mind his father, or to comment on his offended honor. From the pocket of what was now his briefcase he dug out an envelope, and from this a thin sheaf of bills. "Here, José. I give you half now, because I trust you, the other half when you lead me free outside that gate, then much more later because you trust me."

José bowed politely, but his hand was quick and darting as it grabbed the proffered bills. "I must leave now, quickly. We have been too long together; someone might have questions why. *Adios, señor. Muchas gracias.*"

He bowed again, went to the door. Before opening it he turned his smile on Roger, "You will see, *señor*, that José is a trustworthy man—most trustworthy."

Alone, Roger thought, Trustworthy! Trustworthy indeed! I imagine he has a police record somewhere six feet long and that the big bastard holds it over him. Might even be wanted for murder. If I were a betting sort of fellow, I'd ask nice long odds on José. Had to try it though, only damned thing there was to do; might work out, might not.

Early that same evening Don Henrique made everyone's position crystal clear.

"I am not surprised, Señor Storrow. I am not even displeased. Of course you wish to escape. But this is most undesirable. Now that I see you will try, I must make it more impossible. I have now instructed José to carry a pistol. And he is, as he has said, most trustworthy. José!"

"*Si, señor.*"

"You will remove the personal belongings of our guest, all of them, and you will guard them well. The other dollars you will keep for yourself. You have earned them well."

"*Mil gracias.*"

199245

The big man stood for a moment, reflectively stroking his moustache. "And, José?"

"*Señor?*"

"You will also remove all the shoes of Señor Storrow. Yes, also those he wears. It is at this season far too hot for the walk. His trousers? For now I think we permit that he keeps his trousers, and his wristwatch. The passing of time is more interesting if it can be counted, and I do not wish that he should think that we are really thieves."

Until now Roger had been sitting. Now he rose to his feet. José's hand dropped to the butt of the revolver at his side. But Storrow simply stood ramrod straight and still, facing Don Henrique, his face now livid with lines of mortal anger.

"Yes, you are thieving bastards, filthy murderers of women, traitors. You're not fit to spit on."

Don Henrique raised a large hand. "Please, Señor Storrow, calm yourself. I am above insults. I do my job, you do yours."

"God damn your soul to hell." The violence in the voice, on the craggy face, made the bigger man recoil. Now Roger's voice dropped lower, the words became measured. "You, Don Henrique, if I find that what I believe is true, that my wife is dead, I swear to you that you will die. You will die at my hands. Then somehow I shall escape. So why don't you just kill me now?"

"I think not, Señor Storrow. We need you alive. There are certain details we must learn from you from time to time to help the man who, if you will pardon, is in your own shoes."

"Don Henrique, you're a fool. You're fools, all of you. Your man, as you call him, will be caught. So will you when they come to look for me. It's as simple as that."

Again the hand to the moustache. "Perhaps, who knows? But if the other Roger Storrow is too soon suspected, you will, as I have said, be of no more use and quickly dead. As for me, why Don Henrique will have ceased to exist. I can go far, and most happily, on what will be left of your 50,000 nice dollars."

"Not if the Aparat suspects you. You do belong, don't you? They do not like failures, old boy, nor what you say you

92

are not, thieves. You even stole my grandfather's gold watch. Why that, by God, why?"

Don Henrique shook his head. "You would not now believe me if I said I did not know. But I do not. So I tell you this. Yes, I am of the Aparat, and I follow orders, no matter how distasteful. And it was not I who harmed your *señora*. But if I am betrayed, then you, Señor Storrow, you will be food for the vultures and for the worms. *Buenas tardes, señor*."

It was a bad night. Grief and anger alternated with desperate and discarded plans for escape. He was very lonely, and could not help being afraid. Any company would have helped, especially that of a woman. He thought of Evita. But there was no woman, no Evita, for Roger Lowell Storrow, and there was no sleep—not until the stars were washed away and the pale gold of morning touched the bottom edge of the sky. But during that night he thought long and hard.

After José brought his breakfast tray, Roger removed the small alcohol lamp used to keep the coffee hot, and hid it in the bathroom cupboard. He would wait and see what happened next. When José came in to remove the empty dishes, he either did not notice the absence, or if he did notice, he did not care. The lovely North American dollars felt beautifully warm in his pocket. For once he had really been paid for being a most trustworthy servant.

James Chapman had stayed up to await von Tetlow's return. This was not because it was the duty of a proper houseman and valet but because he had been instructed to do so. In point of fact, he had stayed at the house until 11:15, then had driven the Storrow car the relatively few blocks to La Parisienne and spoken to the doorman, "Please inform Mr. Storrow that his car is waiting."

Von Tetlow had been annoyed. As a real Teuton, or bogus Argentinian or false Bostonian for that matter, when he said, "I will not need you any more tonight, James," he meant exactly that. Therefore he raised his voice. "Dammit, James, I gave you the night off. I don't want you following me around. I am quite capable of taking care of myself . . ."

But James took him quietly by the arm, exerting pressure at a point near the elbow and causing a numbing pain. "Yes, sah—very good, sah. I was afraid you had forgotten, sah, the late call you were expecting from the Secretary."

He tried to pull away, but the pain was too great. Meekly he began again to follow; the pressure relaxed. "Thank you, James. Did forget. Busy day and all that, you know."

"Here we are, Mr. Storrow. You will require the robe, sah. It has turned most chilly."

The doorman of La Parisienne did not think anything of this interchange. He did not ponder on it nor speak of it to anyone else. He was quite accustomed to VIPs who had drunk a little too much.

At home, James brought hot, black coffee to von Tetlow. There was now in his manner no deference whatever. "You will drink this and quickly."

"I don't need it. I'm quite sober now, you know."

"It is possible, but we have work to do."

"What d'you mean, work?"

"In the first place, I have the answers to questions about some people you meet with tomorrow. Mr. Storrow has been asked about them under drugs and gave the information. It is most important you should make no more mistakes like tonight."

If von Tetlow had felt a cold weakness in his bowels before, he now felt it again. "How do you mean, mistakes? How do you know?"

"It is a most serious mistake, Mr. Storrow. I call you Storrow so you will remember who you are. It is very bad to take too much drink. Also, I saw myself the face of Miss Monique. She has looked at you most strangely. We must repair this if possible. But there are some things I do not know all about."

"James, I don't believe it."

The Jamaican's face bore no trace of a smile. "This is not a joke. I do not make jokes."

He made no comment. No, it certainly was not a joke. Nor was it amusing to be lectured by this damned arrogant mulatto. He tightened his jaw, "And so?"

"And so, give me your silver case. There are a few things I

94

must add to your report, some more questions I must ask. Then I must get this in the last mail."

"Where will you mail it?"

"I will tell you when you need to know. Now, give me the case and listen carefully."

It was a strange feeling for von Tetlow to sit in what was in a way his own library while the houseman dictated an efficiency report on his master, a report detailing his value as a Communist agent in the United States. The most enraging part of the whole thing was that he knew that James was right about his mistakes in behavior and that he, a late Colonel of the Waffen SS, was wrong. Nevertheless, since he was himself a highly trained man, he forced himself to listen and to learn. And he learned well. He would never be conscious of making another mistake—none, that is, until he made his last. And even that would not be the result of failure to think, or of failure in judgment.

In his bedroom that night he was again reminded how worthwhile it was for him to avoid any such errors. On the table next to his bed still stood a silver-framed photo of a tall, distinguished girl in a wedding gown. He studied it closely. On the silver was engraved "M.J.S., June 11, 1957." Her only error had been to be in the way, and as a result she was buried now. She had been a member of a socialite family, in her own right of society, and the wife of a VIP. She had been removed so efficiently that no one had even questioned the manner of her passing—at least, not yet.

He, however, had no rights at all—not any. There were those on the side of the law who would welcome his passing, even in violence, as an act of overdue justice. The others, those of the Aparat, would crush him like a cockroach if he in any way endangered their plans or even seemed likely to embarrass them.

Von Tetlow did not sleep that night, not even when the murky Potomac sun rose slowly to chase away the much paler Northern stars.

CHAPTER XI

THE DAY, BORN surly, grew steadily worse. Clouds blocked out the sky, the wind grew more chill and cut more deeply. Eventually a sort of snow began to drive through the empty caverns of the Sunday streets. It was not a proper snow at all. It did not even look white. Rather, it was grayish and somehow dirty, like the day itself. It was a spiteful snow, stinging when it hit the face, freezing to dangerously slippery thin sheets of ice.

It was, in a way, lucky that it was Sunday, or else the massed traffic of the nation's capital would have slithered at last to immobility. The whole city, its trade and its government would have been paralyzed. As it was, suburban householders helplessly stalled their cars on very slight grades and thus avoided going to church. In fact, everyone who could find the slightest excuse escaped doing the things he should have done. It was the kind of day when most husbands and wives would have sat five rooms apart had they had the five rooms.

Weary and sleepless, von Tetlow could not escape. Furthermore, his eyes stung and scraped painfully as a result of his forgetting to remove those damnable contact lenses last night. But, weary or sleepless, freshly brighteyed or achingly hungover, the Storrows had always, at least in Washington, gone to church on Sundays, under the soaring, echoing masonry of the National Cathedral. So on this dreary, ice-swept day von Tetlow attended church, somberly as suited his state, returning nods and tentative smiles to those who nodded or smiled to him as he moved toward what James had told him was the Storrows' regular pew.

96

It was a strange feeling. It had been a long time since he had attended religious services. He found himself compelled to glance surreptitiously at his neighbors to discover when to stand, to sit or to kneel. He started to leaf through the unfamiliar hymnal and Book of Prayer for the proper verses, the right responses. Then he sensed that Roger Storrow would never have used textual aids. He would have known the words, known them since his second-form year at Groton, completely and never to forget. Quickly he slipped the book back to its rack and remained, henceforth, head slightly bowed, lips moving in silence.

It was now an empty ritual, a parroting of phrases, the repetition of ancient outworn forms. "Blessed are the meek." Well, millions of the meek had recently died. Because they were the meek? Perhaps. "Blessed are the peacemakers." Where were the peacemakers now? Then again, where were the makers of war, the warriors themselves, his beautiful father, for instance—blinded, despondent, now dead—or himself, or those who had been his leaders?

Then had come the sermon. He had tried not to listen. Sermonizers were men who say too easily what others can or must do. They could never do these things themselves. That's why, he felt, they were preachers. Nevertheless, words, sentences, flowed from the pulpit to strike against his ears, to penetrate unbidden to his brain. "He that serves only his needs, his own greeds, his own desires . . . whereas he that is indeed his brother's keeper . . . the brotherhood of man. He who stands resolute for his nation and his God. He may, in the eyes of the world, have failed. But let him look into his own heart and he shall see that he has won." By an effort of will von Tetlow almost drove the words away, willed the sonorous voice to silence. He must protect himself against such voices in this alien land.

Blessedly the sermon was a short one. Then all were standing for the final hymn. Measured and grand the organ chords crashed out. The voices soared, "A mighty fortress is our God." He closed his eyes, shivered. The music rolled on, carrying Martin Luther's majestic words to *"Ein Fest Burg."*

For a defenseless moment he was again little Karl standing as tall as he could stretch, to the same chords beside his uniformed father under the vaulted magnificence of the

97

Cologne Cathedral, his father also standing tall for God and country. He shook his head. And what had he now? No God, no faith, no fatherland, nothing except his own life to preserve, and it was forfeit. No, these things did not bear thinking upon. . . . Ah! Here at last, the recessional. He could file out with the rest, move as quickly as was seemly to his waiting car and James.

He had almost forgotten. There was more; there was worse play-acting to endure. James had bought the flowers yesterday, and now he must take them to place on Marjorie's grave at Arlington Cemetery, Arlington because of Roger's wartime service as a combat intelligence officer. Even to his armorplated conscience, his buried sensitivity, this seemed almost too much. But it had to be done. "Very well, James. Let's go. But you must lead me directly to the grave, without seeming to, of course."

They drove over the ice-slick asphalt, between the giant Italian-given gilded horses standing beyond the Lincoln Memorial, then down the wide highway to the crescent-shaped marble entrance to the cemetery. High and white against the leaden sky stood the porticoed Lee-Custis Mansion. He knew that nearby, but not quite visible, was also the eternally guarded tomb of soldiers "known only to God."

Their progress was halted by a funeral cortège preparing to enter the cemetery grounds. He told James to stop the car and stepped out to move a little closer. Yes, there as he had read were the old white horses, the empty saddle of the charger, the flag-draped coffin. Here was the military escort from the Honor Company of Fort Myer, the muffled drums and the dirge from "Saul." Here was another soldier being laid to rest with the full honors his country afforded. Slowly the procession wound its way through the left-hand entrance and up the first rise.

He turned back to the car. "Come, James, bring the flowers. We will go on foot."

"Very well, sah."

Well up the hill, beyond the mounted figure of Sir John Dill, beyond a thousand white crosses, they came to the grave, a large but plain marble slab. Raw wet earth still showed. The tamped down squares of sod were brown and sere. The chiseled inscription was simple, short. "Marjorie Jackson Storrow, Beloved Wife of Roger Lowell Storrow, April 23, 1914—March 15, 1963. I will lift up mine eyes."

He noted that other flowers, given brief immortality by the freezing rain, lay beside the grave. He turned to James. "This is a shameful charade. Why do I have to do it?"

"Mrs. Storrow had many friends, sah. Someone might wonder why you did not come out." The dark, usually impassive face looked somewhat sick, seeming unable to fix its gaze near the new grave. Suddenly the man tensed; in a low voice he said, "As right this very minute, sah!"

A tall, slim man in a dark belted raincoat, hat-brim pulled low against the weather, was briskly nearing them. Who the devil? he wondered. There was something fleetingly familiar about the figure. Now he was only a few yards away, lifting his head so that the face was visible. For a second it was a strange face.

Then recognition came, chillingly. This was the Gestapo. This was Charlie Joyce, a security officer. What in hell was he doing here? For a moment he could only stare, unable to move. Had they discovered so soon? No, it was impossible. Or was it? But how?

The newcomer raised a hand in greeting, but said nothing, merely walked up to him, extended a hand in silence. Roger took it briefly in his left. The tension eased from his body. But of course. Had they been coming for him, they would not have sent Joyce by himself. Still, why was he here? Why? He forced the warmth of a smile, and after a slight return of pressure dropped Joyce's hand. "What brings you here, Charlie? Looking for me, old boy?"

Vainly he sought the emotion hidden behind the face. He felt that his own question had been wrong in tone. He was afraid. He felt that this must show. Then suddenly he was certain that he did not look at all like Roger Storrow and that Joyce knew it. Automatically his left hand moved to cover the lower half of his face. In so doing he felt the tape and gauze dressing. Thank God for this partial mask, he thought, and dropped his hand.

Seemingly Joyce had not noticed his momentary distress.

99

"No, Roger. I certainly didn't mean to intrude at a time like this. Just came out to pay my respects. I couldn't attend the funeral. I was all tied up with that funny business in Mexico."

He froze—"Mexico," "funny business." He did not dare ask anything, or to even speak. Surely his voice would give him away. He just nodded stiffly. This time clearly Joyce did stare at him fixedly for a moment, studying his face. "Marjorie was so very kind to Martha, you know, long before she knew me." The alert eyes did not leave his. "Roger, you worry me. You don't look like yourself at all. Your eyes look terrible. You'd better get in out of this damned weather and have a big drink. Do you feel sick? Is there anything I can do?"

Von Tetlow took a handkerchief from his pocket, coughed into it. "No, Charlie, thanks. Quite all right. It's just that . . ."

The brightness of inquiry had left the eyes. They softened in sympathy. "Of course, Roger. Well, I'll be off." Quickly he placed the flowers he had been carrying beside the headstone, jammed his hat back on, turned and strode away. Von Tetlow stared silently after him.

A sharp staggered detonation ripped the quiet apart. He started convulsively. Then there was a second, a third. He shook himself. Of course, it was the crash of rifles above a grave. Hastily now he took his own flowers from James, placed them next to Joyce's, turned to walk back to the car.

James apparently had noticed his worry. "You do not need to bother yourself about Mr. Joyce, sah. He was fond of Mrs. Storrow, precisely as he said," a slight pause, a lower voice, "and so was I."

"Yes, they told me. And so I will have to invite him over some day soon. It will be delightful," and to himself, delightful as a robin inviting a rattlesnake into its nest.

A new sound now came to his ears, muted a little by the dampness. Torn a little at the edges by the wind there came the first farewell notes of taps, then the fainter echo of the second trumpet, lonely sounding almost beyond loneliness. Were he Roger Storrow, he mused, he would, as an old soldier of this land, also be buried here to the sound of rifles and the tears of trumpets. He wondered where they would bury a spy without a country.

100

CHAPTER XII

VON TETLOW HAD spent a miserable forty-eight hours. This was not too unnatural for anyone forced to remain in Washington over the weekend. On a Sunday, especially during bad weather, the city is dead, deserted and desolate. There is nothing to do.

Nearly all the passable restaurants are closed. Even in those which remain open it is impossible to buy a cheering glass. As a matter of fact, Saturday, as well as the rest of the week, a man cannot stand up to a bar and order a drink. That great male prerogative has been outlawed by Congress. So a man must sit down at a table to nurse his lonely beer. He will be ejected with the full approval of the law if he moves himself or his drink to a table where there is company. This, of course, serves to protect the morals of every good Washingtonian.

He had discovered this for himself. Of course, he had been told earlier but found difficulty in believing that it could be true in the capital city of the United States. In so far as female companionship was concerned, the situation was even worse. If a man did not know an available girl, or know someone who knew one, he could and must sit alone. In this respect, also, Washington was most uncivilized.

Somebody had mentioned, possibly the young Attorney-General, that in the late 1930's there had existed in this city a convenience named the Hopkins Institute. Its services were reportedly excellent and its clientele very select. Since it is a federal offense to transport a female within the District of Columbia for the purpose involved, someone had complained

101

and the FBI had been called in. The Institute had closed as both official and social Washington shuddered at what might be revealed by an examination of the record of the most faithful customers. Several federal agents had reportedly resigned because they felt that it was going too far to invoke the full majesty of federal law in order to destroy man's inherent right to relaxation. Perhaps this was not too surprising. After all, this was the nation that created gangster rule by outlawing whiskey. Even the Gestapo would not have gone so far; Himmler would have been lynched.

So von Tetlow had sat alone, most of the time at home. Twice he had been called to the phone by sympathetic friends of Storrow's, but had begged off from an invitation to lunch and one for cocktails. He did not feel secure enough yet to handle the normal, social chit-chat. Of course, given his recent bereavement, the callers had not insisted. General Jim O'Donnel ("Air Force retired, golf companion, excellent bridge player, married, two married sons, liked three martinis before lunch, spoke Spanish and French"—so read his mental file card) had, however, said, "Look, Roger, I mean damn it all. Everybody's terribly sorry and, of course, they understand, but you'd best start getting out. Bad for you just to sit in that damned office or alone in the house. No good at all. Better get with it soon."

"You're right, Jim. Thanks. I'll try real soon, as you put it."

Jim certainly was right, he thought, but not in the way meant. If he, von Tetlow, did not try very soon, it would become increasingly difficult to begin. Unease, self-doubts, fear of exposure would grow to a dangerous point. Admitted, but today was just not the day to begin, not after his visits to the church and the cemetery. He had tried the television programs. Today one had featured two tense and silent golfers, an announcer breathing in conspiratorial tones, interspersed with commercials for underarm deodorants. He had wandered about the house, paying particular heed to the library and the examination of its books. This had been more interesting. From them, from the flyleaf inscriptions, from those well-read and those few with virgin spines, he had learned a lot more about Roger Storrow. He had grudgingly

102

admired the man during the many weeks he had studied him, both in reports and through the one-way mirror, whether normal or under the influence of drugs. Now he came to admire him more as a cultured, an educated, certainly a courageous man. Idly he wished that he could meet him some day, and on some neutral ground, if such existed.

How much longer would they choose, or need, to keep Storrow alive? Certainly they wouldn't if he, von Tetlow, failed. But then, of course, he would be dead also. It was an interesting thought. *The longer I get away with this, and the more questions I have to ask of him about people and things here, the longer Roger Storrow stays alive. If I ever become perfect in this role, if that is possible, then probably he dies. Too bad, perhaps, but no need to think of it now. I must not waste any time worrying about him. I have troubles enough for myself.*

In idle curiosity, he drew from a shelf a red morocco-bound copy of Kipling's poems. He had had to read many of them at school in England, he remembered. Some were awful tripe, but some he had felt truly great. There was a faded red silk ribbon bookmarker separating the pages of this one. He flipped the volume open and saw the title "Ballad of East and West," and without effort the refrain came back to him:

> And there is neither East nor West,
> Border nor breed nor birth,
> When two strong men meet face to face,
> Though they come from the ends of the earth.

Those had been happy days between the wars. He and his fellow students had been of the West, solidly of the West. Now he was of nowhere. The twain now would never meet except at Armageddon. And was he in reality a strong man? Until recently he had never doubted. Now he was not too sure.

Carefully, feeling somehow that he had just intruded on the privacy of another, he slipped the book back into its place and flipped on the FM band of the big radio. There should be some good music on one of the stations this Sunday. Waiting for the tubes to warm, he dropped heavily into an easy chair. He was tired. *My God, how tired he was.*

103

Smoothly the music rose in pitch, strings, brasses, tympani. Dimly he recognized the *Choral Symphony*. He leaned back, his eyes closed. He was half asleep.

Thus he remained until the last movement. Then the crashing chords, the quartet and chorus brought him more widely awake, or a little less asleep. There were the soaring words of Schiller's *Ode to Joy*. He remembered having read that the great poet had originally titled his work *Ode to Freedom* and surely the verses made it clear that freedom for all mankind had been the theme. This, however, in the days of its writing had been a thought too revolutionary for the authorities. So, as to the title at least, the author had bowed.

At the music's end came the usual station break, the repetitive and boring commercials. He ceased to listen but was too comfortable to rise and turn off the radio. Half drowsing he became dimly aware that a panel discussion had commenced. It was only a rumble of voices until, quite sharply, names and phrases edged into his consciousness. "War crimes, genocide, six million helpless victims, men like Eichmann, Borman, Steigmuller, von Tetlow—" Then came a powerful voice, "I disagree with what Mr. Jackson has just said. No, certainly not as to guilt, nor as to his deserving harsh punishment. It's simply that I cannot agree that the death penalty was correct."

"How do you mean, Dr. Kramer? You think such a man did not deserve to die? That . . ."

"Of course, he did. But then we all must die. No, execution, a quick clean end for him or any others like him, is too good, too merciful."

"Then what would you suggest?"

The voice deepened. The syllables hardened like cooling lava. "Yes, quick death is too good for such a beast. This the court should have realized. Find him guilty, as he was, guilty of these dreadful things, then turn him loose, free him, free him to run, to hide if he could, to run and hide for the rest of his life, however long that would be, to live with his conscience. This would be the most terrible, most just punishment of all. There was, they say, the wandering Jew. Let him be the wandering Nazi superman, let him hide if he can, let him . . ."

This was too much. He rose to his feet, flipped off the

104

switch, shook himself. Suddenly from behind him came the soft accents of James. "That man, sah, he was very right, you know."

Von Tetlow started, whirled on the servant. "How dare you come in like that? Get out of here, you Jamaican bastard."

James never changed expression, merely spoke a little more firmly. "No, sah! I shall not depart now, sah. You and I, we have some work to do."

The days which followed were in some ways better, more interesting. But in at least one respect they threatened to be much worse.

At the Security Council meeting much of the discussion centered on the notorious wall separating East and West Berlin. The Secretary of State had used that word, "separating." The Chairman of the Joint Chiefs had interrupted, "Let's call it what it really is, the prison wall around East Berlin. The poor bastards can't get out and the Westerners can't get in without the say-so of a Commie warden. Makes much better propaganda that way. Although, God knows, I'm sick to death of propaganda. What we need is some action."

"Do you mean that General Jeffries ought to knock it down with guns and tanks?"

"Hard to do today, but we certainly should have done so when it was half put up, and kept right on knocking it down as fast as they tried to rebuild. But we've got to do something."

"Agreed, but what would you suggest?"

The General barely smiled. "As a matter of fact, I do have something to suggest. But I'll give credit where credit is due. It was not my idea. It came from Colonel Stapleton, a bright young officer on my staff, Air Force, although I hate to admit it." He turned to the CIA Director, "Art, you remember that tunnel or bunker or whatever it was under the city you fellows were accused of spying with?"

"For the record, no. But you know damned well I do. It was a pretty good idea. We get blamed for everything spooky that happens, or goes really sour. We even took it for Cuba.

Old Allen told the truth, exactly. His evaluation was one hundred percent correct. And he had the guts to keep quiet when the headhunters were turned loose, that . . ."

"Oh, come on, Art. Let's not rehash Cuba again, please. We're talking about Berlin."

The President grinned briefly, nodded. "I more than agree. What was your idea about the wall, General?"

"Well, Mr. President, there are already various tunnels and such under Berlin—subways, the sewers, water-main channels and so on. Of course the Russkies have grilled them off at the border. But the boys on our side could use them as departure points and dig some more to right up under selected points of the wall, plant TNT charges, and blow holes in the wall from beneath, maybe in fifteen or twenty different places all at once."

The Secretary of State was unhappy. "Good Lord, General, you certainly go in for drastic measures, don't you? How many Berlin burghers will you blow up this way, a thousand? Or more?"

"Stapleton's thought that out, too. I asked him the same question. We use spots under street intersections. A trained dynamiter won't get any houses that way. Also, we could start a few major demonstrations at other spots, draw people away from the places we plan to blow."

He reached for his briefcase, drew out a folded paper, spread it on the table. "Look, Stapleton even drew a map for us, using a city street plan and aerial photos."

Everyone, von Tetlow included, drew closer to look. The General went on, pointing with his pencil. "He used to be Air Attaché over there. The red x's mark the places he picked himself. I guess the idea's been kicking around in his head for quite a while. I like it myself."

The Secretary of State shook his head, tapped his pencil lightly against the tabletop. "I'm afraid it is a fairly violent solution. And even if we succeed in not killing anyone, which I greatly doubt, what good are the holes going to do if the East Berliners don't dare cross over? They've been shot while trying to escape before, you know. We must think of the effect on the uncommitted neutrals, and . . ."

The General smashed down a fist on the outspread map.

106

"Damn the neutrals. But these Berliners, by God, they'd risk it again. But think, gaps in a dozen places, maybe more, the other team caught by surprise. We set up big loudspeakers all over and invite escapers to our side. We drop leaflets and what's more, we line up troops or tanks as protection for them. And anyway, I doubt that the Vopos will mow down a whole stream of their own people."

This time it was the President. "What happens when they move more of their troops in to block off the streets and start to rebuild?"

"Mr. President, I know what I'd do."

"Yes, General."

"Well, sir, before they get started, use the loudspeakers and leaflets to say other charges are still primed, that the wall will blow again, but that the West boys don't want to kill any of their Eastern brothers, but will do so if they are forced to."

The President nodded, turned to Jackson of the CIA. "What do you think, Arthur?"

Jackson took off his glasses, seemed to study them for a moment, and finally said, "I think, Mr. President, that it is a splendid idea. Of course there are risks. There are in everything. But this, sir, is one worth taking. The Berliners blow the holes. We protect the refugees. I think we come out ahead."

"All very well, Art," this from the State Department, "but we'll be blamed for the dynamiting as well and for anyone who gets killed—man, woman or babe in arms."

The General's only comment was, "You said that before. So?"

Von Tetlow had returned to his seat, committing to memory as exactly as possible the proposed locations for the breaching of the wall. It was not too hard. He knew the city well, and the spots were mostly those he would have chosen himself. Here was something in which Moscow would be really interested. He wondered what would be the decision of this group, and of the authorities in West Berlin. He really had no doubt about the latter. It might take time, but in the end these people would certainly vote to take the chances and to go ahead.

As a German, he certainly favored the idea, but then he

was no longer a German. He had betrayed his Fuhrer in the summer of 1944. He was hunted for war crimes, for genocide. He had run for his life. He had no country. But he had new masters to serve. He must find out the final decision, and if favorable, the date set for action.

As he passed out the papers covering the next item on the agenda, "Evidence of Possible Sabotage at Missile Sites," he realized that he was feeling increasingly unwell. His head was aching and hot, his eyes watered and burned under their lenses, his throat was raw. Obviously lack of sleep, tension, plus the freezing wind and rain at the cemetery, had taken their toll.

Suddenly an irresistible tickling began high in his nose. Doggedly he fought to ignore it, to stifle the lurking sneeze. It was useless. The pressure mounted too fast, his lungs sucked in a great gout of air. No more than in time he pressed his handkerchief to his face as the sneeze blasted forth, seeming to lift the top of his head, to squeeze his eyeballs in their sockets.

He looked up quickly in embarrassment. His "Sorry" coincided with at least two *Gesundheits*. Why say it in German? he wondered. He was briefly conscious that Charlie Joyce was staring hard at him. He looked down again in reflex to the linen in his hand. In horror he saw between two folds a tiny semi-sphere of green-tinted, paper-thin plastic. Quickly he forced a strangled cough, and pressed the handkerchief again to his face. "'Scuse me," he mumbled through it. "Be right back."

It was a difficult business, he found, to replace the little lens with hands that were shaking so.

Charlie Joyce found it difficult to credit what, in that quick flash, he thought he had seen. Red-rimmed and blurred by moisture as they had been, surely one of Roger's eyes had seemed a steely blue. He shook his head. This was insane. Men's eyes just did not change color. It was an idiotic thought, one to be banished. He found, however, it was a thought that would not easily go away.

When Roger returned, Charlie studied him covertly. No doubt about it, the two eyes were an identical shade of green. He was a highly trained man, and not one often to doubt

108

even the most fleeting evidence of his senses. Somewhere there remained also the impression of this man at the cemetery, for some reason trying to hide his face behind a hand. Dammit, Joyce, he thought, you have been seeing things. Let's forget about it.

CHAPTER XIII

HIS HANDS MOVING rapidly, Roger slapped five cards, one after the other, on to the little stacks in the center of the table. The last one was the king of clubs. He now had none left in front of him. At least twenty remained in front of José. He sighed, scratched his head. "Never, I am afraid, will I learn this game so fast."

Roger smiled, picked up the center cards, began sorting them out. "According to my count, José, you now owe me twenty-three million pesos. Do you wish to play again and double the stakes?"

José smiled and shook his head, "No, *señor,* you are too much clever for me. Also, now I must go to meet Don Henrique at the *aeroporto* from the midnight plane. So again I must lock you in." He rose, went to the door. "Again I say, *señor,* you are too clever for me. *Adios.*"

"*Adios,* José." He thought, I sure as hell hope I am. I'd better be.

Roger had had much time to think, too much time when most ideas led only to frustration and almost, but never quite, to despair. For over a week he had been in a locked room with barred windows, shoeless, without money or identification, and without a weapon. The room was pleasant; he was not mistreated except for occasional druggings. The food was excellent, for Mexican food. He now had plenty to read. Still, this was no more than a prison cell. His sentence was indefinite, but however short or long, it was certainly for whatever was left of his life.

Perhaps the words "life sentence" and "prison cell"

110

had given him the idea. That is, they had in conjunction with something he had been reading one day, a rather pedantic article about the problems of Mexican agriculture.

In addition to the normal lack of sufficient irrigation and fertilizer, the new Secretary had denounced the huge, unproductive landholdings of the few very rich. "The answer seems to me a land reform to create small productive individual farms, where the individual owner will have incentive to produce since he can keep the fruit of his own labors. The answer is not, as I see it, in the giant collective, the kolkhoz of the USSR—that system. . . ."

Kolkhoz. This rang a bell. This word had suggested something. Something he had read a long time ago when he must have still been in his early teens. What in the devil had it been? Finally he remembered. Now he could see a thin brown book, illustrated on every page by line drawings of unusual things and strange people. It was Ripley's *Believe It or Not*. Suddenly the book had flipped open to a long forgotten page. There was the bearded, fanatic face, the powerful hands holding on to the ends of a short, slender object. And the name, there it was also, Louis Kogloscz, anarchist and murderer, locked in a jail cell, condemned to death. That was it. This man had escaped the gallows, but at the cost of his own life. Well, he would have to do better. It was then that he had decided upon a plan of action.

There was an excellent chance, he felt, that he would not survive the attempt, but it must be made. Tonight seemed as good a time as any. José would certainly be gone for nearly two hours, and it was most unlikely that he or Don Henrique would come to check on him very late. The whole scheme still seemed improbable. He wondered if it had really worked, or if the author had gladly accepted as truth some jailer's often repeated legend. Well, there was no time to worry about that now. He must set about collecting his slender supply of unlikely tools.

First were the bed sheets. He knotted these tightly together

111

and tied one end of this "rope" to a foot of the heavy mahogany bed near to the wall. He hoped it would hold solidly, but there was no use in worrying. That would be the least of his problems.

Next the bathroom. Thank God its fixtures were far from modern. The washstand was a low portable one, from the underside of which projected a three foot length of pipe, its end centered directly over a porcelain-circled opening in the floor. Some days ago he had begun working on this pipe, forcing it backward and forward to the limit of his strength. At first it had refused to budge. However, hours of effort had finally weakened, then loosened the pipe's soldered adhesion to the metal drain ring. Now two or three powerful lunges proved enough to break it loose. He carried it back to the table, set it down next to the pile of cards.

He seated himself at the table, picked up a card, tore it methodically into small pieces. Even now he was able to grin at himself, Bite-size pieces, by God! What a sight this would be for the press photographers.

He stuffed the first dozen pieces into his mouth and slowly began to chew. They tasted not only dry, but of some foul-flavored dye. It took longer than he had expected, even the pieces of a single playing card. At last, however, the ace of spades was reduced to a saliva soaked mash. Using a pencil he pushed it as far as possible into one end of the pipe, tore up another card, distastefully placed the bits in his mouth, begin to chew again.

Nearly one hour later it seemed he had scarcely made a dent in the first pack. Four times he had taken a large drink of water, and his jaw muscles ached horribly. My God, how would he ever finish on time, in fact, how would he ever finish at all? The answer was simple. He had to finish. Achingly, doggedly, he continued his strange task.

It must have been another hour later that he was aware of the sound of an automobile, the probing flash of headlights, then the opening of a gate, the crunch of gravel under the tires. There were voices, the thudding shut of the front door. Quickly he slipped the pipe under the bedclothes, kicked the knotted sheets under the bed, rolled himself beneath the blankets and waited.

112

First one, then another set of feet thumped measuredly up the stairs, clacked down the passageway outside his door, then were still. Two minutes later Roger Storrow resumed his task. Two dreadful hours later the pipe was packed nearly full, and the first part of his task was finished.

He took from a drawer four of the aluminum tubes which had once protected his cigars from moisture. With the use of considerable force these could be made to fit the aperture of the pipe. He did so, making as little noise as possible as he drove pipe and tube against the tiled floor. Then he forced the tubes further in at each end, using the wooden handle broken from the bathroom mop. Carefully he repeated the process with two more cigar containers. Finally he snapped the handle in half, wadded each end with toilet paper until it would but barely fit, then drove the wooden plugs in also.

This completed, he stood two heavy books on end, about four feet apart, up against the wall, then set the protruding wooden ends carefully on top of the books. The pipe now rested some ten inches from the floor. Too high. He laid two books flat on each other directly beneath the pipe's center. That looked about right. Next he placed the lighted alcohol lamp on the books. Now the bluish flame lapped gently around the curve of the metal. His last act was to drag the heavy mattress from the bed over to a corner of the room, lean it on its side against the wall, and lie full length behind it.

He glanced at the luminous dial of his watch. Three-thirty in the morning. Whole sentences came back to him from the sad story of Louis Kogloscz, among them, "No one knows for how many hours this desperate man sat with his head bowed over his infernal machine, how long it was till head, arms and brains were blasted apart, and the concrete walls of the cell dripped crimson."

Huddled, protected he hoped by the mattress, he found there was still too much time to think. Suppose the bomb never exploded at all, or just seemed never about to do so? How long must he remain crouched, not daring to lift his head? How could he know, otherwise, if the lamp still burned? How many hours should that half-pint, more or less, of alcohol last? Suppose hours later the whole business just

113

went harmlessly *phoomp!* like some of the Fourth of July experiments he had tried as a youngster? Suppose, on the other hand, the force was sufficient to kill him by concussion or else send a sharp shard of metal slicing through the ticking to sever his spine or pierce his heart?

No, these things did not bear thinking about. Still, even for a man as capable of self-control as he, there was no possibility of forcing himself to sleep. He first tried doing complex calculations, attempting mentally to visualize the figures and equations. No, he could no longer do this. Next he went back to the counting rhymes of his childhood. He had used them with his sister Annie, now so tragically dead, to kill the endless hours between the time of waking and their parents' permission to rush pajama-clad to the living room to see whether Santa Claus had really come. Of course they knew he must have, and yet "Ninety-six bottles hanging by the wall, one of the bottles had a great fall."

He had worked his way down to twenty-three and could not resist another peek at the watch dial a few inches from his nose. The hands had hardly moved. One thing, however, his eyes were now accustomed enough to the dark for him to know that the alcohol flame still flickered, casting its tiny bluish light, less bright than half a candle, to the ceiling and the walls and finally to him behind his doubtful shelter. Now, nearly imperceptibly, this illumination seemed to be coming stronger. No, this was not possible. There was no way the flame could increase. The answer was clear. The added light came from the pale darkness of the predawn sky. Time was running out.

Somewhere in the house there was a stirring, the opening of a door, the creak of floorboards. Good God! The footsteps were nearing his door and he heard a man's cough. He had been holding his breath for some time and did not dare let it go until the steps creaked into silence down the corridor.

He had to pass the time somehow. Doggedly he searched his mind for lines and verses of poems he had, a thousand years before, been forced to memorize. Strangely, perhaps because of the adrenalin of tension, they came back easily, with a minimum of effort. Triumphantly he marched down the hexameters of Macaulay, to

Oh Tiber, Father Tiber, to whom the Romans pray,
A Roman's life, a Roman's arms, take thou in charge
   this day.

That had been in the third Form at Groton, he recalled.
Too easy. Now he'd try something harder.

Arma virumque cano, Troiae qui primus ab oris
Italiam fato profugus Lavinaque venit Litora—multum
   ille et terris iactatus . . .

Good old Virgil. What in hell came next? . . .
In one terrible meeting the door slammed against his body.
The breath was driven from his lungs, his mouth. Twin sand-
bags of pressure drove the sides of his skull together, and
blackness wrapped about him.

Groggily he shook himself. Had he been unconscious?
How long? His head hurt. Blood was pouring from a slash on
the back of his right forearm. He was sure he was deaf.
Scrambling toward the far end of the room, he smelled fresh,
cold air, then saw a jaggedly formed patch of pearly light.
Thank God, part of the wall had gone. Was it enough?
Grasping the loose end of the knotted sheets, he squirmed on
his belly, thrust his head through the opening in the stone
and stucco partition, and pulling with one arm, driving with
his feet, he squeezed his shoulders through, dimly conscious
of the skin being torn from his back by a jagged point of
something. Then, at last, his hips pulled free. Quickly he
grabbed the sheet with his other hand and dropped, crashing
painfully into the house wall below, scraping across it and
falling finally the last few feet to the ground.
Stunned as he was, he realized that lights had already
begun to come on in the house above him. He dared not look
back. Somehow he had to get over the wall or the iron gate,
and damned quick. He ran to the wall, looked to its top. It
was at least two feet higher than he had estimated, much
higher than he could jump up to and grasp with his hands to
lever himself over.
Desperately he ran to the gate, easily eight feet high
between its stone posts. This he saw was topped by long
lance-like points. He grasped at the cold iron. Somehow,

115

somehow he must climb. He could already hear voices and saw that the ground floor lights were on. His hands groped for the latch-bolt—locked, he supposed. But no! Almost weeping with relief he found it moved easily under his hand, the gate swung outward on its hinges.

Now his brain was kind. It ordered him to look to his right. Twenty feet away stood the black limousine. Daring to waste precious seconds, he darted to it. There was no time to climb in, try to start the motor. Reaching through the window his hand touched the ignition keys, jerked them from the lock. Without looking he threw them as far as he could over the wall into the unknown of the night. Turning in the same motion, he sprinted on bare feet which did not yet register much pain. He lurched out onto the roadway, running toward the dawn.

He knew he could not run far. He prayed they did not have an extra set of car keys, or bloodhounds.

Where was he? Where was he heading? His feet by now hurt dreadfully, especially when one hit a pointed pebble on the road's hard surface. He'd best get off that road, and soon, but where? Where could he seek help? Suddenly he came to a crossroads: to the left nothing, to the right, about two hundred yards away, was a building showing a light, and what seemed a tower against the brightening sky. He must take a chance; he headed toward it.

His chest was agonizingly painful and he breathed with difficulty, but he was nearly there. He looked up. Yes, he'd been right. The building was a church, a little one to be sure, but a church for all that. For there rose its cross. Roger reached the door, pushed it wide. A short man stood, back to him, silhouetted against the candles he was lighting for early Mass.

Slowly Padre Fortunato turned to face Roger. What a weird sight! This tall, gray-haired gringo, barefoot and clad only in trousers. He saw the man raise a hand, try to speak, saw him clutch at his chest with the other, heard the words forced between gritted teeth, "Help me, please . . . I am . . ." Then the tall man stumbled forward, fell to his knees, rolled over and lay still.

Padre Fortunato was neither an unkind man nor a stupid one, quite the contrary. This stranger was surely in trouble.

116

That he was very ill was obvious. The priest placed his hand on the chest, at the sternum, then to the hollow beneath the ear. Yes, the heart still beat flutteringly, the man still breathed. But his color was ghastly. He might very well be dying, might die right here on the pavement of the Padre's church.

Yes, the gringo might be in trouble, even with the police, but he had no love for the police. This man, consciously or not, had sought sanctuary. He would have it, especially since it was well known that although gringos were crazy they were also rich. No, his lips and the lips of the church would remain sealed, except for one thing. He shouted to a barefoot boy who was propping himself up on the handle of a broom. *"Hola,* Carlos, run like the wind to fetch the Doctor Alvarez. Quickly, and speak to no one else, otherwise I promise to strip the hide from your unsanctified body. Run, now!"

Casting only a passing glance at the long, inert form on the ground, Carlos did as he was told.

Roger struggled back to semi-consciousness. A terrible nauseating pain gripped his chest, tore at his heart with fingers of steel. His left arm was numb. He gasped for breath. Now there was, somehow, a cool hand on his forehead. Dimly he heard the voice, a voice in Spanish, "Peace, my son, do not move. The doctor is here."

He only half felt the sharp needle pierce the flesh of his right arm. Gradually, blissfully, the pain transferred itself, as if to someone else. Roger could see from a dimness the other man lying there, knew that the other was suffering terribly, but did not care. His own pain was leaving him. That was all that mattered.

Dr. Alvarez nodded in satisfaction. "It is the *Norte Americanos,* Padre, who gave this drug its name. They call morphine 'G.O.M.'—God's own medicine. They are right."

"Will he live?"

"Quién sabe? One thing is certain. We cannot move him now. I will inject adrenalin, then I must send for oxygen. Have you here a telephone?"

The little priest shrugged gently, "For me, a poor servant of God—no."

"Then Carlos must run again. I cannot leave this man now."

Carlos ran again and Roger Storrow lay asleep on the stone floor; for the time being his strong heart refused to die.

CHAPTER XIV

FOR ONCE THE GOVERNMENT of the United States, or at least its executive branch, had reached rapid and courageous agreement. Because of the pressing nature of events, or in spite of them, it required but forty-eight hours for Security Council approval of the plan to blast holes in Walter Ulbricht's infamous Berlin Wall.

Colonel Stapleton had been flown back to Berlin on a special mission and with instructions to co-ordinate the whole matter with the German authorities. The latter had been delighted and had gone rapidly ahead. In short order tunnels had been dug, shafts raised from them to selected spots beneath the wall. The sound of the work was masked by heavy building demolition, road repairs and the like. Thus any East Zone acoustical devices were deafened to what was being done underground.

Von Tetlow had learned all this at a special meeting, attended by only five members of the NSC. At that conference was decided the precise time at which the wall would be breached. The consensus was Sunday, the ninth, at exactly noon. Sunday, because more East Zoners would be away from their jobs and hence free to be on the streets, later to make a bid for freedom; noon because all those who had wished or been permitted to attend church would by then have left the services.

Afterward von Tetlow dictated the full scheme, including the exact location of each planned explosion, into the tiny microphone of his recorder. He did so with mixed emotions. Here was a real coup of espionage. Here was news of the greatest possible interest to the Kremlin. Still, no matter how long his absence, he felt a deep sympathy, even a community of purpose, with the people of the divided German city and nation who wished again to be one.

He wondered what action or counteraction the Communist command would take when its members digested the news. Probably, he imagined, they'd move in many more troops, tanks and guns along the Zone frontier. Also, there would probably be speeches and articles announcing that any attempt to breach the wall would be regarded as an action justifying closing the Berlin ground corridor or airlanes, perhaps both. Certainly there would be some threat. It really was much better to try not to think about it at all, just carry out his assignment and report the facts. His personal feelings must be shoved aside.

Physically he felt miserable. His cold had become considerably worse, and he knew he was running a fever. James was away for the day. But he realized that despite the cold drizzle outside, the report he had made was so important that it be mailed at once and by him. Accordingly, he carefully packed the little spool of wire in another jeweler's box, and stuffed this in turn, surrounded by cotton, in a strong cardboard container which fastened with wire clips. It was already stamped with the words "Fragile" and some fainter letters reading "Insured."

He unfolded a square of paper tucked into a hidden recess of the desk and studied it. Let's see, what was the address to which James had mailed the last package? Yes, here it was checked off. The next one down the list read Julius Stein & Sons, on East Forty-Sixth Street, New York City. This he imagined was, as the others, a one-man, one-room watch repair shop used occasionally as a mail-drop, and then only for communications of the greatest importance. He printed carefully with his left hand. Damn, how long would it be before his right shoulder would again be of any use. Merely dressing without help was almost impossible. And this miserable weather made the still present aches more painful.

How many stamps did this little packet need? James had never told him, or, if he had, it had slipped his mind. If he did not put on enough, and if he dared write on his correct address, the package would come back to him in a day or two. But that would be too late. No, he would not use his own address. The best thing to do was to put on what would have to be more postage than necessary. He dug around to find stamps of sufficient value, glued them on. Then he had another thought. Suppose the postal service lost or mislaid this package? Such things had happened. He'd best make sure, since this information was of such a vital nature. He would record his report on a second tape and mail that at the same time. Shouldn't it be to the same address? Yes, all things considered, that would be the better way.

Twenty minutes later, overcoat collar pulled up about his ears, the brim of his hat lowered against the wind, he stepped into the street. There was, he remembered, a mail box a little more than a block away. Despite the warm coat, he shivered. No doubt at all, he was sicker today. God, what horrible weather. If he'd never met that damned Meyer woman on the boat he'd be comfortable and warm somewhere in Southern Europe. What a terrible fool he had . . .

"Great scott, Roger." He started, looked up. "What are you doing out in weather like this?"

It was Charlie Joyce. What was he doing here, for that matter? Every time he saw the man it made him freeze a little, tightened his nerves in fear. He tried to act and to talk normally, "Going to mail this damned watch to be repaired. Quit on me again, don't you know."

"Why, hell, Roger, why trust it to the mails? Plenty of good watch repairers a few blocks from here on Wisconsin, or downtown. Want me to take it with me?"

Quickly he asked himself, how would Storrow have answered? Oh, yes, of course. "Never, never, Charlie. Shreve's in Boston has mended, or claimed to mend, every watch I ever had since grammar school. Can't change now."

He dug into his pocket for one of the packages—the other one would have to wait—and covering the address with his hand he dropped it into the box.

Joyce was looking at him quizzically. "Roger, you look terrible. Go home, make yourself a hot drink, crawl into bed and call a doctor. Promise?"

"Don't need a doctor, old boy. But I'll take some of your advice. I'll kill this one with whiskey."

"Kill yourself, more likely. I came over to call and see how you felt. Now I know, so I won't bother you any more. But, believe me, if you don't call a doctor, I will. I mean it. Uncle can't afford to lose you yet, you know."

"Righto, Charlie, thanks. I'll do just that."

He turned and walked back toward Storrow's house. It was an effort to appear brisk and partly healthy. His legs felt heavy and very weak. He did not turn to look back, since he believed he would meet those cool inquiring eyes studying him.

Charlie Joyce stood by the red, white and blue mailbox for quite some time. What the hell, he wondered. What's his hurry about mailing his watch to Boston to be repaired? Faithful Miss Kelly usually takes care of that kind of thing. And he looked nervous, like a schoolboy caught sending away for a dirty sex book in a plain wrapper.

That evening Charlie Joyce was alone. Martha had gone to Chicago to assist at the birth of her sister's first baby. What earthly good she would be, he had no idea. Well, women were women and there was no use seeking to find out why they acted that way. Also, both his children were away at schools which cost too much. One thing was certain. He hated eating alone in this house. Therefore he would eat out, and by God, he'd do it at an expensive restaurant.

Not only was he lonely, he was tired of puzzling himself with an absolutely impossible theory. He did not have the kind of mind that could, like Alice's friends, believe one, never mind two, impossible things before breakfast, or before dinner for that matter. The devil with it! He owed himself La Parisienne and a few words with lovely Monique.

Every time, which was far too seldom, that Charlie Joyce went to the restaurant, he was liable to twinges of regret that he was a government servant and not a foreign diplomat, a filthy capitalist, an influence peddler or even a successful crook. He did not wish he were unmarried when he saw Monique, but he did upon occasion wish that there existed in this country a more continental liberality about sex. Martha knew this and had even smiled some approval, "If you stop looking, Joyce, that's the day I'm sending for the ambulance.

You'll be through." Then she added, "So will you be if you touch."

He had only half finished his first cocktail when Monique came over to his table. "Good evening, Monsieur Joyce. Long time I have not seen you. How is Mrs. Joyce and the big children?"

"Très bien, merci. On parle francais?"

The impish grin, "No, we do not. You speak French like an Irishman. This is not good. I practice my English instead."

"Oh, all right. How's your love life?"

"That is my affair, no?" But there was only friendliness in the remark.

"Then, where did that ring come from? It shows up like a searchlight."

She extended a slender hand, studied the stone with admiration. *"Touché.* It is from my friend. I think he will marry me, perhaps."

The bald proprietor, Corsican and resembling not a little his most famous compatriot, who had joined them for a moment, grinned an evil smile and made what was clearly a most improper remark, but one quite untranslatable to Charlie Joyce. The girl lifted her fine nose and, looking down it, said clearly, "You are a pig, a cow and a stinker." Joyce's French was just good enough to understand the words.

"Dammit, Monique, I wish I could handle the language and the French slang well enough to keep up with you two. I wish I could speak it like Roger Storrow, for instance."

There was a tiny wrinkle of puzzlement, a pout of thought, "Oh, him!"

"Why, 'Oh, him!'?"

"Well, the proper Mr. Storrow was in here the other night and was quite a little strange. I do mean strange, do I not?"

"How do I know? What do you mean? What was strange about him?"

"Oh, it was nothing, Monsieur Joyce. I should not have mentioned it. Let us say only, Mr. Storrow was just not himself. That is simply all, nothing more."

"Not himself!" That was it. Those were the words that brought the absolutely impossible theory flashing back full-formed into his mind. Yet, how could it be. Not himself. Charlie Joyce's hand shot out and grabbed the girl's wrist too hard. Automatically she tried to draw away, looked a little scared into the suddenly too unsmiling gray eyes. "What's the matter with you? You're hurting me."

He dropped her wrist. "I'm sorry, Monique." He noticed that two diners at the next table were staring at them. Better to drop the whole thing at this time and place. "I guess I'd better have another cocktail. Now go away. You're too pretty. I don't want to make your friend jealous."

"It is okay. I still like to flirt a little with tough black-haired Irishmen." But she turned and walked away. The view was just as alluring as it had been when she approached.

He asked his waiter to bring him the plug-in phone. Two night-duty officers would have to stop reading their who-dunits, or bosom and bourbon novels, to arrange interviews on the morrow with two very important persons. And I know, he thought, I know bloody well they aren't going to believe me. As a matter of fact, I'm damned if I can believe it myself.

First he had gone to the Director of the FBI, not to his boss the Attorney-General. Years of service and of habit had deeply ingrained in Charlie Joyce that one did not go over the head of the Director. He was a great man, a dedicated one, but very, and quite justifiably, jealous of his prerogatives. He had earned them. He was probably the ablest, most honest security chief in the world, and the one least contaminated by politics of any kind. Since it was Sunday the building at Ninth and Pennsylvania was officially closed. So Charlie Joyce, despite his White House credentials, had to obtain a pass. He remembered a not apocryphal account from the first year of the war. Then Attorney-General Francis Biddle had also entered this door on a Sunday. Asked to produce a building pass which he did not have, he said, "But I'm the Attorney-General." The guard's retort was simple: "I don't care if you're J. Edgar himself, you don't get in without a pass." Riding the elevator, walking down the echoing halls, Joyce remembered his first tour of the building as a boy. The electric sign moving like a giant odometer on a car's dashboard to record each new set of fingerprints filed. By now there must be almost two hundred million. Next there was the arsenal of captured weapons; the death mask of John Dillinger or Pretty Boy Floyd; the gleaming crime laboratory with its mysterious instruments; and best of all the shooting-range in the basement where soft-talking men calmly placed each bullet in the "kill" portions of man-sized silhouettes. One of the men had let him pull the trigger of a loaded tommy-gun and let him pocket the still warm, acrid-smelling empty shells. It was on that day long ago he had decided in his secret heart that he would be a special agent of the Bureau when he grew up.

Now he was once again in the reception room to the Director's office. The same receptionist he had always known led him across the hall, beyond the Bureau Shield, reading "Fidelity, Bravery, Integrity," then into the big handsome office, toward the desk flanked by its flags. The room had never failed to impress him.

The Director rose to his feet, came forward to shake hands. "I'm glad to see you, Charlie. Sit down, please, and tell me what's on your mind."

This man had, in his long career, seen and studied nearly all that could exist of the criminal, subversive, natural or perverted. But this, this hypothesis of Joyce's had taxed his credulity, gone beyond his imagination. He had raised a heavy, square-chiseled head, placed his fingers steepled beneath his chin.

"Good Lord, Charlie, I've known you for how many years? At least twenty-three by now. And I'll admit I've never," a quick smile, "well, hardly ever, known you to go off on a wild goose chase. But this time I think you've hit some kind of jackpot. What you need is a vacation. You've been around the White House too long."

"But, Chief, listen. You always trusted my eyesight. Did I or didn't I spot two of your most wanted fugitives and one of them in a race-track crowd? Was I or wasn't I one of the select few who shot possibles with every damned firearm? I tell you I saw one blue eye and one green on the man."

A shake of the massive head. "Well, I was there too and I didn't, and neither did you. Neither of us is getting any younger."

"All right, Chief, all right, granted. But how about going

out, sick as a dog, in that filthy weather just to mail a watch? How about that fishy story of falling off a ruin and smashing his shoulder all to hell, but getting only a cut on his upper lip? How about the proper Bostonian, and I checked this with a waiter, the proper Roger Storrow, widowed only a few weeks, making a public pass at a blonde? How about that?"

"Now you're making sense, Charlie. A busted shoulder hurts, a broken heart hurts, alcohol sometimes helps. And, I hate sounding like a psychiatrist—phony head-shrinkers, all of them—but how do you, how do I, know what repressions the poor man's had? I've met the late Mrs. Storrow. Wouldn't surprise me if he was cold at night. But she wouldn't let him go out in the snow without his—what's that fine New England word?—galoshes. And he wanted to mail his own watch, so what?"

Joyce did a thing that would have terrified him years ago. He pounded his fist on the three-yard desk top. "Dammit, Chief, you can find an answer to anything. But I'm sure I'm right. Don't laugh. Call it Irish instinct, if you will. Can't we at least have a phone tap, a mail cover, maybe an electrician's check of the wiring with a mike left behind?" the voice became even more earnest. "I know I've got a suspicious mind, but remember that hit-and-run of his wife, not a single, solitary trace, not a clue, even a tiny one. Too damned professional, too slick to be just an accident."

"Don't pound desks at me, Charlie. No! No phone taps, no mike, no surveillance, nothing. And that's final. Was there anything else?"

"No, dammit." The habit of years returned, "I mean no, sir." There was no point in losing his temper. He managed a grin. "But I'll make you a bet—at least even money."

"You're on. Dinner, and of course cocktails, at Harvey's."

"Done, and do you know, I hope I lose."

Charlie Joyce's colloquy with the Attorney-General was even less rewarding. That crusading young office holder was deeply concerned with the vast variance in the prices of seemingly identical pills. Not only that, he was busy rewriting a speech to be delivered to the American Legion in Biloxi, Mississippi. It still contained a section outlining desegregation

126

of the membership of certain private clubs in Washington, D.C. Should he take it out or leave it in? In either event he would be wrong.

He had been impolite, and he was hardly ever impolite, except intentionally. He had said, "Oh, for God's sake, I'm just as Irish as you are, and I've yet to see a leprechaun. Now, get out of here and let me work."

The CIA buildings used to be readily accessible, somewhere behind the old red brick brewery. Now they had built big and beautiful new ones near the town of Langley, Virginia. This annoyed the natives, made communication in person harder and created horrid traffic jams on Chain Bridge and Canal Road at rush hours.

The reception room, however, was attractive, the Director's number one secretary even more so as she arrived smiling to escort Charlie, who asked, "What are you doing here working on Sunday, Ellie?"

"Oh, all kinds of hell's breaking loose, and anyway my boyfriend's out of town."

"How about me?"

"Ask that again and it will cost you a dinner. Now come on. The boss is having a busy day."

Once in the office he noted his usual favorite exhibit. It was a long framed strip photograph of Communist leaders. Across the faces of Stalin, Beria, Malenkov, Zhukov and two others had been drawn big red crosses.

Arthur Jackson noted the direction of his gaze. "Still too damned many of the bastards. I'm having another rogue's gallery framed of our Chinese friends. Want some coffee? I do."

"Yes, please."

"Ellie! Get the nice man some coffee."

She tossed her head. "I don't see why I should, sir, when he won't buy me dinner."

"I didn't say I wouldn't, you did. Now, Arthur, I need your help."

"Ask and it will probably not be given you."

Arthur Jackson was more receptive, but scarcely more convinced. This was not surprising. Already that day he had

127

been told—no, instructed to believe was the proper phase—that a nationalist, anti-Communist African was an enemy, and that a two-faced South American leader who had shared bank deposits, assassination and chicken with Fidel Castro should be treated as a trusted and valued friend.

He did, however, have suggestions to make. "Look, Joyce, there are two things certain. In this beautiful city a good man's closest friend on earth is his secretary, especially if he's not sleeping with her. Second, I've never trusted a single Jamaican in my long and evil life, especially one who smiles all the time and says 'Yes, sah,' meaning, 'If I had my way I'd castrate you, you white bastard.' So you're on your own. Officially, I'm out of it. That's internal security, and not my business. But if you dig up anything worthwhile, I'll see you get help."

"You mean you believe me?"

"Of course not. I don't believe anyone—not any more—but I suspect everybody. Good hunting!"

Good hunting, he thought on the way to his car. Good hunting be damned! No hounds, no gun, no horn, nothing, not even his old gold badge or framed Bureau credentials any more. He looked up to the wispy crescent of an early moon poised too theatrically above the point of the Washington Monument. He shook his head. So maybe the man is just poor, sad, sick Roger Storrow after all; and as for you, Charles Xavier Joyce, maybe you're sick, too, sick in the head. One thing is for sure. You're a tired, tired man and it's bed for you.

CHAPTER XV

NOT ONLY TIRED, von Tetlow was sick. His fever had risen alarmingly by late evening, and his chest was congested. Even the normally impassive James, now returned, was alarmed. "I had most certainly better call the doctor, sah. He will know what to do."

He did not like the idea. He had thought about it quite a lot. Doctors were probing and inquisitive. That was their business. Not only did they look down throats and into ears, they also sometimes shone little bright lights into the pupils of patient's eyes. There was no reason why Roger Storrow should not be wearing contact lenses. Still, he had not owned any before, and it seemed unlikely that he would have acquired them on a ruin-hunting expedition to Yucatan. Also, doctors quite often took blood samples. A too radical variance in chemistry pattern might make even an internist suspicious. A cardiogram could be just as bad.

A good doctor knew his patient by certain medical fingerprints as well as by physical features. He did not want to see a good doctor, at least not Storrow's personal doctor. He told James. "Your people must have some man we can call in, or at least someone who never knew Storrow."

James agreed. "You just rest there easy, sah. I'll go down to the drug store to use the pay phone."

The work week of the Party Aparat is seven days and the day twenty-four hours. James had no difficulty in making his contact. He recognized, however, the accent of trouble. His question had been, "I know it's Sunday, but the set just won't

129

work and the boss will miss his favorite program. Can't you send your man over?"

The answer was, "Sorry. No can do. Our best man just called in sick. He says it's some kind of virus infection. There's a lot of it around these days. So you'll have to get someone from another shop. You don't want any viruses in your house."

So, he thought, the Aparat's local doctor was under suspicion, possibly under surveillance. He would have to find a physician with the aid of the local medical society.

The practitioner who arrived was young, eager and a little nervous. The large Georgetown house obviously belonged to the rich. He had never before been called to one like it. Also the patient was a big shot. This was a man who sat at least at the left hand of Presidents. It didn't make much sense that he had called in an unknown, a medical blind date. He must take care to remember all he saw and heard. It might impress some of his young colleagues at the hospital.

A quick examination of his patient convinced him that Mr. Storrow should be in a hospital. If he did not yet suffer from pneumonia, it seemed probable that he would shortly. The man, however, already apparently lightheaded from his high fever, categorically refused to be moved.

The doctor had concluded, "Very well, sir, I cannot force you to go to a hospital, but I must warn you that you're taking a grave risk by refusing."

Lightheaded or not, he was in complete control of his role. "Balderdash, young man. Hospitals are only for dying. Do your stuff with the old needle, then leave quietly." Roger Storrow would have been proud of him, he thought.

"Yes, sir. I will give you penicillin now, more tomorrow. I'll leave these sleeping pills in case you're too restless. And you must take a lot of liquid."

"Whiskey?"

"Water and fruit juices, clear soup, such as that. You really should have a nurse. In fact, I insist."

"James can take care of me. Always has."

"Perhaps so. But I consider it my duty to send a nurse. I'll call the registry. One will arrive. If you wish to send her away, that's your business. You will only have to pay half a day's salary."

"All right, doctor. Bully for you. Good night, doctor."

James Chapman did not like this idea of a nurse or any other stranger in the house. But by the time the nurse rang the doorbell, von Tetlow was half delirious. James was scared. So Rita Bernstein took over the care of this distinguished patient. She was neither young, pert nor pretty. She was, however, experienced, mature and, in her way, beautiful. Her dark eyes were sad. She had looked on much misery, including her own. Soul and body alike would for ever bear the scars from the dreadful world of concentration camps.

She had, perforce, developed that instinctive recognition of danger which had been necessary for survival. Strange that here in a spacious bedroom in peaceful Georgetown she was conscious not only of the smell of sickness, but also of some scent of evil. This man with the fevered eyes and deep-flushed skin came directly from somewhere in her past. She felt a reluctance to be near him, to touch him even in the course of professional duties. Once or twice during the night she could have sworn she had heard him mutter in German.

Von Tetlow made reasonably rapid recovery. He was required, however, to remain in bed for nearly a week. It was enjoyable. He was resting. He felt safe for the time being. From telephone calls and personal visits he was learning more and more about the character of Storrow's friends. When he was once more free, he would no longer hesitate to accept a few invitations. In short, except for one thing, his confidence was returning.

He had enjoyed the ministrations and the sight of a fine-looking nurse. What he could not understand, though, was her nervousness, the fact that more than once he had caught her staring at him when she felt he was unaware of her scrutiny. Nor was she much of a conversationalist. God, how he hungered for companionship, particularly feminine companionship. Certainly there was little cheer from the taciturn, ever-watchful James; and there was little from this starched efficient creature bearing thermometers, wash cloths and pills. He was glad when, after three days, she left.

James, who also had a fine instinct for survival, was definitely pleased. He had not liked the woman. She was danger. He knew it. And danger enough existed already. He mentioned this to von Tetlow, who briefly considered the matter, then asked, "Well, what was it about her, James?"

"The eyes, I think. Yes, sah, it was the eyes."

Yes. James was right. The German shuddered. Now he knew; it all came back. There had been something in the eyes which reminded him of that damnable Hilda Meyer who had trapped him on the boat.

Von Tetlow did a great deal of reading from Storrow's library and the two daily papers. He even watched more TV broadcasts, offensive as many were. Particularly he watched and read the international news. It was strange to be lying in Storrow's room, in Storrow's bed—or was this one—rather, had this one belonged to his wife? How, he wondered, could man and wife, especially if still of vigorous age, sleep thus apart? As a matter of fact, in such a narrow couch, how could they ever sleep together? He now knew Roger Storrow very well, and he felt sympathy for him. It was clear that he was well-respected, even liked, in official and social Washington. It was also quite plain that he was respected but not at all liked by the press. Probably this was in his favor. Von Tetlow rather hoped he was still alive, even if a prisoner; though if alive he provided another added danger.

He wondered about Charlie Joyce. The man had come to call once when he was still quite sick, had made a few friendly inquiries, left a book, *Masters of Deceit*. "Dull reading but interesting. Maybe you've already studied it."

A strange gift this; a book by the Director of the FBI. A strange remark, also. Would Storrow have read it? No, probably not. There was, as he knew, little love lost between the two men. Damn Joyce anyway. He kept showing up. At the cemetery, that was accident, but at the mailbox, what of that? And now this last visit? He made him uncomfortable. He acted so normally, so affably. Yet he always seemed to be watching so intently, studying him so carefully. Was Joyce suspicious of him? Had he seen that contact lens business? If he was suspicious, how much so? On what grounds? What else did he know? Perhaps he was letting his imagination get the upper hand, causing him—what was that phrase?—to run scared. Probably, he thought, there isn't really anything much to worry about.

Charlie Joyce was a persistent man. Even after his trying day with officialdom, a long night's sleep had made him feel much better and more determined than ever to prove his suspicions valid or lay them to rest for ever.

To any trained investigator, the personal physician of a subject is a valuable potential source of information. The physician has, of course, the duty to protect the confidences and privacy of his patient. He has also every citizen's duty to uphold and assist the law. Therefore, Charlie had gone to Dr. Fisher, not with any specific questions in mind but simply to discover whether the doctor had observed anything unusual in the recent appearance or actions of Roger Storrow.

He hadn't even seen his patient. "I can't understand it. Comes back all bunged up. Nearly comes down with pneumonia, and doesn't even try to call me. Makes no sense."

It made sense to Charlie Joyce. He had now, of course, no investigative personnel at his command. So he went himself. A nurse, even one who had never before treated the patient, probably would have noticed certain things. Contact lenses, for instance. No she had not. There was a look of displeasure. "I certainly was not that much interested in the man's eyes."

Then, gradually, his tactful questions had released the nurse's recollections. He took her over the same ground again, starting with the first hours in the Georgetown house. Yes, she was almost certain she had heard him mumble or dream or something in German. Yes, she understood German, But the words had been too indistinct to decipher perfectly. No, she couldn't be sure it was German. It could have been Dutch. Yes, his manner had completely changed after the fever broke. Was there anything else, any words, any actions that seemed strange? She had to think. Yes, yes, there was one thing. "When I went to hang up his clothes, of course I emptied out the pockets, put everything neatly on the bureau. Suddenly he was looking at me, angrily I thought, as if he wanted to stop me, but he didn't say anything."

"Think carefully, Miss Bernstein. Can you remember what was in the pockets?"

"Wait, let me see. The usual handkerchief. I left that. Wallet, keys on a chain, two fountain pens, some envelopes, cigarette lighter, and a little package, quite heavy. The valet took it."

"Stop right there. What did it look like, this package?"

"How do you mean? It was just a package—square, cardboard, let me see—oh, yes, it was stamped for mailing, to some jeweler, I think."

"Can you possibly remember where?"

A shake of the head. "No, I don't study other people's personal things."

"Sorry, of course not." To himself he thought, well, I'll be damned. I'll be just plain damned.

For days, von Tetlow had wondered if the Berlin report he had mailed would reach its destination. He had wondered what the Soviets would do. He found his answers in the black headlines in the *Washington Herald,* and he learned the details from the story beneath.

In an attempt to do something about the Berlin Wall, the Western Powers have committed a most ill-advised act. Using huge charges of explosives, they have blasted holes in the Wall at some dozen places. Unhappily, the explosions also killed over a thousand people. The number of wounded is not yet known. It is known, however, that the dead and wounded include many who were leaving Sunday worship in the East Zone, or had come to chat with West German relatives across the wall. While we appreciate that it was the intention of the Western Powers to facilitate . . .

Weakly he dropped the paper to the floor. *Pravda* could hardly have written a better piece for the Communists. So there it was. Clearly, just as clearly as if the real truth had been printed, instead of this distortion, he could read what had happened. The tactics, the technique of totalitarians never changed. A life was worth less than a pfennig, not so much as a kopek. The explosions had been massive. Apartment houses had been destroyed. Crowds in the streets had been massacred. What had happened was plain. The Communist authorities had been fully prepared. They had heavily mined the streets and basements on their side of the demarcation line. Then, at the noon hour, using some lure, they had herded people to their massacre. The Communists could and had already blamed the West. They would be believed. The shattered wall, the collapsed tenements, the torn and bloody corpses were their witnesses—mute for ever and so doubly eloquent.

And he had done this, and under orders as usual. He was still weak and ill and was very much alone. Perhaps this is why he wept. James saw this when he came into the bedroom to remove the breakfast tray.

"You appear sad, sah," his eyes dropped to the headlines. "Nothing there to be sad about. Not for any of those dirty Germans. They did this thing themselves to each other. How many, sah, will it take to pay for six million Jews?"

Damn the man! "What the devil are you talking about, James? My head hurts like hell and my eyes water. Bring me some coffee."

"Certainly, sah. But I'd be most careful, for I do not want to make a bad report. It might reflect on me. I would not like that."

He started angrily to protest. He'd fire the insolent bastard. He stopped himself, sighed hopelessly. No, he commanded no one. There was no one to whom he could really give orders, not even to himself.

CHAPTER XVI

THE LOYAL AND efficient Miss Kelly felt terrible. She had been subjected to further harassments, more obscene whispers, blind phone calls. She had suffered screaming nightmares. Her priest had counselled peace of mind through prayer and meditation. He had also advised forsaking the world, the flesh and the devil. This was really of no help at all. Her doctor, and she put little faith in doctors, had been more specific but no more helpful. He had told her quite frankly that she was fast becoming an alcoholic and must pull herself together. In her heart she knew all this to be only too true. For this she gave the poor doctor "a piece of her mind," then flounced in outraged dignity from his office.

She had a hangover again today. She felt, therefore, that all her friends seemed to have deserted her and nothing but self-pity remained for company. What is more, she had had a very trying morning at that house in Georgetown, working on Mr. Storrow's correspondence. He had been uncommonly irritable. Not only that, she had had to put up with his damned insolent houseman. Not that she had anything against Negroes, but after all there was a limit. Now she was able to tell that nice Mr. Joyce all about it. There really was, when you came right down to it, something about the Irish.

"I know you'll think I'm crazy, Mr. Joyce. Everybody else does. Sometimes I'm not sure about it myself. Maybe I am off my rocker. But I want to tell you what happened today, if you don't mind listening."

Charlie Joyce crossed one long leg over the other, rocked back comfortably in his chair. "Mind? I should say not, Mary Margaret. Carry on."

"Well, I was sitting in Mr. Storrow's bedroom taking dictation. Some of it very complicated. You know, usually I can write shorthand without half looking at the paper or the man dictating. Why, heavens, I can practically write what Mr. Storrow's going to say before he says it. But somehow it was more difficult this time."

She quickly lit a cigarette, exhaling a nervous mouthful of smoke. After all, it was bad for you to inhale, wasn't it?

"Right in the middle of a long paragraph there's a voice from the hall. It's dark out there, you know, and I almost jumped from my skin. It was that bastard, James."

"Ooh!" Her hand flew to her mouth. "I'm sorry, Mr. Joyce, but that's what he is as far as I'm concerned. But as I was saying, it's so dark out there, about all you could see was a great tall shadow and sort of the pale outline of a face. But that's not the point. All of a sudden I was sure it was the same voice I heard that terrible night—that terrible night when those flatfooted cops wouldn't believe me," her voice was rising toward hysteria. "Why, they practically insulted me!"

Charlie Joyce did not move except to raise a hand gently. "Relax, Mary Margaret, please relax. Tell me what night you're talking about. I don't know, don't you see. Start from the beginning. Do you have any whiskey anywhere about?"

"Why, Mr. Joyce, you know better than that."

He grinned. "Ah, come off it, Mary Margaret. Four to one there's a bottle in your desk. I would like a drink. Water from the cooler will do. And I never drink alone. It'll do you good. Just a light one."

The drinks poured, Joyce noted that Miss Kelly grabbed at her glass a little too avidly. Maybe he hadn't had such a good idea after all. Oh, well, it would help for the moment to take some of the tension out of her. He waited. Sketchily at first, then in more confident detail, she told him everything that had happened—well, everything except about the one obscene thing she had seen. After all, there had to be some limits. She told also of the disappearing letter, the men following her, the whispering in theaters, all of it.

When she had finished, she felt much better. He felt much worse, although more firm than ever in his convictions. Arthur Jackson had certainly been sound in his offhand suggestions. Seek out the loyal Miss Kelly's suspect, the untrustworthy Jamaican—the one who called you "sah," but with murder in his heart.

Back in his own office Charlie Joyce sat down to think. He knew what he knew, but he had no way to prove it. He was up against a ruthless, efficient organization. He must work alone—at least until he had some really tangible proof. What did he now have that was new? An immigrant nurse had seen a second jeweler's box. A woman some thought to be nearly insane was sure she recognized her prowler as the servant of Roger Storrow. He knew he was certain, but how could he prove that the National Security Council itself was harboring an imposter, certainly a spy? The only sure proof he could imagine would be fingerprints. Handwriting was out with that mangled right hand. And, dammit, you just couldn't walk up to a special assistant to the President and ask him for another set of prints.

There were various things he could think of. He might, for instance, go again to Storrow's house, enter under some pretext, and try to remove some object the imposter had recently handled. No, that would not work. The man was still housebound and was certain to be on his guard. If he waited until he went back to work, there still remained the suspicious James.

If only he could gain one little minute in the house by himself it would be enough. No complex equipment was necessary to lift a fingerprint, just a pinch of any fine powder and a piece of scotch tape would do. The powder would stick to the minute dots of perspiration exuded from the pores of the fingertips. And the tape would pick up the powder in its patterns.

Then there was Storrow's office. There was no glass top on the desk since the man disliked glass tops, and the tooled leather desk pad was not much good. Let's see, what else was there? A bronze pen stand, the brass corners of the leather pad, a fancy paper knife, two telephones. If he knew Mary Margaret as he thought he did, those objects would be useless also. He would find out. He dialed her office number, asked the questions.

"No, I'm sorry, Mr. Joyce, Mr. Storrow's been out so long, I cleaned everything. I always do, but this time I did a specially thorough job. I even used polish on the metal things. I don't think Dick Tracy himself could find a print. Who are you looking for, anyway?"

"I'm damned if I know myself."

"Now people including me are going to think you're a little crazy too, Mr. Joyce."

"Maybe they won't be so wrong. Tell me something else, Mary Margaret. Does Mr. Storrow have any magazines on his desk, or on a side table? I can't remember."

"No, sir. He thinks it's unbusinesslike."

He thanked her and hung up. Damn! The cover or pages of a slick magazine could have picked up a very clear print. All he needed was one little print, just one. If there are 30,000,000 individual fingerprints in the world, no two appear identical under magnification. And of course those of the genuine Roger Storrow are on record.

Yes, Charlie thought, the fingerprint business could be difficult, but there is one thing I know I can use—a photograph. With a miniature camera, indistinguishable from a cigarette lighter, he would record the man's face, then blow up the picture to a size where it could be compared with one of the genuine Storrow. Surely then some flaw in the impersonation should be recorded. The idea pleased him.

In the shelter of the Mexican priest's little house, waiting came hard to Roger Storrow. Fortunately, for a few days he was too heavily drugged to think out many problems. In fact, and this is why some victims of coronaries live and others die, he had said nothing to himself other than, I must not die; I am going to live. In this way he had devoted every atom of conscious, and thus subconscious, strength to staying alive. He had had to stay alive, and had done so. He was, however, very weak and realized he dared not try to move too much. He must not become too excited, and somehow he must not despair.

In any bed, at first balanced between life and death, then edging closer and closer to full life, there is time for long, long thought. He had finally come to a conclusion. His impersonator, unless he had assassination in mind, could only do a limited amount of really serious harm in a short period of time. If he were discovered, well and good, if it were done quickly. If this did not happen right at the beginning, the longer the man succeeded in his masquerade, the greater were his chances of getting away with it indefinitely. If too much time passed, there remained only one sure and certain way of stripping away the mask. He himself had to survive, not only the occlusion of a coronary artery, and with it the partial death of the great heart muscle, but also the certain attempts of the Aparat to track him down. They would surely work hard to find him and eliminate him, preferably without trace. Therefore, it behooved him to do but one thing—make haste slowly, with extreme caution.

He called Padre Fortunato to his bedside, looked weakly up at the kind, round face of the fat little priest. "Padre, you are aware that besides this thing with my heart, I am in bad trouble, so bad that it could bring danger to you and to your house?"

There was a gentle, pitying smile, then a more humorous quirk of the lips, "You will, I hope, pardon me, my son, but seldom does a man run at full speed down the Grand Calle at night, with bare feet and clad only in trousers, unless he is in some little trouble. But I must say you speak our language well."

"Thank you. I have had much practice lately, enforced practice, you might say. But this trouble is more than some little trouble. This is very bad trouble. Padre, I am not of your church, but I am a Christian. I must throw myself on your mercy."

A benign nod of the head. "You have sought sanctuary, my son. You were afforded it. And so it shall be."

"I am not a criminal, Padre, except in the eyes of those who would destroy your church, everything in which I think you believe. This I must tell you, although I am afraid."

"Speak, my son."

"My enemies, those who held me prisoner, are the Communists. And before my God and yours, they will not rest until I am dead. This is why I speak of bad trouble, of danger. It is for your sake, for that little broom-sweeper's sake, for that of the good—what was his name?—Dr. Alvarez, and I need not mention, it is for mine."

Padre Fortunato shook his head gently, unbelievingly. "Are you certain you are correct, my son? These Communists are not of the church and, granted, cause political trouble and sometimes riots. But to assassinate a visitor from North America and cause the death of a poor, small priest, surely it is that you exaggerate?"

"In this I do not exaggerate, Padre. These men are of the Kremlin's International Aparat. You have heard of the Mafia, perhaps?"

This time the expression was apologetic. "Indeed, in fact, asking your forgiveness, it is often said that they control your country. This is what one hears. But what have the Mafia to do with Communists?"

"Sometimes much, but this was only as an example. The Mafia has important figures in many countries who control all activities. So with the Communists. These who held me, who would kill, are important, ruthless men. And now talking has made me very tired, Padre."

"Then you must sleep again. These pills . . ."

Roger raised himself on one elbow, very slowly. "But there is one more thing. Tell me the truth, Padre. Isn't it true that since I came here men have asked whether you have seen anyone answering my description?"

A slow nod. "That is true. I, however, thought they were of the police, in fact they so indicated. So, of course," quickly he crossed himself, "I lied."

Roger grinned. "I am sure you will be forgiven, perhaps even rewarded if I live long enough."

"This too had occurred to me. And mine is a very poor church, I trust you forgive me for saying this?"

"I forgive and understand. But, Padre, these men will be back. Word will spread in the neighborhood that I am here. Inevitably the news will leak out. You must decide how to protect yourself, perhaps send me to a hospital."

"No, my son. That would be even more public, and perhaps, if what you tell is true, of more danger to you. Now you must rest. For some reason I believe you. I will think of something. So, take your pills."

He took them and soon rested in a heavy and dreamless sleep. He did not waken until the following dawn. Shortly

141

thereafter the good priest, bearing a self-satisfied smile, brought him hot coffee.

"Why so happy so early in the morning, Padre?"

"It is because I have told you I would think of something, and I have. More than this, it has been acted upon most expeditiously. I must admit it was with the help of the estimable Dr. Alvarez. What hour is it now, by the way?"

"What has that to do with it?" But he instinctively had glanced at his left wrist. The watch was gone. Maybe he'd put it on the chair beside the cot. He reached over.

Padre Fortunato put out a restraining hand. "No use, my son. You will never see that handsome watch again. But you may live to buy another."

Roger was becoming annoyed. "Come on, Padre, what is all this play-acting?"

The priest leaned forward in appeal. "Please, I apologize. I do sometimes love a little drama."

"So?"

"And so, as I have said, your watch, this nice platinum watch, is gone. If it has not already been, it will be found very soon around the wrist bones of a body so charred that no one could recognize any feature at all."

"How in the devil's name . . ."

"I will tell you. Dr. Alvarez, with no difficulty, obtained a pauper's body. We have many paupers, you know. After the moon was down this morning we left it, wearing your watch with its letters R.L.S., in an abandoned railway shack. This shack, most fortunately, has just burned to the ground. The man was of your height, or almost."

"My God, Padre, you took this risk, you and Alvarez, for me? You will never get away with it."

Again the soft smile. "Yes, my son. We took the risk. I, because I believed you. Dr. Alvarez, because he received his education on a North American—how do you say *premio*? —prize?—no, not this."

"Grant?"

"Exactly, on a grant to the medical school of the university at Harvard."

"I am a very fortunate man. But how did Alvarez know he was not shielding a criminal?"

"Because, my son, I told him he was not."

"I am doubly fortunate." He shook his head in wonder. "But tell me, will my friends know this body has been found?"

"From the police, assuredly not. The police have the brains of pigs. They will assume that the body was of some vagrant who had stolen the watch but had, as yet, been unable to sell it. Then they will conveniently forget the whole matter, but keep the watch for its value in metal."

"Then, how?"

"Oh, this is simple. Dr. Alvarez is also the medical examiner. He will have inquiries made concerning the body and the watch to see if some relative would claim them. Your friends will most surely hear of this. I doubt they will claim such a heap of burned meat and blackened bones."

Roger disagreed. "I'm not as certain. These are very thorough people. They might, for instance, claim the body just to make sure I am really dead."

"How will they do this?"

"By examining the teeth. They are very familiar with my teeth."

"Then I will tell Dr. Alvarez to delay somehow."

"How could he deny the body to these men if they claimed to be relatives?"

Padre Fortunato looked less sure of himself. "Frankly, I do not know. Have you any idea?"

Roger was silent for nearly a minute, then turned his head to smile directly at the priest. "Do you know, Padre, associating with two such upholders of law and order as you and Alvarez makes my mind work deviously also. I think I have something."

"And this is?"

"Some such reasoning as this. If these Red friends of mine claim the body as a relative, no one would believe he was a common vagrant. If he was not, what was his body doing in an old shack. The presence of the watch lends an added doubt to the vagrant theory. If then it is thought that the corpse is of an important man, more inquiry must be made on suspicion of what we call foul play. No, it will not translate."

"Do not trouble yourself. I understand."

"Good. Something about even what is left of the body may

cause Alvarez to consider the possibility of poison or something. He will tell them he must keep the body to make certain chemical tests. He might even send specimens to a laboratory in Mexico City to be certain. This idea might succeed in giving us quite a lot of time."

This time the priest laughed in genuine pleasure. "Congratulations, my son. But now I am not so very sure that you are not a criminal."

"I thank you most graciously. Frankly, I do not believe even this will wholly satisfy them. It will, however, throw them off the scent, give us a little time. Time, Padre, I must buy time. God grant I get back my strength and quickly."

"Alvarez thinks you will, and I, I think that God will grant it."

Roger bowed his head. The priest looked at him fondly. "Was there anything else, my son?"

"Yes, you could call the counsul in Merida to ask that he come to see—no, that would not do, it would attract too much attention. No. I will write him a note, trying to tell him the truth. Damn it anyway, I've only met the man once. Why should he believe me? No, I'll just write a letter saying I am too ill. No, none of it is any good."

"You are right. But if you should write this letter and I should take it in and explain to this man all that you have told me," a quick smile, "and perhaps you should tell me quite a lot more, then we might cause some action to be taken."

"I am an idiot. I should have thought of this a day ago. The consul would not wholly believe the story, even from a priest, but it would, I think, make him curious enough to investigate, and I hope with some armed help."

Then Roger told the little priest much more, and wrote an appropriate letter. Since there was nothing to do but wait until his host returned from the city, he slept.

The vice-consul was on a five day fishing trip and could not be reached. The Mexican girl who handled the telephone and discouraged visitors during his absence was, to Padre Fortunato, obviously not the person with whom to discuss the matter. He was afraid that she could talk and he knew that she lacked any authority to take action.

When he heard this, Roger felt no anger, only frustration

and discouragement. He cheered considerably when Padre Fortunato brought him a reasonably large drink of Castillo Rum. "The good doctor is a humane man. He says this is excellent for the arteries."

Roger agreed. "It is very good indeed and fine for my heart, even for my mind. Do you know what I am thinking?"

"No, my friend. When we drink together I say 'my friend,' not 'my son.' No, I do not."

"I think, Padre, that this is what we North Americans call a do-it-yourself job. But I'd feel much happier if I had a gun. I'm still afraid those men might come back before I am on my feet. Can you get me a gun?"

The priest nodded happily. "Yes, even in the house of God. Even a poor priest can still occasionally eat broiled quail, that is if he shoots them himself."

For the first time in so very long, Roger laughed. "Then you had better leave it by my bed. Birds may be acceptable to the church, but if someone must shoot Communists it is better that it be on my conscience alone."

Padre Fortunato laughed also. "We will all three have things on our consciences before this is all over, I am afraid. We have been body snatchers, thieves, arsonists and liars. No, and this time I repeat, my son; this is not exactly—what name did you give it?—a do-it-yourself job."

CHAPTER XVII

CHARLIE JOYCE HAD believed the loyal Miss Kelly. He had told her so, and had thereby given her a most precious gift— the ability to believe in herself again, and in her own sanity.

He had not, however, mentioned to her his certainty that her beloved Mr. Storrow had been replaced by an imposter. That might have been most harmful. Well along the road to recovery and trusting the evidence of her senses, she could be an invaluable ally. This was as it should be. Charlie Joyce had trusted in and believed Mary Margaret Kelly. When the time came, she would trust in Charlie Joyce, and trust completely.

But what about the untrustworthy Jamaican? What in the name of great Gilhooley had he been doing prowling in the Kelly apartment, exposing himself to the terrified woman? How did this fit into a pattern of espionage? He would have enjoyed invoking the methods of the old third degree to get answers from James. Or would he? After all, the man had been the houseman and chauffeur of Roger Storrow for a good many years. Charlie Joyce did not doubt for a minute that Miss Kelly had seen an intruder. He was much less positive that her identification of his voice was accurate.

There was a way, of course. He could see if the lady was willing to swear out a complaint, to appear at a line-up officially to restate her identification. If she were willing, if in this way she could identify him, James could be held and would be questioned. Still it had been some time ago and he would have the skeptical police report to deal with. Also, he did not want to upset Mary Margaret Kelly all over again.

No, on the whole this was not the answer. He would have to do better.

In his frustration he even considered physical violence. Action would have given him pleasure, to beat the true story out of James Chapman. This thought caused him to smile wryly to himself. He was nearly fifty-two years old, and although he played squash sometimes in winter, and golf in summer, always badly, most of his life had been desk-bound. Soaking wet he weighed in at 165 pounds. His proposed victim was at least ten years younger and carried his 190 with the menacing grace of a big cat. The idea was ludicrous, unless he could find two other men to hold the Jamaican. Not only that, he had a feeling that this was not the kind of man out of whom a confession could be beaten. Mental torture or dread of the Jamaican Obeah might be more effective. He was, however, not only out of patience and short on time, but entirely without powdered dried embryos and bat's blood. . . .

There was one thing he could do. No one was going to help him conduct an investigation, or conduct one for him, into the bona fides of the man now lying in Roger Storrow's bed. Right now that was certain. He could, of course, have a national agency and police file check run on the man's Jamaican servant. He doubted that this had ever been done, at least since some cursory checking at immigration time quite a few years ago.

For a security-minded government, he often thought, we did some weird things. Chauffeurs, switchboard operators, even interpreters for our top officials overseas were nearly always natives of the country where these officials were stationed. They were checked, if at all, only by the security services of their own country. At the best they might be working for those very services, at the worst for the Communist enemy.

He remembered that in 1947 the Chief of US Army Engineers in Greece had an excellent chauffeur. He spoke passable English and could repair American vehicles. He had other affiliations, including high rank in the Communist Aparat. This his employers refused to believe. It was, however, amply proven. The man was caught late at night by Greek military police while kneeling with a lighted cigarette

147

lighter in his hands. This in itself was no crime. What was questionable was that the lighter was being held against a fuse. The fuse was connected to nearly a ton of dynamite stolen from the Engineers' Supply Depot, and the dynamite lay in the center of an arsenal of US arms and destined for the Greek National Army.

At home? Well, such a check for servants would most probably be done through the files of some employment or credit agency.

He went to his desk, sat down and typed out all the data he could recall about the man, plus as good a physical description as possible. He grinned to himself when he recalled his early days in the Bureau on the hunt for Negro draft dodgers. Height 5 foot 8 inches, build medium, eyes dark, hair dark, complexion dark, and usually known by at least four different names from as many addresses. He tried to do a little better. Then he suddenly remembered something which might prove useful.

Roger had mentioned that the invaluable James had once served in the Merchant Marine, and at a time when Communists seemed welcome while Nazis were out. Somewhere, therefore, there existed some accurate identifying data, including fingerprints and photographs. These would help in the check here and perhaps with the authorities in Jamaica. He completed the memorandum and signed it. His name was enough authority at least to cause investigation of the servant if not the master. He stamped the envelope and decided the fresh air could do him no harm. He would walk to the mailbox three blocks away. It looked more patriotic these days in its bright tri-color. The service, however, was no better.

The mailbox, the fresh air, or both gave him a further idea. Instead of returning to his empty house—damn the slow arrival of his sister-in-law's baby anyway!—he walked briskly another four blocks north and two west, mounted the steps of a square brick house and rang the bell. To his pleasure, the owner himself answered. "Charlie Joyce! What revolting combination of circumstances brings you here? Wait, don't tell me. Your Martha's out of town, and Irishmen don't dare drink alone."

148

"Right, and also wrong, General. You should know better. After all, together we helped liberate France for de Gaulle and the Folies Bergères."

"Well, don't just stand there. Come inside. I have some vintage ice."

The two men walked into a small library. General Scanlon headed for the compact built-in bar. Joyce put a hand on his arm. "None for me right now, Jack. I have a tale to tell, believe me, and I'll be thirsty only after I get it off my chest."

"So be it, you miserable gumshoe. I shall listen because I have no choice. But I shall also have a drink, maybe two."

Twenty minutes later General Scanlon sat twirling an empty highball glass between his palms. "Curiouser and curiouser, as Storrow would say. And you, my old super-sleuth, have bats in your belfry, or should I say, C. X. Joyce, you are suffering, perhaps, from the hallucinations of male menopause . . ."

"Goddammit, Jack, now just listen."

"Down boy. Relax. I still enjoy needling you. Does me good, probably doesn't hurt you. You're too serious, always were. You just said Goddammit, listen! Well, I have. And for some inexplicable reason I almost believe you—almost but not quite. This is not because it's believable. It is not. But because the little people and the leprechauns have always seemed to be on good terms with you, and whisper strange truths in your shell-like ear. So let's assume I swallow this, what can I do to help? But first let me ask you another question."

"Shoot."

"You and I've been at this business quite a long time. Still, I'd like to ask you how any man, no matter how clever, can get away with the impersonation of another?"

Joyce rubbed the back of a hand across his forehead. "Well, old friend, we both know it has been done, and done well, but not how often. So, if it has been once it can be again. I won't belabor the point of Arnold at, and even before, the Battle of Cowpers, or of Major André. There is, however, a good reason man sees, sometimes even hears, only what he expects to."

"How do you mean?"

149

"I'll answer you with another question. A lawyer, let us say, has walked into the same office, even his own den, five days a week for five years. One day someone has changed one of the three pictures on the wall. How long would it take the average man to notice the difference?"

"Damned if I know, Charlie. I'm no test case, but my wife says I wouldn't even note a change in the pattern of our living-room rug."

"Mine says the same; but women are different."

"So they are, so they are, and so?"

"So that's why they had to wipe out poor Marjorie—and do that Kelly business I told you about."

"Go on."

"All right, now suppose that picture in the office was a forgery, not even a very good forgery, what then?"

"I get your point—but how about voice, manner of speech, and so on?"

"O.K., General, I'll try that one too. God knows I've given it enough thought. You like music, right?"

"Within my cultural limits, a little narrow, I'm afraid."

"So be it. You have friends in for drinks. You've got a Beethoven symphony on the player. In the middle I switch just one record on you, from a different Beethoven work?"

"I'm not sure. I might notice, even if not at once."

"Maybe, Jack. But what if I just put one in, same symphony, but played by a different orchestra?"

Scanlon held both hands over his head. *"Touché,* you Jesuit. You win. I believe you."

Charlie Joyce exhaled gratefully. "Thanks, Jack. I'm even convinced myself. Now, tell me. Do you still run from your lofty post, or have something to do with the plain clothes detail of the CID?"

"For my sins, yes."

"Your boys are still sent on practice missions around town, tailing people, trying to plant dummy bombs in restricted areas and so on?"

"Naturally, that I'll never officially admit. But let's say there's an awful lot less of it than there used to be." The General thumped his near-empty glass on his knee; the ice

150

cubes tinkled. "But no matter, you just wait a minute. None of them, by God, is going to tail any special assistant to you-know-who."

Joyce raised his hand. "O.K., so now you relax. But couldn't you have them try a test run on that damned Jamaican houseman?"

"Why my boys? Didn't you all do that kind of thing in the Bureau?"

"You know better than that, General Scanlon, sir. We went out with orders, 'Never lose your man, but don't ever be caught.' Pretty tough instructions, but they were always for real."

"Why the grin, Charlie?"

"I was thinking of one time when an agent friend of mine was called on it. He acted mad as hell, walked up to his subject and said, 'You're damned right I'm following you, and if you don't keep your dirty hands off my wife, I'll do much worse.'"

"Did it work?"

"It worked perfectly. But now, Jack, I'm being one hundred percent serious. I know the Office of Special Investigation of the Air Force does this kind of thing. Let's say I've read about it. They even used to try to plant dummy explosives in Curt LeMay's big bombers. So, it's still being done. Can you help me or not?"

Scanlon stood to refresh his drink, raised the glass to Charlie Joyce. "I'll help you, you know that."

"Yes, General, I was sure you would."

"Very well," with an inquiring grin, "and more, I know you too well. I know there's still something."

"There is. I'd give my remaining hairs to know what in hell Storrow's mailing in little square jeweler's boxes—or, rather, what that Jamaican is probably mailing for him."

"Now wait a minute, Charlie. Robbing Uncle's mails is a little beyond . . ."

"Don't get jumpy, General. My idea is this. Your boys aren't too damned expert yet. You'll pardon me, of course. James William Gordon Chapman, that's really his name, may spot the tail and grow nervous. That can help, especially if you'll put on replacements at once. But what I really want is this. If he's about to put something in a mailbox, two of your boys can grab him and take it away."

"Great! He yells, the cops come, the NAACP screams, the boys are in trouble. I can already feel them snatching those hard-won pretty stars off my shoulders."

Again he raised his hand. "You, General Scanlon, sir, are the one suffering from hardening of the brain. Your boys can either tell the truth, they're on a practice mission, pick-pocketing potential spies, that they were clumsy, etc. Or, even better, two clean-cut American youths are out walking when up to them comes swishing this Caribbean queer, and so like good mothers' boys they were just teaching him a lesson . . ."

Scanlon slapped his knee with an open hand. "All right, all right. I quit. You haven't lost your devious and degenerate touch." He stood and saluted with his raised glass. "You win. I am at your command. Now, you black Irishman, will you have a drink?"

"Thanks a million, Jack. Yes, I'll have a drink. Scotch and soda, light on the soda—but there's still something else."

"I'd never have guessed it. What?"

"Can you get us a mail cover?"

"Never mind the 'us' business. But the answer is, yes, I think I can. But how much good will it do you?"

"Maybe not too much, but at least we can get a listing of return addresses on all mail addressed to Storrow's house. Also, if the mailman co-operates, the addresses of all stuff sent from the nearby mailboxes. There's nothing sacred about what's on the outside of envelopes."

"Charlie, I know all that. As long as a piece of mail is in private hands, Uncle Sam doesn't care if you open it. The second it's in his possession he has no right to peek. But didn't you ever?"

Joyce took a long final swallow, grinned over the glass brim. "For shame, you should know better. Narcotics peddlers, kidnappers and spies are protected by our laws. Why, hell, with a court order you can tap their wires, but you can't tell in court what you heard. And now, sir, a little dollop, if you please."

Scanlon handed him the brimming glass. Charlie Joyce took it in his fingers, raised it to watch the bubbles scooting upward. As he felt the cold surface against his skin another idea came to him. He asked, "How could I have been so damned stupid for so long?"

Scanlon grinned. "What a question. Shall I answer it?"

"No need to, Jack. I have just figured out how to trap the so-called Honorable Roger Lowell Storrow."

"Bravo!"

"Bravo, indeed, but damned if I can figure out what speaking German has to do with the whole business."

"What in the devil are you muttering about, speaking German?"

"I was merely conferring with my little people. Still, thank you more than I can say. I mean it. And now I go to prepare confusion for mine enemies."

During the final days of von Tetlow's convalescence he found reason to dictate another tape. The content was not particularly startling. It was what would have been termed a progress report.

Between the lines, however, ran a countermelody of worry, not so much in the actual words but registered, even on thin metal, in the timbre of the voice.

For once, James had not been present at this recording session. He had been trying to prove to his own satisfaction whether two young men were actually trailing him. Using normal evasive tactics, he had soon found himself free, at least apparently free, of his followers.

James, once he had wrapped and addressed the little spool of wire, walked confidently, without a backward glance, toward the mailbox on P Street. It was one which he had not used recently, near the bridge over Rock Creek. This was not the bridge favored by would-be suicides. Rather it was the one below which the hopefully prurient often gathered in the semi-cool of the District evening. To James' credit, this evening he had no such thoughts. Right now he was carrying out orders, and this evening was not just cool, it was bitter cold. Because of the cold he almost hurried. This made him less alert to sounds and movements other than his own.

153

He had just reached the mailbox, stopped and was reaching into his pocket when two men broke from the shadows to pinion his arms. They almost succeeded in catching him off guard. Charlie Joyce had been correct in his estimate of the big Jamaican. He moved with the explosive speed of a big cat. Rather than try to pull away from the man holding his left arm, he followed the pressure, catching the other off balance. James then pushed him in a stumbling fall across the high curbing. To save himself the man let go, staggered two steps away. The second man now held the left arm in a firm grip, a grip quickly broken by two quick agonizing blows to a tensed biceps muscle from the hard edge of James' right hand.

The second he was free, he ran the three steps to the parapet, threw a small object far out into the dark of the Rock Creek chasm. Since it was early spring the waters were high, turbulent and muddy. The spool of wire would never be found, not even with a dragnet or mine detectors.

The two embryo detectives stood uncertainly. There was no point in searching their quarry now. They had seen him throw. There seemed little reason to hang around at all. This was a very big man, and in his hand glittered a six-inch blade.

James closed the clasp-knife, and slipped it back into his pocket. Robbers? he wondered. From the too-quick glimpse and sudden contact, he rather thought not. Still, one couldn't be sure. G-men? Even more doubtful. They would have been much more skilled. Nevertheless, he felt that the instinct that made him throw away the jeweler's box was correct.

Von Tetlow had been present at the next meeting of the Security Council, still a little weak, a little pale, but very much alert. No one present could have failed to be otherwise, because the main item on the agenda was a discussion of Albania. It was not the usual talk about how real were the ideological conflicts with Moscow. The Council wanted an answer. Was this or was it not the time and place to create a Laos in reverse, to do all that had not been done in Cuba? If it was and if it succeeded, this would give the West its first

154

real victory since Guatemala in overthrowing an established Communist regime.

Today most of the men present felt the risk was well worth while, that Russia would not care to intervene directly by armed counter-invasion. Von Tetlow was not only interested, he was impressed. This was realistic thinking. This was taking the offensive, not merely reacting. Even after the disaster of the Berlin Wall these men still showed courage. They were, in their way, admirable.

Silently he admonished himself. This was no proper line of thought. His was to report not judge, to record not think, especially since thinking recalled the Berlin deaths already on his hands. He heard the President say, "Very well. I want an estimate of exactly what we'll need. And how soon, at the latest, we can be ready—and from you, Mr. Jackson, an evaluation of how much support we can realistically expect from within. I no longer care what world opinion, especially India's, will be. And I want this one week from today."

He rose to leave. Everyone else rose. "I must go. Carry on with the rest of the agenda. Good day, gentlemen."

"Good day, Mr. President."

"Wow!" exclaimed Arthur Jackson. "I guess you all heard the man."

Jackson, still standing, reached over to the water pitcher and poured himself a glass. Charlie Joyce, sitting to von Tetlow's right, said, "Don't stop now. It's good exercise for your tennis arm."

Jackson poured three others full as well. Joyce then turned to his left. "Roger, pass me some of that stuff. I know it's undrinkable, but it's the best we have."

Von Tetlow's left hand moved toward a glass, the fingers open. He sensed that Joyce was watching him too intently, and simultaneously he let his hand jerk spastically against the glass, upsetting it and sending water flooding across the table toward the lap of the Secretary of State. "Damn, I'm sorry. Still clumsy with the left, don't you know. Guess you'd better get your own, Charlie. I'm not to be trusted."

"You said it, not I."

Charlie Joyce was sorry the moment these words escaped

155

him. Had he put the man on his guard? No. Of course, he already was. That damned James would probably have reported to his master the incident at the bridge. Still, just a simple request to pass a glass of water—should that have triggered so quick a reaction to avoid leaving prints? Or had it been just an accident? No accident, probably. The hunted quickly develop strong instincts of self-preservation.

There was one more thing he could do. Charlie took a cigarette from its pack, placed it between his lips and raised a heavy lighter to its tip. He looked directly at his quarry. With a click the lighter flamed to life and at the same time stored within itself a tiny likeness of the hunted. Yes, the man was now just that. And now he must know it, know it irrevocably.

CHAPTER XVIII

ROGER STORROW STILL felt hunted. There was, of course, a chance that Don Henrique and his comrades had been permanently thrown off the scent by the business of the charred corpse: a chance, but not a very good one, at least not for very long. To men of Aparat intelligence it should quite soon be recognized as too pat, too coincidental, and the hounds would be on his trail again.

He was much stronger now, and was even allowed to walk about his little room. He did not dare step outside, and wouldn't until he was prepared to make his move, and that must be very, very soon.

He was also thinking more clearly. The vice-consul at Merida was not the answer, and he himself could not get safely to a phone. Maybe a personal letter to, for instance, Arthur Jackson of the CIA would do the trick, especially if it contained reference to events or personalities which only Roger Storrow could know about. Yes, that was one answer, but not the best. Arthur was so damned busy and so often on a trip.

The best answer was Mary Margaret Kelly. How in God's name had his imposter managed to escape detection at her capable hands? Then the thought struck him. Could they have done to her as they had done to his Marjorie? Rage momentarily seized him, and with it an agonizing pain beneath his breastbone. Grimly he forced himself to relax, uncapped the little bottle Dr. Alvarez had given him, slipped a nitroglycerin tablet under his tongue. The pain ebbed slowly, at last was gone. He must stay cold and logical. Too

157

much anger could quite literally kill him. Muddled thinking could do the same.

He would write three letters. To Arthur Jackson, Charlie Joyce and Mary Margaret Kelly. If only one, any one of them, were received, it should do the trick. Let's see, Merida to Mexico City, Mexico to New York, New York to Washington. With luck three days—without, five or six. Probably too long, but what other choice had he? At least he had pen and paper. When Padre Fortunato returned he would ask him to take care of the envelopes and stamps. When he began the letter to Arthur Jackson, some puckish instinct intruded. He began, "Dear Art, I bet you can't guess where I am. . . ."

About half-way through the letter, it did not seem so very amusing after all. He was glad he kept a loaded shotgun at his side.

He had just about finished his writing when he heard the softer clip-clopping of unshod hooves. They came nearer, and slower, accompanied by some very unpriestly language. It was, nevertheless, Padre Fortunato. His round brown face appeared in the doorway a minute later. It did not bear any trace of the customary smile.

Roger greeted him. *"Buenas tardes,* Padre. What has your noble steed done to merit such language and for you to look so glum?"

Wearily the priest seated himself. "Poor Joselito has done nothing except be a burro, but I, my son, I do not at all like the look of things."

"How do you mean? Didn't my friends buy the story of the charred vagabond?"

"At first, yes, from what Alvarez has told me. They came, as you had suspected, to claim the body—not as that of a relative but of a trusted servant. The good doctor told them at once of his suspicion of poison."

"Did he know the men who came?"

"One, yes. A rich one, a big man with a moustache who calls himself Don Henrique. The other he did not know, one dressed in the uniform of a chauffeur."

"Those are my friends, all right, no doubt of it. What happened next?"

158

"The two men talked together in a low voice, seemed satisfied and departed. But then later came the bad thing."

"And that was?"

"Yesterday afternoon Miguel, who sometimes helps Dr. Alvarez at the morgue, did not appear for work. That night he staggered home almost paralyzed drunk on tequila, wearing a new silk shirt and, more extraordinary, a fine pair of shoes. Naturally, Alvarez was angry, and demanded to know where Miguel had obtained the money. Had he stolen it, perhaps? If so, he would call the police at once. In fact, he would call them anyway. Miguel, terrified, or merely drunk, babbled he had done nothing criminal, had simply given a little harmless information to the kind chauffeur of the rich Don Henrique."

"For God's sake, what information could he give?"

The priest rubbed a hand across his scalp. "Enough, my son, more than enough. The man asked whether the body in question had several gold fillings and a bridge of three false teeth. Miguel told him that, quite the contrary, the corpse had hardly any teeth at all, and what there were were worn and black. Certainly there was no gold. Alvarez is very sad about this. He feels he has failed."

Roger shook his head as if to clear it from a blow. "I'm very sad about it, too, but Dr. Alvarez has nothing for which to reproach himself. He did much more than his share, as did you. In fact, you both did brilliantly. No one can think of everything. I am now worried about your safety and his—not to mention my own."

For the first time since coming in, Padre Fortunato smiled, a rueful, not a happy, smile. "So am I, my son, so am I. But after all, what can they do to me? I merely performed my duty as a priest and gave refuge to a sick stranger."

"Padre, let us be practical. They want me, dead or alive, preferably dead. You are hiding me. That is more than enough for godless murderers. Do you think they suspect you of any part in this?"

A shake of the round head, an upward movement of the palms. "How can I know? But I think a little, yes. People are curious, they have wagging tongues. Why would a poor country priest ride into the city to the North American consulate. And also I have a feeling that men are watching this place. I thought, on the way back, that I saw the gleaming of such glasses as hunters use. What are they called?"

"Binoculars?"

"Yes, that is the word. From the top of the hill across the road."

Roger stood up, placed a hand on the little man's shoulder. "That settles it. I leave as soon as possible, as soon as it is dark. I will not bring my enemies down on you. But I'd better take the gun. Someday, somehow, I'll pay you back."

The priest gently pushed the hand aside, stood up in turn. The top of his head came barely to Roger's chin. There was, however, a curious calm dignity to his square stance. His voice took on a ring of authority.

"Not so, my son. This is part of the house of God. It is also my house and I am His servant. Here I command under His will. I order that you stay. Were I to let you go now out into danger, I would be denying the will of God."

"But, Padre, I am a stranger, even a foreigner."

There was something majestic in the small figure. "Silence, my son, do not argue. You are not a stranger or an alien, for we fight the same enemy, you and I. I see that you have written letters. They are important?"

Quietly, "Yes, Padre, they are."

"Then, when it is dark, I shall take them through the fields, not along the high road, to Alvarez. You will remain here with all doors locked. When I return we will think of something." He paused, then slapped his hand lightly against his forehead. "But I have been stupid. I have not really thought. The solution is most simple. I believe I know the best, the safest idea."

"I wish I did."

"It should be without difficulty. I will return with Dr. Alvarez by automobile. We will move rapidly, arrive with the lights out. You, my son, must be ready. We will drive at great speed to Merida, then place you in the hospital, or perhaps a hotel. You should be quite safe this way. Also we mail your letters more directly, and you will have available a telephone."

160

"Padre, you are a brilliant man. You should have been a field general. But I think a telephone would be nice but useless. Who would believe me?"

"I believe you."

"True, but you had the opportunity to observe my honest face. But, all jesting aside, you are right, and I obey your orders."

When it was solidly dark, Padre Fortunato prepared to slip quietly from the house, to ride his burro back of the hedges and through the fields. Roger took his hand. *"Vaya con Dios, Padre."*

"Take great care, my son, while I am gone."

The Padre's house had been watched, as had the entrances to that of Dr. Alvarez. The little priest was suddenly rushed and dragged from his mount to the hard surface of the road. One man held him, while the other began to search his clothing.

"Where do you go so late, fat man? Talk and talk fast." The first man had begun to twist an arm painfully behind his back.

Padre Fortunato struggled valiantly. He fought upward, managed to stand. Then he lashed out effectively with his feet, sank his teeth viciously into the shoulder muscle of the man who held his arm. With a curse, the other let go, and before his companion could stop him, picked up a rock and smashed in the little man's temple. He crumpled limply to the roadway.

The taller of his assailants cursed the other. "You damned ignorant fool. You've killed him—and I wanted to question him." He bent over the motionless figure, found the letters, stuffed them in his pocket, commanded, "We must get away from here fast."

The other hesitated, pointed to the inert form. "How about him?"

"He fell from his burro. The animal has already rushed home. They'll find the body. This poor fellow hit his head on a rock. Happens all the time."

"I still don't like it. He is a priest. Maybe we should move . . ."

161

"Don't be a fool. It does not matter whether you like it or not. You were the one who lost control and hit him. Come on, we must quickly take these letters to Don Henrique."

By the roundabout way it was about thirty minutes to Dr. Alvarez' house, certainly no more than ten to organize that able man, then another ten to be back. He no longer had his watch, but felt that nearly an hour had elapsed. God, how he wished he had a cigar, tobacco of any kind. Maybe there were some cigarettes around. . . .

His ears suddenly caught the scurrying hoofbeats of a frightened animal. He moved to the window. It was the Padre's burro skittering into the yard, stopping by his favorite cactus. The pack-saddle was empty. He had to believe the worst, and act on this belief. It gave him very little time. He put on a pair of the Padre's sandals, wrapped a serape about his shoulders, found a flat-brimmed hat. Picking up the shotgun, he started for the door.

Then he knew he had no time at all. Through the window he caught the brief flash of a flashlight parting the darkness, seeming for a split second to stare right at him. Then quickly it went out. Straining to hear, he made out the muffled voices of two men, then nothing but silence. They were very close to the house now and would no doubt separate and come in from different directions, one by the door, the other by the window. But there was no time for guesswork. Quickly he backed into the corner farthest from both, and sank to a sitting position, his left hand on the forepiece and the right index finger touching the trigger of the Padre's quail-gun.

Dimly he again heard the whisper of voices, the shuffle of stealthy feet. Then he noted a moving but much dimmer light, probably a man trying to shield the flashlight with his hand. Roger looked to the window. Outlined by the pale illumination of the sky, head and shoulders became visible. Wait! He forced himself, wait! That's only one. Sweat ran down between his shoulder-blades, along the hollow of his spine. Where in hell was the second man?

There came the soft clicking of the latch, then with a crash the door swung open. A figure rushed in. Simultaneously the window shattered inward. In that same second Roger executed the prettiest right and left double of his life, and the most important. Birds shot in the brush at such short range end up so shredded as to be inedible. Human heads explode like rotten melons dropped from a height, only they spread a little thinner. They almost become unrecognizable as heads, but are still quite unpleasant to look upon.

Roger did not bother to look. He was in a hurry. Two for you, Padre, he said to himself, and stepped out into the warm Mexican night.

CHAPTER XIX

AFTER JAMES CHAPMAN had reported the main events at the Georgetown bridge to von Tetlow, he reported in minute detail to his Aparat chief.

This time, after the phone call, his report was in person, but not face to face. His superior sat on one side of a one-way mirror, he on the other; the only face he could see was his own. This had happened before, three times, and always at a different address. They had been given him but once, just before each appointment. Even these he had forgotten, by intent.

A well-trained man can teach himself to forget, as well as to remember. That is, he cannot make himself forget a thing entirely. It will remain imbedded in the subconscious, from which it can be dug under hypnotic influence or narcosis. A person who must hear many secrets which he fears he might inadvertently let slip can say to himself each time a certain one rises to the surface of his mind: This I must forget, this I must not remember. Repeated often enough the fact will, in the sense described, be forgotten. In this way, an espionage agent teaches himself to remember a cover story which is wholly untrue until, for his purposes, a lie becomes the truth, even to the extent of answering automatically to a name not his own. Even under highly sophisticated interrogation James Chapman could not have furnished the federal authorities with any useful leads to the higher echelons of the Aparat.

The voice coming through a speaker concealed in the air-conditioning vent had been neither pleased nor displeased, simply cold and inquiring. "You say you suspect you

164

have been under surveillance for several days? Is there any possible reason, any little thing which could have made them suspicious? You worked for Storrow for five years. Has this man done anything, said anything, too much out of character?"

"No, sah, hardly anything. He has kept to himself a little more than Mr. Storrow. He tells people it's because of Mrs. Storrow being dead and all."

"What do you think, Jim?"

"I think maybe he's a little bit scared to go out, sah."

"Anything else?"

"Just one thing, sah. One of the very first nights he was here he took too much gin, and acted a little indiscreet."

"How do you mean, indiscreet?"

"Out of character, sah. It was my impression that he may have propositioned a lady he should not have."

"Has anything like this happened since?"

"Nothing at all, sah. But there is another thing I do not like. That security policeman, Mr. Joyce. He keeps showing up."

"Not unnatural. He and Storrow were friends. You know that."

"Yes, indeed, sah, but that Mr. Joyce now acts like he is hunting. It's something you feel more than see. He moves sort of more light-footed, more careful-like. I can't explain it any better."

"I'll have to take your word for it. Now, Jim, here are your instructions. Your employer has been sick and is still weak. That is your excuse whether he likes it or not. You will stay close to him at all times, unless, in your judgment, this would cause suspicion. We will use one or two men on both of you to spot any surveillance. I tell you so that you will not be looking for tails yourself and appear nervous to any federal agents who may be watching. You will tell your employer to act naturally no matter what, accept one or two invitations, go to the Metropolitan Club, Chevy Chase and so forth."

"May I ask a question?"

"Yes."

"Who is this man playing the part of Mr. Storrow?"

Here the voice did change; it became steely. "You may not

165

ask and you will never know. Also, any signs of sympathy for Storrow or regret for Mrs. Storrow might lead us to no longer trust you. Is that clear?"

It was clear all right. "Yes, sah."

"Don't forget it. Now, if you see or hear anything that doesn't look right, you know how to call us. Call us, anyway, as near to every four hours as possible, in case there are further orders for you. Incidentally, do you have a gun or a switch blade?"

"Yes, sah."

"Are you carrying them?"

"Yes, sah."

"Why, you damned fool! That's all they'd need to hold you, cut us off from your boss, and maybe beat a story out of you. Get rid of them, and quickly. No, better leave them right here before you go."

"Very well, sah. But I'll feel naked without my knife."

"So? You will feel naked. Now get out. No, stop. One more thing. How do you think Miss Kelly's bearing up? Is she still in a state where no one will believe her?"

"I don't know, sah. The other day when I took some packages to the office she seemed more cheerful, not so hung over. I'm afraid she's making a comeback, sah."

"We'll have to do something about that."

"Sah, do you wish me to . . ."

"No, by all means no. You stay out of it. You've done enough already, maybe too much. And, Jim?"

"Yes, sah?"

"Do you know where she usually eats lunch?"

"Yes, she usually has it brought in from the Diplomat Café, down the street."

"Good. That will be easy to take care of."

Von Tetlow was not surprised at receiving new orders. It did, however, irritate him to be told to act naturally, unworried and not nervous. Psychologically it became an invitation to act in precisely the opposite way. The authorities were clearly suspicious of him, he knew. That is, Charlie Joyce was suspicious, and that was more than enough in itself. Also someone, and it could reasonably be only some security

166

people, had been following James, had tried to snatch the jeweler's box from him. If the Jamaican had not acted so quickly and decisively... Even now, could they find the damned wire spool? No, he guessed not, not in a muddy, swollen creek.

"So, James, we're all to act naturally. You follow me, the FBI follows you, and your friends follow the FBI. A fine parade. Like a string of mongrels trailing after a bitch in heat. And I am to accept invitations, go to my club and act naturally."

For once James did smile. "I do not blame you, sah. Not at all. But we have no choice, not now. I think, if you will pardon me, the best idea's going to the club. Nobody can follow you in there, especially me. It's not like the Cosmos. No colored need apply."

"It's a good idea, perhaps I will have a steam bath and a massage." He felt his shoulder. "Still aches like the devil. I have forgotten exactly: what are the names of the men who manage this health department? One I know is Eino Kallinen. Who's the other?"

"The little one is Kallinen. He is a Finn. They say he hates Germans, Russians and Swedes all the same, sah. The big one is Joe, Joe MacCarey. He amuses himself, sah, by insulting the members. This they say. If the members do not like it, too bad for them."

"Did he insult Mr. Storrow?"

"All the time, sah. But Mr. Roger he was a very hard man to insult, sah. He often came back laughing about some bad joke. He told me almost the first time he went there Joe watched him walk over to the toilet and said 'I thought all Bostonians sat down to do that.'"

"Not very funny. Maybe I had better learn to be more amused. What time is it now?"

"Five-fifteen very nearly, sah."

"Well, in that case get the car, and we'll go to the club. Let's see," he picked out one of Roger Storrow's best cigars, nipped off the end, "the evening doorman is Teddy; front desk Carlos, an Ecuadorian. The other, yes, the other's George; bartender, Nazarino, been there almost forty years. The others—oh, the devil! Now I remember, one's Karl." He

167

recalled being told that Storrow indiscriminately called all the other Latins "Chico," no matter what their real names.

"You took lessons in this thing, not I, sah."

"Don't be insolent, damn you. Am I right?"

"You are right, sah, both ways. I apologize. We are skating together on the same thin ice. We certainly are."

"Remember your instructions, James. We are not nervous. We act natural, we do not worry. And that, you Jamaican devil, goes for you as well as me. What was that line—'Big Brother is watching you!' "

"I do not think this amusing, sah!"

"Neither do I. Shall we go?"

Karl von Tetlow was at home in the Metropolitan Club, since all good men's clubs are the same—or nearly the same—everywhere east of Hong Kong and west of the Elbe. Here, however, there was a jarring note. Since it was after five the presence of women in certain clearly defined areas was permitted. This tragedy had smitten many male sanctuaries all over the world. Some blamed it on taxes. Some on the fact that women now drank openly. Some on the decline of masculine independence. But whatever the genesis, the proximate cause was without question—the clubs were no longer able to exist without the revenue from the patronage of members' wives—not girl friends, but wives. Both von Tetlow and Storrow regarded this development as a bloody shame.

Otherwise, the Club was most satisfactory. Quiet, comfortable furnishings, a really fine library, two priceless and beautiful chandeliers and a great deal of history—both past and living. Senators, cabinet officials, leading newspapermen and ambassadors from many lands could be found every day but Sunday. On Sunday a graveyard could be as cheerful. Leading lawyers, physicians, engineers and men of business patronized its bar. It differed from the Somerset Club of Boston. In the Somerset Club it was once said by a member, after a remark that young Roger Storrow was doing very well, "Yes," grudgingly, "I suppose so if you mean on a national scale."

In the Metropolitan Club a more likely colloquy would be, "Good to see you looking so fit, George, been out of town?"

"Yes, for three years." "Doing what?" "Been Ambassador to Belgium." "Oh, really! Come on, I'll roll you for a drink."

Furthermore, this Club has had the same doorman for twenty-five years. He remembers the faces of over two thousand men; he is a reverend in some mysterious church; and has been arrested for participating in the numbers racket. And it has the Health Club, recently redesigned by a humorless house committee as the Athletic Department. This is said to be because its walls are decorated by the city's outstanding photograph collection of beautiful undraped girls.

Von Tetlow elected to walk the two long flights up to that establishment. At the second floor he paused to look around the big room with its scattered glass top tables, leather upholstered chairs, bad portraits of bearded and long forgotten admirals, and early drinkers. Several looked up to wave casually. He swung his left hand in reply. A few of them he recognized from his mental file of often studied photographs. There, to the right, for example, sat an assistant secretary of state earnestly, but *sotto voce,* declaiming to the Washington Bureau Chief of the *New York Times.* The latter seemed to be listening, but clearly did not believe. This was normal. At the back of the room was the Chief of Procurement of the Armed Forces. He was being somewhat more attentive to another man who held before him what looked like an industrial brochure. Members were not supposed to use the Club for business, but that they did so was likewise normal.

Upstairs in one of the cubicles von Tetlow undressed with some difficulty. It was only the second time he had done so without Chapman's assistance. Still, he did not want to ask either Joe or Eino for help. He felt it would not have been in character for Roger Storrow. Joe MacCarey was, however, totally in his. He looked up from his gin rummy game. "My God, Mr. Storrow, you look like hell. I warned you about those Mexican girls, but damned if I thought one of them strong enough to kick you that far out of bed."

This was no way for a servant to talk. Nevertheless, he forced a smile. "They're not, Joe. I was kicked by a mule."

"I'm ashamed of you. Girls I go for myself, but not mules."

He checked an angry retort. "Have it your way, you miserable Irishman. Now, how about giving me a massage?"

"You didn't call for an appointment," he spread ten cards in a fan. "Can't you see I'm busy? You just go in and take a nice steam bath and then we'll tear you apart."

They nearly did, Eino at the foot, Joe at the head of the rubbing table. Some of it was pleasant, much of it painful. He grunted and tried to pull away from the powerful fingers probing the muscles at the side of his neck. Joe spoke. "Dammit, Mr. Storrow, stop wriggling like an eel. How do you expect me to do my work?"

From a recumbent sheet-draped figure on the next table came an amused, "Sadists, both of these men. And yet we pay to be insulted and tortured." Von Tetlow roused. Where had he heard that voice? It echoed familiarly far, far back in memory. It was definitely Germanic. There was something faulty in the memory, some flaw in the picture which he tried to call to mind. The man was speaking again. "Joe, please, in one minute I plan to sleep. For twenty minutes precisely. I wish just a glass of water, if you should be so kind."

The powerful hands on his shoulders halted, lifted away. "Yes, sir, Mr. Ambassador, right away."

Mr. Ambassador? That did not help very much, or did it? Yes, of course it did! It identified and at the same time sickened him with fear. Still, fascinated, he turned his head to look to the next table. Although instinctively sure whom he would see, he tensed spasmodically. Eino Kallinen felt it. "Snake bite, Mr. Storrow, or is it the brandy yips?"

He made no answer. He was, for the moment, incapable of speech. He found himself staring into the serious, probing blue eyes of Rupert Wilhelm von Tetlow, son of Uncle Konrad in Dusseldorf, his own cousin and now Ambassador of the Federal Republic of West Germany to the United States.

He felt the blue eyes staring back at him. He clenched his hands. He could feel sweat between fingertips and palms, taste the salt in his mouth. He wanted to get out of here and in a hurry.

CHAPTER XX

ROGER STORROW STARED angrily into the glassy black eyes of
the stubborn burro. He had just demonstrated the certain but
little noted fact that almost no one can be as vocally vulgar as
a proper Bostonian. It had done no good whatever. The
burro, unmovable and silent, stared blandly and balkily
back. This was Padre Fortunato's burro. He had been a long
way tonight. He had had a scare on the road. He was now
home and he intended to stay. Roger could feel the sweat of
urgency and of anger and some pain in his chest. He could
taste the words he had just uttered. He wanted to get out of
here and in a hurry, a damned big hurry.

This man had, in his time, played polo, ridden races as a
gentleman jockey and belonged briefly to a cavalry regiment
before the Department of the Army had bowed to Congress
and outlawed horses. This did not alter the fact that Roger
was quite ignorant of the management and dressage of
donkeys.

He was, however, resourceful. His favorite cousin had once
said, "Roger, you really don't know a damned thing, but you
never forget anything you ever heard or read." This time
Roger remembered a regrettable incident of his youth. He lit
one of the Padre's black cigarettes, which his fingers had
found in the pocket of his cloak, and climbed, not too
nimbly, to straddle the animal's back. Gripping tightly with
his knees and to the halter rope, he drew strongly on the
cigarette, reached behind him and held the glowing ash to the
rear end of his mount. Long before the scent of scorching
hair reached his nostrils there was action.

171

Anyone abroad at this hour would have seen a startling sight. Neither Boston's Beacon Hill nor the Capitol's George-town would have believed its collective eyes. Oddly enough, Beacon Hill would have been the less surprised. Nothing really shocks or much surprises Beacon Hill. Its inhabitants merely pretend. In any event, within seconds after the application of the self-starter, a tall, gray-haired figure, wrapped in a Joseph's-coat serape, partially crowned by a flat, round hat and clutching an ancient double-barrelled shotgun, was clattering down a Mexican highway atop a brutally offended peace-loving burro.

As it happened, the only people visibly abroad at the time were two who had been testing the devirginizing effect of raw one hundred proof pulque on semi-ripened señoritas. They saw, but did not fully believe what they saw. Still they felt it safer, in the long run, fearfully if not too devoutly to cross themselves. Roger Storrow, joltingly uncomfortable as he was, appreciated the gesture. A lineal ancestor of his had been hanged near Salem as a witch, and such a man does not laugh at others who still suspect that dead men ride by night.

It was a miserable trip to Merida. Roger was still weak. He had little faith that his damaged heart could support the strain, but knew it must. More and more he admired the brave fat Padre who had made his constant lengthy rounds by this primitive means.

Having at last slowed the burro to a sedate pace, he had had some time to think. What an outrageously ludicrous spectacle he must present, a modern—well, not so very modern—Sancho Panza going to his wars. He wished that Marjorie could see. A wave of pain hit him, not anginal, but still so acute as to be nearly physical. There was no Marjorie now. There never would be again. For a moment tears blinded him as he rode along.

Men who have suffered coronaries, in the early days of recovery weep very easily. Doctors do not know exactly why this is so, but they recognize the fact. The patients, however, know that they weep because of weakness. They are mortally tired because they have fought so desperately for their life, in silence and alone.

Roger Storrow was not yet aware of this. But he knew why

172

he wept. Part of the reason was irreparable loss, the other, quite simply, rage. At least in the company of rage he was no longer lonely, and its heat soon dried his tears. With the flight of tears came the return of thought. Here he was, robed, sandalled, hatted and mounted on a shaggy burro. Into oncoming midnight, he rode toward a city he did not know, without money, passport, credit or even the smallest tangible proof of identity. Again he thought of Cervantes, and now he was more Don Quixote than Sancho Panza. What windmills could he tilt in this scented Mexican night? There were none. Where could he go for belief or refuge? There was nowhere. To whom could he recite his three-times unbelievable tale? Not to a living soul. Rest, sleep, he must have. Safety? Refuge? There were none nearby.

Thank God, however, that the good Padre's church had stood off by itself beside that road. The muffled shotgun blasts might have passed unnoticed. How many of what Leslie Charteris had called "the ungodly" were still at large? Everything had happened so suddenly, and the light had been so dim, that he could not be sure that one of the men he had decapitated had been Don Henrique. How many others might be on his trail again? How could he know? What could he do about it? One thing was sure. It was much too late to wonder, and he was much too tired to think. To save his life, he must rest. His legs chafed abominably, his back pained, and in his chest rose the premonitory, doom-foreboding ache.

And for the first time since, as a little boy, he ran away from imagined tyranny at home, Roger Storrow took his longed-for refuge in deep, deep sleep on the sweet-smelling layers of a hay-mow in an alien field. That first time the fears of childhood had kept him long awake, but this time the lead-heavy weariness of man, which can more than drown out fear, dropped him mercifully to sleep under the tropical stars.

The good Padre's burro munched contentedly, then, too, went to sleep, if sleep it can be called, still standing, thick coat bristled against the coming chill, yet prepared with brassy bray to greet the dawn.

In that latitude morning comes early and in one gilded

173

rush. For some reason, perhaps the lack of haze, perhaps the nearness to the equator, the sun seems to climb the sky faster than in the north to bring the heat of day earlier.

The warmth was welcomed by the tall man lying by the edge of the hay-mow. He was still weary, itched abominably and was stiff. However, he was no longer cold and above all he was still alive. He stretched creakingly and pulled himself slowly to his feet. To his surprise, the burro was still there, gazing at him placidly, fur-lined ears cocked inquisitively. Roger Storrow walked over to the animal, extended a hand slowly and rubbed the velvety nose. "Good morning, friend, so you stayed. Right now it's nice to have a friend."

The burro merely flapped its long lower lip. "Yes, burro, but you've had plenty to eat and I am hungry as hell."

There was little he could do about food at the moment, and he wondered what he was going to do next without any money. Maybe by now his appearance was so woebegone that he could pass as a beggar. He lit one of the little Padre's evilly coarse cigarettes. For some reason a smoke always eased hunger pangs, at least for a little while.

It must be very early, he thought, far too early for any establishment to be open except a very late bordello, or some very sleepy police station. Sleepy police were inclined to biliousness of temper. In any case, so far as even the chief of all Mexican police knew, Roger Storrow was five thousand miles away. He rubbed a hand across his chin, a crew-cut length of beard at least, then around to the nape of his neck. His hair by now was well toward the collar. He must really look like the devil.

There was the consulate. Again a useless haven, given the consul's absence. Anyway it would not open for hours. Doctors, travel agents, Red Cross—was there a Mexican Red Cross? A hotel where, with his Yankee accent, he could per-haps cadge some money from a sympathetic Northern tourist? That seemed sounder, but for this, too, it would be much too early.

The best idea seemed to be to lie down again. He patted the burro a second time. He had nothing with which to tie it. "Stick around, old friend. Don't leave me now. I must think about something and maybe sleep."

174

He did think, and he slept a little, but fitfully. When he awoke, things were not much different. The sun was higher in the sky and warmer, and it was now the rear end of the burro which faced him. He, however, had decided where he would go. He would go to an office whose employees were told, and even sometimes believed, twenty incredible things every working day.

Hours later Roger parked his conveyance on the outskirts of the city and slapped it on the rump. "Goodbye, friend, we must part company here." The burro moved away two steps, then stood again to gaze at him as he strode off toward the center of Merida.

He paused for a moment, studied the padre's shotgun. He'd better leave it here, hide it perhaps. No, by God! He would not go unarmed. He unsnapped the forepiece, and, extracting the shells, took the gun apart. He placed the shells in a trousers pocket. He felt a little foolish carrying the gun in pieces. Still he hoped he would attract less attention from the local law.

The office he sought had opened. The sleek but sleepy clerk did not believe him when he announced that he was a very important North American who wished to see the local American manager of Pan-World Airways. When, however, the bearded, oddly-garbed Yankee added that he had been drunk in a low house of ill-fame, drugged, rolled and robbed of his clothing, this he did believe. Such things, he knew, had happened before.

"The señor," said the man with rather contemptuous scorn, "should report this occurrence to the police, to the Guardia Civil, to the consulate, but not here, not to me here at Pan-World, because I, the number one clerk, as anyone can see, am a most very busy man. I cannot concern myself with such a matter."

It was at this point that a Roger Storrow known to the press, federal officials, ranking officers during World War II, even to ambassadors and certain foreign ministers, came to the fore. The Padre's hat was gone, the tri-colored serape tossed aside, the muscular arms crossed over the tight-shirted chest.

"Why, you miserable little bootlicker, you number-three

175

boy, you Pan-World pimp, you don't know what trouble is. You do not even hold the slightest idea."

One arm uncrossed, straightened, its index finger pointed like a pistol barrel, he said, "I have already killed two men to get here and I would gladly kill you. Go, instantly, and alert the director that I am here. Now, at once. I want to see him."

The very busy, very important, clerk started to protest. At "Look at me when you talk, by God," he made the mistake of doing so, and he no longer noticed the bearded chin and jowls, the grimy skin or unkempt hair. All he could see were the cold commanding eyes, and like other much more important men before him, he simply nodded and mumbled, "*Si, señor,* at once. I shall go to him, to inform him . . ."

"No need, my man. Take me with you!"

"*Si, señor.*"

Bill Walters was not assigned to Merida because he was the airline's most able Latin American representative. He was good enough, however, so that his next scheduled position was to be in the nature of a promotion. Proving his ability, it took him only two minutes to recognize the sort of man confronting him.

He had met components of the type before; once a Long Island mother whose two children had been off-loaded short of destination because of seat oversale; another one had been a wiry Negro minister refused a first-class seat in Brownsville, Texas. One more example was a pig-tailed twelve-year-old from Richmond, Virginia, with a Siamese cat in her arms, who asked why her well-behaved pet was refused while smelly, screechy babies were allowed aboard to bother everybody else.

Having once studied the set of the head and shoulders, and heard the voice, Walters knew enough not to send this man to the Guardia Civil. He did, however, begin to utter the word "Consulate." He was quite shocked to hear his visitor's concise opinion of that office. It was uttered in a rich, nearly British accent. But it used what George Patton had once called "Anglo-Saxon sporting terms."

Who the devil was this tall, heavy-bearded stranger? That

he was a somebody, at least a mad archaeologist, seemed clear. "But, sir, at the consulate . . ."

A silencing wave of the hand. "Stow it, young man. As I said, no one of any use at the place. Now listen. I am from Washington," then came the product of thought beside the hay-mow. "You mustn't tell anyone, don't you see, but I've been doing some very delicate undercover work for the CIA," he almost whispered the initials, "ran into a bit of trouble, you know. Some of the dirty buggers almost did for me. I must telephone Washington, at once. No money with me of course, but the government will reimburse you."

Bill Walters somehow believed the man. But calls from Mexico to Washington were expensive. This was not his phone. It was the company's and the company was most miserly about expense vouchers. He knew this from sad experience. "I'd like to help. But, sir, do you have any ident . . ."

"Certainly not, not on an assignment like mine. Don't you know anything?"

Walters scratched his head, pondered briefly. Then he saw the light, the way out. "I understand. I'll be happy to let you use our phone, and you can reverse the charges, I mean, can't you?"

"Of course, young man. Can't expect you to pay out of your own pocket." Walters now saw a most engaging grin. "But could you send out your boy and trust me for the price of some coffee, a big sandwich and a razor? Yes, I see you could. Now, which phone do I use?"

It is a slow, painful process successfully to place and complete a call from Merida in Yucatan, Mexico, to Washington, D.C. It is fraught with interruptions and a lack of understanding which even Roger's Spanish found hard to conquer. His patience suffered most. Still, he refrained from using the harsher words of his eclectic vocabulary. He had shaved, eaten and smoked half a package of American cigarettes before the call to his own office, to Mary Margaret Kelly, at last went through. She, no matter what, would recognize his tones, he was sure of it.

A totally strange voice answered the telephone. "Mr.

177

Storrow's office." No, Miss Kelly was not in; no, she did not know when she would be in. What? Oh, Miss Kelly was in the hospital, very bad food poisoning, she'd heard. "No, operator, I certainly won't accept any call from Mexico. No, of course not."

Roger Storrow cursed soundlessly. What now? He asked if the operator were still connected to the Executive offices' switchboard. When he found she was, he knew there was one more thing he must do. He smiled to himself a trifle grimly and told the girl, "Well, leave a message that Mr. Storrow called. Mr. Roger Lowell Storrow," and hung up. He thought, if it does nothing else, that ought to panic the bastard in my office a little, whoever the hell he is.

CHAPTER XXI

NEAR PANIC, VON TETLOW did not dare to turn his face away too quickly, nor did he dare undergo this close blue-eyed scrutiny. Did his cousin Rupert recognize him? Or did he see a resemblance to family he had once known? After all, it had been many, many years. Had Storrow known this ambassador? He could not remember what he had been told. Dammit, he must keep calm—control himself. By great effort he forced his muscles to relax, put a hand to his face and sat up. "Blast it, Joe, bring me a wet towel. You've put some of that bloody liniment in my eye."

The Teutonic voice at his side was raised again. "Insult, torture, and now they blind you. They have not managed to blind me, at least not yet."

Von Tetlow wiped at his face. He could not look back at the man, not right away. Still, he would have to soon. If this was the moment of unmasking, let it come quickly. He turned to cousin Rupert, forcing a grin. He hoped it did not look as false as it felt.

The other man rose to his feet, stepped toward him, extended a hand. Automatically, he took it. Then the man was speaking, "I know who you are. You are Roger Storrow, of course. Permit me to introduce myself. I am Rupert von Tetlow, the new Ambassador for West Germany, here but recently."

"Glad to meet you, Mr. Ambassador."

The blue eyes still studied him, "Do you know, for a moment you looked so very much like someone I used to know. Pardon that I say it, but your hand is cold and you do not have good color. Aren't you feeling well?"

179

Thank God, he thought. Aloud he said, "Afraid you're right. I think I'll lie down a while. Had rather a rough day, you know."

The next day began badly. There had been some improvement two days ago when Mary Margaret Kelly had been taken to the hospital—seriously ill from food poisoning, they said. This made at least one less person before whom he must exercise extreme caution. He wondered if someone had caused the illness deliberately. It really didn't matter. The new girl assigned to his office had never known Storrow. She was younger, prettier and had a more attractive body. This made the day more pleasant.

Her first news of the morning did not. Mincingly she came into his office, leaned over his desk to place the morning mail before him. "You just won't believe what happened right before you came in. It was the craziest thing ever. You really won't believe it, I tell you."

"Well, don't just stand there, Miss Pollard, pushing your front in my face. Tell me what happened."

The girl stepped back, flushing, obviously hurt. Von Tetlow did not like himself, but at least he had stayed in Storrow's character. He did not apologize, but smiled broadly at her. This seemed to help.

"Well, I just got a long distance call from some place I never heard of in Mexico. They wanted me to accept it collect. Of course, I wouldn't, and then the operator told me it was from a man with exactly your name, Roger Lowell Storrow. Why, whatever's the matter with you, Mr. Storrow? You look just like you'd seen a ghost. Didn't I do right?"

With grim effort he kept his voice level. "Yes, Miss Pollard, you did just right. Now, go shuffle papers or something. I have thinking to do."

"Yes, sir. But don't forget you have an important meeting coming up, and soon now."

"Yes, I know," he said. My God yes, he thought, I certainly know.

Quietly the girl left the room. Desperately von Tetlow tried to think rationally. It was hard. Ideas, questions, crashed back and forth through his mind. They would not line up in any logical sequence, lead to any solution, to any escape.

And now, fully emerged from the background where it had lurked before only to peep out occasionally, stood fear, stark inescapable fear.

Fear he had known intimately before. It was no stranger to him, but it was a ghastly hindrance to organized thought. Fear can be overcome, or at least neutralized, by action. It is all but impossible to banish it merely by thinking. But he had to think. How could Roger Storrow possibly have escaped? How could they have let him? Could they have left him alone in that house and allowed him to reach a telephone? Maybe he had been able to telephone but was still a prisoner? If he was, the call to this office had done no harm since the new girl had dismissed it as false. Even so, he could not count on her not talking about the call, and that damned Charlie Joyce would certainly hear about it.

Whom else had Storrow called? Would anyone have believed him? Perhaps it hadn't been Storrow at all. Yes, here was the most comforting idea. It might have been a hoax. But who did it, and why? Perhaps Storrow had some friend in Mexico whose calls Miss Kelly would accept in her employer's name which the new girl did not know about. No, that seemed unlikely. Then there came another thought. Could this telephoning have been arranged by Charlie Joyce to jolt him into some precipitate action which could finally betray him? Yes, this was possible. Along the same line, could this be another attempt to make Mary Margaret Kelly doubt her own reason? No, of course no. The Aparat agents certainly knew the woman was sick.

Dazedly he shook his head, got up, opened the window to breathe deep of the fresh air and to think. No, von Tetlow, stop deluding yourself. The best is to believe the worst. Storrow has escaped somehow. The hounds will soon be on your trail. Even this minute they may be close. You are trapped. This is the end of the line, unless—here a faint ray of hope—unless they, whoever they are, have some plan to get you out of the country and to safety. Certainly, it would be better for their own security if they did.

Well, there was no time left, no time even to worry about telephone taps. Resolutely, he picked up the instrument. "Get me my house please, Miss Pollard." Then, after a short wait, "James, things are going to move fast now. Your old friend

181

from Mexico tried to call me this morning. Yes, yes, that is what I said. It is in your hands now. I will be home after the meeting. I think I will walk." He replaced the receiver.

Damn the man! There had been shock, of course, but also a note of satisfaction in James' voice. He probably was a little glad that Roger Storrow still seemed to be alive. Strangely, he himself felt something akin to pleasure. He now knew the man well. He had read his books, listened to his music, studied his paintings, talked with his friends, slept in his bed. He had come reluctantly to admire the man he had coldly studied in person for weeks, watched and listened to but never met. It now seemed probable that Storrow had escaped. No, he could not yet bring himself to believe it probable. But certainly it was possible, yes, quite possible. If Storrow had escaped, then he, von Tetlow, would also escape, in flight, into prison, or more probably into death. The Aparat wouldn't dare leave him alive.

Mentally he had been through all this before, and it profited nothing. He glanced at the bronze desk clock. Good God! It was past time for his appearance at the Security Council meeting. He gathered up the papers, slipped them into his briefcase, stood up. Squaring his shoulders caused a painful twinge. Ignoring it, he strode from the room toward what he felt would be the last scene of the last act of his last role. This play has certainly had a very short run.

For the first time since assuming the job, the Special Assistant to the President was a few minutes late to a Security meeting. The people in the room turned when he entered and gave looks ranging from surprise to amusement. The punctuality of Roger Lowell Storrow had become a Washington legend. He had lived forty-three years as a bachelor and had acquired meticulous habits. It was said if a neighbor saw him leave for the office at any time other than exactly ten past eight, the man would doubt his watch enough to reset it.

They were all there—all, and for this he was thankful, save Charlie Joyce. He, for reasons not divulged, had left on what he described only as a short hop to a warmer sun. He had said his sinuses hurt. Thinking on this in light of what he now more than half believed, that Storrow was alive and free somewhere in Mexico, von Tetlow decided there was probably nothing for which to be grateful after all. Quietly he seated himself, placed the briefcase in front of him, withdrew the sets of stapled pages to pass around. He again studied in turn the face of each man.

He had known these faces, so to speak, for a very short time. Of course, he had studied them intently and at length before accepting or being inescapably forced into this mission. It was not, however, wholly from this earlier study that he knew them so well. It was because he had lately watched and listened carefully to the slightest change in expression and nuance of a voice. He had done this as part of his job as a spy. He had done it also out of curiosity as to what made these people act as they did.

He oftened wondered what drove this strange, aggravating, sometimes uncultured country to feel it must be conscience as well as benefactor to the world. How could its leaders be so intelligent yet naïve, so generous yet politically greedy, so strong yet somehow ashamed to wield that strength effectively? He had, of course, also watched and listened so attentively in order to save his own life, and in this he would probably fail. But he had learned a lot.

There at the head of the table sat the President, no longer so jaunty or so sure of himself. He had aged, but for the better. He was no longer certain that he was always right. In fact, about some things he was no longer certain at all. He doubted, and he was quite often afraid. But he had now and for ever made up his mind as to the line he would follow. His eyes were tired and hooded. His jaw, however, was set. His public voice was as before, but it commanded more than it cajoled.

Next to him sat the Secretary of State, suave, polite to a fault, but still not quite a gentleman. Intelligent, well educated, he was still lacking as a man of action. Von Tetlow recalled the old joke, the State Department's definition of rape: an unnegotiated piece. Here was a man sarcastically critical of John Foster Dulles' mis-called brinksmanship but unable to replace it with anything better. He would go along, but he would not lead. He could sometimes bulldoze a small Central American country, but lacked the courage to knock down a wall. Von Tetlow thought again of that catastrophe at the Berlin Wall, that terrible defeat for the West. He had caused it himself, almost alone.

Next sat the Secretary of Defense, bland, brilliantly efficient, unimaginative, a little scared of his generals and admirals, perhaps not quite trusting them, and therefore inclined to treat them as inferiors, a good man really, but trying so hard to play a game whose rules he would never quite understand.

In this room sat some of those officers. One had floated for three weeks on a waterless, foodless raft in the blazing South Pacific. Another had been deputy to the man who years before had answered "nuts" to a demand for what seemed inevitable surrender. Both had been rescued by George Patton's Third Army in a feat of logistics and command unequalled since Hannibal had crossed the Alps. And here was another who had fought under a great admiral into the very mouths of the Japanese battleship guns, and silenced them for ever. Shortly after that there had been no Japanese navy left.

Yes, the Secretary of Defense was a good, honest man, sometimes compelled by politics to say that these officers, proud in the traditions and insignia of their services, were not fit to decide what should be the military posture of their country. Von Tetlow saw the man shake his head, somewhat as a badgered bull, and knew one thing—the Secretary had also made up his mind. Politics was out. Patriotism was returned to favor.

Next down the table was the Attorney-General, young, brash, politically ruthless. He had been, and probably still was, too ambitious. At one time he had quite patently desired to be Secretary of State or some form of Deputy President. Fortunately his wings had been clipped just enough and in time. Now he was attending to his job. There could now be no questioning the genuineness of his interest in the downtrodden and the disenfranchised. This was largely true of all those here. In this they represented the heart of America, one very different from that advertised across the world by her enemies.

Also there was the Director of the CIA, tough, pragmatic,

widely experienced in the power politics and secret in-fighting of competing nations. His was a voice of courage and determination, of willingness to take risks and to assume personal responsibility for the failures as well as the victories.

Beside him was that tenacious older bull from the FBI. He had been right for so long about internal dangers to the country that too many who should have known better too frequently failed to listen to his voice. This had, and would again, cost dearly.

There were others, less important, less impressive because they more clearly represented the political and the factional. But, in their way, they too were men of good will, if of insufficient caliber. All were meeting today on the General Agenda of the nation's business, with particular attention being devoted to details of the military budget and, in general, to a study of the impact of proposed action in Albania. Another meeting, consisting of only four of these men plus Special Assistant Storrow, was scheduled for the morrow to consider and plan the operational details. He thought it unlikely that he would be there.

More and more he found difficulty in concentrating. He wanted to get out. Sitting here in this familiar room he could almost hear the hounds baying ever nearer, and sense the trap's closing jaws. Where was Storrow now? What in the devil was Charlie Joyce up to? Had James contacted his superiors? What action did they plan? Escape for him or fatal "accident"? The two hours lasted for ever. But finally the President looked at his watch, rose to his feet. "Thank you, gentlemen. Good day."

They all rose. Von Tetlow trembled inwardly when the President walked over to him and rested a hand on his good shoulder, "I meant what I said the other day. You'll have to come over for dinner soon. By the way, that pneumonia's no joke. You still look seedy, Roger. I think you'd better quit for the day."

"Thank you, Mr. President. That is exactly what I shall do."

CHAPTER XXII

BECAUSE OF HIS mental turmoil, to help counteract it, and to further avoid what the Spaniards call the moment of truth, von Tetlow had earlier elected to walk the three miles home. In walking, he did not remember that this had also been a habit of Roger Storrow's, a habit which amused but still caused envy among his more flabby contemporaries. It did occur to him, however, that he might be followed. He thought of it, but dismissed it as unimportant. What could anyone find out now? Only that he walked the evening streets of Washington filled with almost-spring, that his wide-spaced strides brought him to Georgetown and to Roger Storrow's front door.

Nevertheless, he occasionally turned to look behind, to the greening lawns where happy shirt-sleeved men with rakes scratched away at the brown debris of winter passed, cleaned and polished window-panes against the last red-gold of the setting sun, lovingly caressed with chamois rags the new-gleamed surfaces of their cherished cars. He also saw house-wives carrying home heavy paper parcels, the women's faces perhaps reflecting outrage at prices paid, annoyance at the cooking tasks to come, but, withal, satisfaction that they had the wherewithal to place a meal before their men and their young. Most of all, he noticed the children, children of all ages, drunk with the sweet damp scent of the season. They were playing in puddles, roller-skating, throwing things or shyly daring to touch, not really hold, another's hand.

There was no trace of the hounds. Yet von Tetlow knew they could not be far behind. From one pack or another, they had been after him too much of his adult life. He knew he had long been their quarry in what, from their viewpoint, had been a legitimate hunt. Some cried out for vengeance for his ruthlessness to hapless Jewry, some demanded the heads of traitors in the dying days of the Third Reich. And others today sought vengeance in the name of outraged humanity.

And this time there was irony. Those who this moment hounded him could only be security officers of a free nation, or, just as probably, agents of a land which had no God, no ethics, no morality at all.

It mattered little whose were the hounds. It did, however, greatly matter whether he could somehow throw them off the scent, somehow reach a refuge. Were he caught, he would die for nothing. As he thought about this, something from the distant past came to him now at this hour of the setting sun. It was the vision, the memory, of his full-panoplied and beautiful father. Father had lived, fought hard for something, had in the end died for nothing, but he had deeply believed. He, son of that brave colonel, now lived for nothing in which he believed, might die for even less, could only hope for another chance to run. Once more he straightened his back, slowed his strides, lifted his head a little higher. One thing he hoped—he hoped that he would not break and run, at least not yet. There must still be something to try, something left to do.

Reaching the Storrow house he saw the car parked directly before the door, found James waiting for him in the front hall. This was the first time he had seen the big, calm Jamaican truly agitated, much more so than he had been after the assault at the Rock Creek Bridge.

"We have got to move fast, sah. They have called for you twice already. He will give you your instructions."

"Who the devil is 'he'?"

"I do not know, sah."

"What do you mean, you do not know? Out with it, man!"

"That the Lord's truth, sah. I do not know. I have never seen his face, only heard the voice. He talks from out of some kind of mirror."

Von Tetlow had had experience with such mirrors before, many times. "Very well, James. Let's get moving."

187

"No, sah, not yet."

"Why not? You said that I'm wanted now."

"That is right, sah, but if you leave the second you arrive it might seem peculiar. The man says, 'Be sure you're not followed.' " The Jamaican made a helpless gesture of his long powerful hands, "But, how, sah, how do we do that? I got no more ideas, not now anyhow."

"Neither have I. Let me think. First, give me the address where I must go."

"Room 723 in the Bellevue Hotel Apartments. You are to ask for Mr. Ruggles. You are Mr. Dale Johnson from Hartford."

Von Tetlow thought rapidly and with clarity. James went out to the car alone. After a couple of minutes, he, in shirt sleeves, went out of the front door to the car and openly handed James a small, square, jeweler's package. James touched his cap and drove off as von Tetlow re-entered the house. Maybe that would draw the hounds. Three minutes later, now properly dressed, he walked out of the back door, through the little walled garden and into the alley which halved this block. He looked quickly to either end. It was empty. Which way to go? Well, it didn't matter. His best bet was to head for Wisconsin Avenue. He did, without once looking back, flagged down a taxi, and asked for the front entrance of the Bellevue, only to change his mind a minute later. "No, take me to Harvey's Restaurant." This was only a short distance from the hotel entrance.

At Harvey's he paid the driver, stepped inside and walked resolutely across the first floor dining room toward the men's room. He smiled wryly as he went out of the service entrance. He had just passed through the favorite dining place of the Director of the FBI and his deputy. From the back door it was half way round the block to the apartment entrance of the hotel. He remembered something about the apartment suites of this hotel—about other hotels also, but somehow the Bellevue was more famous. Important business representatives, lobbyists and influence peddlers rented many of these apartments on a year-round basis. Allegedly they rented them for business conferences. The true purpose was to entertain men influential in the government—and to provide a sanctuary where such a man could be alone—alone, that is, with some lady other than his wife.

At the door he looked back. The pedestrians seemed more intent on the toes of their shoes or the cracks in the sidewalk than on anything or anyone else. He hoped that what he had acted out had been good enough.

New York, Mexico City, Merida. Quite a junket, thought Charlie Joyce. But after he had learned of the call from Mexico to Storrow's office, it had seemed the logical path to follow. He had talked once more to Arthur Jackson of the CIA, and at length to General Scanlon. Both, by now, had believed him. Officially each man felt his hands were tied, but had nevertheless communicated personally with a top agency representative and a military attaché in the capital of the southern republic. Appropriate, if unofficial, help had been rather eagerly promised. Joyce knew for certain that he was right about the presence of an imposter. He could deal with him in due course, but right now there was something far more important.

He was not at all sure of the fate or whereabouts of Roger Storrow. He and Jackson had agreed that probably he was captive and alive, since right now he was obviously too useful to the Aparat to be disposed of. This state of affairs, however, might not last long. Therefore, the imperative and immediate aim was to locate the man and free him, no matter what means were used, no matter who else was hurt. A live special assistant to the President far outweighed the capture or death of a spy. That, at least, was what Charlie Joyce thought.

Von Tetlow walked smilingly past the desk clerk in the little lobby, entered the self-service elevator to push the button for the seventh floor. Very discreet, he had thought, especially if you could trust the desk clerk. He imagined that a liberal tip from time to time would take care of that. A small sign indicated that 723 was down the hall to his left. He walked to the door and sounded the buzzer. A muffled voice asked, "Who is it?"

"Dale Johnson, the representative from Hartford."

189

"O.K. Just wait a second."

The latch clicked and the door swung open. He stepped into the sitting room of the suite and looked around. There was no one in the room. He noted only the usual furniture. Desk, chairs, a sofa along one wall, a rectangular coffee table before the sofa, a television set. On the table, between two heavy glass ash trays, he noted a small cardboard box. He looked up. There, as he expected, was the mirror, quite a large one with an ornate gilded frame.

"Von Tetlow, you may sit down now."

The voice came quietly, almost in a monotone. He had expected the voice, but still it startled him. He sat down, facing the mirror. "Listen, von Tetlow, listen with great care. Do not interrupt with questions until I have finished. Do you understand?"

"I understand."

"Very well. Here is the situation. Six days ago we heard that Roger Storrow had somehow escaped. With no clothes, no money, no proof of identity, but he has escaped, he did get out."

Despite himself, despite his fear, von Tetlow could not help but smile and say to himself, They don't like it, not one bit. Somehow, my hat is off to Storrow.

The voice continued. "We covered all possible exits from the area, covered them well and thoroughly. Storrow did not appear. Then, for very good reasons, we concluded that he was dead—dead and to be buried, no longer a threat to anyone. But only this very morning there was good evidence that this was not so."

He could not avoid asking, "What kind of evidence?"

The unseen voice rapped out, "No interruptions, I said. That murderer got out, that is enough." That murderer, so! Von Tetlow thought, the proper Bostonian turns out to be a man of toughness.

"Eventually, of course," the voice went on, "we will catch him. It is impossible for him to escape completely. Naturally, we have prepared against this contingency for some days."

Have you indeed, thought von Tetlow.

"We study every possibility, von Tetlow, so we know that Storrow might somehow contact and convince the authorities

190

of his identity. Thus your days, even hours, here are numbered."

"How very perceptive!"

"What did you say?"

"Nothing important. Please continue."

The voice became harsher, less emotionless. "Von Tetlow, it is best that you listen with the greatest care. We have arranged for your escape, but only after you have met certain conditions. If you do not meet these, you either cease to live, or we turn you over to the US authorities. Probably the former. Now answer yes or no—no more. First, do you have a special meeting with the President, the Secretaries of Defense and State, and head of the CIA tomorrow at ten o'clock?"

"Yes."

"Just as we knew already. Now, on the table before you is a square cardboard box."

"Yes."

"Open it."

He untied the string, lifted off the top, picked out thick layers of cotton batting which hid the contents. This just did not make sense. Why had he been called to this secret rendezvous to look at a heavy gold chain and a big old-fashioned gold-cased pocket watch? He picked it up curiously. It was too heavy, he felt, for its size. He held it to his ear; there was no tick.

"Be very careful of that, von Tetlow, very careful. Don't drop it. Yes, it's a watch; in a way, that is."

"What do you mean?"

"I mean it's an exact replica of Roger Storrow's, the one he wore when you saw him in Mexico, and it runs by transmitted electricity. But it is much more. In fact, it is a small fission bomb, powerful enough to destroy half a building. It is now set for one o'clock tomorrow. Neither you nor anyone else can turn it off or change the time. I alone can do it by remote radio control. I can likewise detonate it. The setting knob is a dummy; the hands, however, show the time correctly. You had a question?"

Von Tetlow made an effort to keep his voice steady. "And if it is dropped or struck?"

191

"I would not do so if I were you. Anything else?"

He shook his head.

"Very well. You will take this watch with you to the meeting tomorrow. Should this meeting be postponed or delayed, you will call me here immediately. Then I will be able to reset the timing mechanism appropriately. Now you may ask your questions."

"What in God's name is the purpose of the murder of all those men? What can it possibly accomplish? Does the Kremlin wish to accept the blame for such an act?"

"Come now, von Tetlow, you're not thinking clearly, not clearly at all. Of course, we have nothing to do with this, know nothing of it, will deeply deplore it. What will happen is this. You have written—and we have had it typed for you—a letter on your own stationery. James should have it by now and will bring it to you for signature.

"In it you announce that for years you have been a member of the John Birch Society and the Minutemen. That you have been sickened at the spineless pacifism, the cowardly compromises, the appeasement and left-wing socialism of your leaders. Oh, yes, we know all the phrases. You write that you have come to regard them as no better than traitors to your country, and that you have elected yourself judge, jury and executioner for the true patriots of America."

"My God, man. Do you expect anyone in his senses to believe such a thing? You must be insane!"

"Not at all. Of course people will believe. Assassinating the President has been quite a favorite American practice. Assassination attempts, successful or not, have been made against twenty-five percent of the American Presidents. What an enviable record! You, of course, are well known as being a very strong Republican."

"What has that to do with it?"

He received no direct answer.

"Oh, yes, it will be believed, by all who wish to do so. If Oswald had not been captured the last time, no one in the world would have believed that the murderer was from any-where but the extreme Right. This will make the Right a thing really to hate. It will rip the country apart. It will destroy the moderate right wing of both parties. And both are

192

most dangerous to us. It will cause panic and lead to more killings, and drive the people to a psychosis of fear and despair. It will for some time paralyze the workings of the government of a whole nation. And this country will be utterly detested by the rest of the world."

It was still difficult for von Tetlow to believe that this man was wholly serious in ordering him to commit so outrageous, so insane an act. He protested. "But with Storrow escaped and the authorities certain to learn soon that I'm an imposter—or that I was—they could tell the people the truth about the murders I am to . . ."

The voice broke in, "Oh, no, they couldn't tell. No one would believe them. And even if the government thought that anyone would believe, it would not speak out. Think of the ignominy of being taken in at that level by an imposter. Those people would much rather be hated than laughed at."

There was a pause. Then, "No, we have thought this out carefully. It is our final decision. And it will succeed." The voice rose now in a note close to triumph. "With Storrow's watch you can do so much for Russia in a few seconds that you will be her greatest unknown hero."

"Unknown—and dead."

"Not so at all," the man's tone was now slightly amused. "I can see you have not been thinking clearly. A few minutes before one—you must be very careful in synchronizing your other watch with this one—you will leave the conference room on some excuse, saying you will return. Instead you will walk, quite normally, out of the building. A car painted with the name and colors of an airport taxi will be waiting for you, number 99. James will not be there. We fear he is still being followed. You will tell the guard that you are expecting this taxi. It will take you to the small private commercial airfield near Butler and drive you directly to our company plane. This will belong to the Pan-Mex Oil Company. With two refueling stops we will get you easily to Mexico."

"And just what do I do when I am met there by police and immigration authorities?"

"Very simple. You will once more be wearing your moustache, glued on with a glue that even the hardest tug will withstand. James will have the cement for you. You are once again the Señor Heinrich Schmidt y Mendoza of Buenos Aires, now returning from your four months' European trip. We have kept your passport and other papers for you. The passport contains even the appropriate visas and the various national entry and exit stamps. We have gone to a lot of trouble. We have gone so far as to withdraw money from time to time from your personal bank account to, shall we say, defray the expenses of your extended absence. We also have your police identity card bearing your fingerprints. If there is any question at all, this can prove your identity. We have even purchased an airline ticket in your name from Mexico to Buenos Aires. You do wish to return there, don't you?"

"It might as well be there as anywhere."

The unseen voice dropped all casualness, became once more harsh and commanding. "So be it. So, von Tetlow, you carry out your assignment and we carry out our part of the bargain. In this way you can escape. Fail us and I leave you to imagine the consequences. You really have no choice."

"No. I have no choice."

"Correct. Now go."

Von Tetlow stood up. "One more thing. What if the FBI comes for me before tomorrow afternoon?"

"I doubt they will move that fast. They will want to be absolutely sure first. That is simply a chance we must take. We have done everything we can. Still, no man can be totally sure of what will happen next, can he?"

CHAPTER XXIII

NOT AT ALL sure of what would happen next, Roger Storrow felt he had done all he possibly could. Shaven, fed, washed, although still grotesquely clad, he presented a somewhat more convincing appearance. He had impressed Bill Walters that he was somebody. His appearance brought to mind the famous Peter Arno cartoon, in which the top-hatted drunk, glasses and white tie askew, has just assured the desk sergeant that he can't remember his name, but knows he's someone pretty damned important.

Roger could remember his name. He talked and stood as would someone pretty damned important. But still he had no way of proving it. Mary Margaret Kelly in the hospital, seriously ill; Charlie Joyce away on some southern jaunt—he had been unable to learn more than this. There were no brothers or sisters to identify his voice and take action. Marjorie was . . .

How about James? Well, how about him? There were two obvious possibilities. One, the fake Roger Storrow, whoever he was, had succeeded in hoodwinking James. How the devil could he have done so? James had known him for over five years. This left the second, and in the light of all that had happened, it made sense. James must have belonged to the other side all along. How long had the masquerade gone on? A little over three weeks, and it was obvious from the results of his phone calls that the man had got away with it. Quite an accomplishment! He had a sudden desire to meet his replacement. He didn't really want the man to escape undetected, of course not—but still, he must be quite versatile in his own way.

It no longer mattered to him whether or when this imposter was caught, not to him personally. It would have no effect on his own chance for survival. This would depend on the tenacity of the opposition, or whatever remained of it, and his own skill or luck in concealment and evasion. Concealment, at least, was still necessary.

He had made one last phone call, one he felt could do some good. It was to the president of Pan-World, a man he had known casually over the years. By alternate use of politeness and rudeness, gentle wheedling and angry shouting, he had got through to the man himself. This time he had avoided disclosure of his distant location by persuading the operator to say only that long distance was calling. Otherwise the president's personal dragon would never have accepted the call collect. Nevertheless, the conversation was less than satisfactory.

"George? This is Roger Storrow."

"Good to hear from you so soon again. What can I do for you?"

"Plenty. Now hold on to your hat and listen. I need help and I need it fast. I'm here flat broke."

"Who isn't?"

"Damn it, don't joke, just listen. I'm in Merida. That's in Mexico, and I want you to talk . . ."

"Come off it, Roger, what have you been drinking?"

"Not a damned thing. Now please listen . . ."

Laughingly the voice interrupted, "Oh, that's it. Maybe that's the trouble, withdrawal symptoms and so forth. I knew it would get you some day. Now what I suggest is . . ."

Roger found himself pleading, his voice rising higher. "Please, George, listen for Christ's sake, I'm in Mex . . ."

The other voice broke in again, this time rudely, "O.K. A joke's a joke, but it's a bit too early in the morning for me to enjoy it. I saw you last night wandering around the club, and you were on your way up to the massage table, not to Mexico. Your arm was in a sling; it should have been your head. Good-bye."

Roger heard the far-off click, then the local operator's *"Terminado, Señor, buenos dias,"* and the receiver was dead in his hand. He put it back on the cradle, then picked it up again, once more to signal the operator. For a moment his finger hovered above the dial. Then he gave up. "Oh, hell, what's the use? What else could you expect from a bloody Yale man?"

Shrugging wearily he turned to Bill Walters, whom he had asked to listen on the extension. "You heard?"

"I heard."

"Do you believe that I'm Roger Storrow?"

Walters spread his hands. "Well, you certainly convinced Mr. Big you were. But what's all this about being in some club last night? It just can't be done on any schedule I know of and certainly not in a beard and clothes like that."

"Right you are, and it's just too complicated to explain. Let me leave it at this." He leaned toward the younger man. "I assure you that I am Storrow, Roger Lowell Storrow. I am a special assistant to the President of the United States. I must," he pounded the desk, "it is imperative that I get to Washington as quickly as possible, or faster. It's absolutely vital. Do you understand?"

There was really something about this square-jawed, gray-haired man, weirdly dressed as he was: something which compelled belief. "Yes, sir, I understand you and I guess I've got to believe you. But what can I do now? My hands are tied."

"Well, untie them. When does the next plane leave for Washington or New York?"

"We have a New York flight—changing planes in Mexico City—leaves at ten tomorrow morning."

"Anyone else have an earlier flight?"

Walters consulted a printed schedule. "Yes, sir. Air France at midnight."

"You must have a blank check here. Would you accept it if I made it out to the company?"

To his lasting credit Walters agreed that he would. "I'll accept your check against a ticket. Then you can exchange that one with the Air France people. I'll even lend you a

197

shirt, and find some shoes and a sports coat, though they might be a little tight for you. But what in the devil will you use for a passport?"

"Damned if I know, my boy. If only that miserable consul were around, you and I might be able to ankle over and beat on his head. But he isn't," he rubbed a hand along his freshly shaved chin, thought for a moment. "Know anyone in our embassy in Mexico City? Someone who'd believe you, I mean?"

"I'm afraid not."

"Then how about your company manager up there? He must know someone in the embassy. He'd have to to do his job."

Walters lit a cigarette frowningly, considered for a moment the thin plume of smoke. Suddenly his face cleared. "Sure, that's it. Ted Downs has been there for years. Claims he knows everyone who is anyone. I'll call him. I'll try to explain this set-up and have him get on to someone who'll maybe be able to do something to help."

Ted Downs did, in fact, know several people in the embassy, particularly the air and military attachés. For the time being this acquaintanceship proved of no value since the clocks of the embassy, as all other clocks, mechanical or mental, throughout the country had reached the hour of lunch, and lunch was inevitably followed by an hour of siesta. Walters reported this. "So there's nothing we can do right now except close up this shop and take you out for some lunch. I bet you need a drink as much as I do."

"You are right, my boy, but I'm not going out with you."

"Why not, sir?"

"Tell you why. There are some people after me, most unfriendly they are, too. That's why I carried that shotgun, don't you see? You've been a great help, and I'll not have you getting your head blown off on my account."

Bill Walters looked at him, still with some disbelief. "Are you serious? Here in the streets of Merida in the middle of the day?"

"Serious as hell. Maybe not on the streets as in *High Noon,* but they would spot you with me—not good, not good at all."

He placed a hand on the younger man's shoulder, "No, you go, bring me that drink, anything strong will do, and something more to eat. Also those clothes. Then we'll think of what to do next. Now get going."

"Yes, sir."

Roger walked to the corner of the room, picked up the Padre's gun. "And meantime I'll mind the store."

Somewhat relaxed, Roger sat deep in thought. Obviously the decapitated bodies must by now have been discovered in the Padre's house, and the Padre himself. Some furious police activity must be in progress. There must also be an all-out hunt on the part of the Communist Aparat. It was not inconceivable that certain members of the latter wore the uniforms of the police. In fact, it was probable, since it would have been stupid for the Aparat to have neglected such an elementary precaution.

Roger could not, however, see why either organization should be looking for him in this shuttered airline office. It would seem an unlikely refuge for a man who had just blown off the heads of two presumably respectable local citizens. As for the Communist agents, it seemed more probable they would be covering approaches to the various police headquarters and the American Consulate.

Pedro Jiminez, the front office clerk of the Merida Pan-World office, felt he had been insulted by an insane gringo. He was a man who enjoyed reciting to everyone his every grievance. And there was glamor to this tale. The man had said he had killed two citizens. Before the end of siesta time his slightly colored tale had reached the many ears of Merida.

Left to his own devices, and with a telephone at his disposal, Roger Storrow made several more attempts at communicating with persons known to him in Washington. These failing, he seated himself in one chair, placed his unhappy feet on another, the shotgun across his lap, and leaned back.

Tired as he was, his eyes were drawn to a commercial calendar on the wall. It depicted a blonde in a bikini. Then memory tugged at him, a warm memory of two days when he

199

had not been lonely. He levered himself to his feet, walked over to the wall, peered closely at the photograph. By God, unless it was her twin, it was Evita. Yes, it surely was. She or Felix had said that she was a model. Martinez, that was her last name, she had said, and it seemed so long ago. "I feel that, my Roger, someday you will need me," and "you said it yourself. I am a prophetess."

Well, he sure as hell needed someone now. But what could Evita do? He closed his eyes to think. A square white envelope—"An easy number to remember"—"You will remember only if you want to."

He did and called 333-678 in Mexico City.

She was in her apartment. Her voice at first was puzzled. *"Que habla? Como? El Señor Storrow*—incredible!"

Roger had to break in. "Yes, it is I. But I still cannot dance."

"Por Dios, Roger, of course I will accept the call. You have no money? You must be in trouble."

"Yes, Evita, I'm in trouble. Perhaps you can help."

"Of course I will help. Where are you? Merida. Then I send you money at once."

"No, no, little one, it's not that. I need official help—your government, La Seguridad Nacional, anyone—you must know some important people."

"Of course I do, Roger, one who has been an actress always does. What can I do?"

"Listen carefully. I am in Merida at the office of Pan-World Airways. Some criminal Communists are hunting me. Try to get word to someone who will alert the police here, or better, the governor of this state. Do you believe me?"

"No one else might, Roger, but I do—I also know the Communists. I know some of them too well. I must hurry now. Roger, take care of yourself, please?"

He chuckled. "I'll do my damnedest, Evita. God bless you."

"And you. *Adios. Que Dios te guarda.*"

The connection was broken.

He shook his head, "Perhaps she is a witch after all."

He sat down again, much more relaxed, and drifted into a gentle doze; heartbeat and respiration slowed below the pace of wakefulness. The dreams of half-sleep are strange. Sometimes they resemble pieces of wholly unrelated motion pictures spliced into one long reel. For a moment Roger had been happily awake. But recent days had been too hard. He dreamt in the red of anger, the grays of sadness and the black of despair. None were pleasant dreams, all had a dreadful quietness. Faces quickly changed expression; the mouths opened, but the lips moved in silence. There were faces of friends and acquaintances striving desperately to speak to him, yet no sound came. And there was Marjorie, so very clear. He tried vainly to call to her, strained forward in helplessness, felt tears burning in his eyes. He reached to her pleadingly, found that his arms were leaden and could move only in an agonizing slow-motion.

She was walking away, drifting from him, becoming misty, less clear in outline. She was drifting through a doorway, pausing at the last instant to turn and smile at him over her shoulder. He tried again to call, but couldn't. The door clanged shut. Now heavy iron nails appeared from nowhere, placing themselves point first against the door. They were being driven in blow by thudding invisible blow to seal her from him for ever. Despairingly he watched the nails sink home. One of them suddenly bent double under the unseen hammer.

He fought once more to move, was awake, the thudding sounds were real. They came from heavy fists, boots maybe, against the door of the outer office, the one opening to the street.

Instinctively he gripped the gun, his finger sliding inside the guard to touch the trigger. Better not move, he thought. He was in the best position possible; against the far wall, behind the heavy desk. He would wait. He would let them come in.

He heard the shattering jangle of broken glass. Then it came to him that this was probably the police. Police everywhere would rather kick in a door than pick a lock. It is the ungodly who move in silence. Then came the loud but slightly hesitant voice of authority, "Do not move, *hombre*. Stay where you are, and drop your gun. There are five of us, so drop it at once."

They made enough noise for five, all right. Two charges of birdshot would never stop them. He hoped his instinct about police was sound. Jail was better than the grave. Pressing his thumb against the lever on top of the grip, he broke the barrels open, ejecting the shells, and placed the gun on the floor. *"Entre, amigos.* I have done as you say." He rose to his feet. *"Entre, por favor."*

They looked a little silly, but deadly also. Five uniformed armed men facing one unarmed with hands above his head can look foolish. But there is nothing amusing about nervous gun-carrying policemen who still fear a trap. The apparent leader rapped out, "Not one little move, *hombre,* only extend your hands."

"Of course," and Roger Storrow held them out to the clicking handcuffs. He smiled from relief, almost with welcome.

The *teniente* of the Guardia Civil was disturbed. What manner of criminal was this who smiled at capture? He tried to insist that his fingerprints be taken at once and sent air mail to the North American FBI, and that he was a man of great importance, who must speak immediately with the chief of police and the governor of the state, and that he was entitled to a police escort to the airport. He asked all this in passable Spanish, but it did no good. The *teniente* was suffering from a tequila hangover and grave doubts as to the faithfulness of his mistress; about his wife he had no doubts at all but did not care. And he had little love for gringos.

As a result, all that Roger achieved was to have his prints taken. He was kept handcuffed, the fingerprint card was shoved into a crowded desk drawer, and Roger was kicked into a heat-drenched and smelly cell.

After exhausting his stock of native invective, he sank dejectedly to the hard concrete which must serve him as both chair and bed. He rested elbows on knees, his chin propped in his hands. Perhaps he had let urgency and anger cloud his judgment. Maybe he should have been tactful, gentle, even pleading with the lieutenant. Perhaps he could have won at least the chance of a phone call to Bill Walters. The surly Mexican might have granted that much, or he might not. There was nothing to do but wait.

The feeling that he was being stared at slowly grew. He raised his head. A shabby man stood unsteadily, holding the vertical iron bars dividing his cell from Roger's. He was bewhiskered, his eyes bloodshot. He was grinning, showing missing and blackened teeth. *"Hola, caballero,* what brings you to our happy house?"

"I shot two men. They are both dead."

His neighbor tried a bow, found he still needed the support of the bars. "Felicitations. How very distinguished of you. And I," a deep hiccup, "I have no fame at all. I am just very drunk. I'm almost always very drunk, when I can afford it."

Roger Storrow waved a hand and smiled. "Right now, amigo, I wish I were drunk myself. I'm now no use at all."

The shabby man pulled himself erect and pushed his face closer to the bars. "Cheer up, *caballero.* Do not be of sad spirits. Surely the men deserved to die. I see it in your face. And so," he spat, and wiped the back of his hand across his mouth; "and so, I say, an honest assassin serves a purpose. Even—I'm sure I have your pardon—a nice execution makes a fine thing for the public, every man is happy it is someone else. So many times, *amigo,* I wanted to kill, but I am just a cowardly drunk. Not you. So you see, you say you killed, I say . . ." He took the risk again of taking one hand from the bars and rubbed his forehead with the palm. "What was it I was trying to say?"

Roger could not help him.

"Now I know. Don't be so sad. A good murderer is a good murderer," a stabbing wave of one grimy hand. "Don't interrupt me. A murderer, he has a purpose."

CHAPTER XXIV

THERE WAS TOO much von Tetlow did not know. His mind was full of questions that night. Had the Aparat planned all along that he was to be a high-level assassin? Was this scheme one always in reserve against the day when his unmasking seemed inevitable? Or was this business of the remote control time bomb an improvisation of the moment? On balance the first alternative seemed by far the more probable. Elimination of the heads of a rival government was not for decision by a local of the Aparat, nor ever a spur of the moment action on the part of the Kremlin. No, this must have been in the cards nearly from the beginning.

In the light of this conclusion, should he believe the assurances of the unseen speaker, that he would be spirited from the country to safe refuge in Mexico? He had been given back his Argentine passport and police identity card, plus a considerable sum in local currency—but was this sufficient guarantee? Why should the Aparat wish to keep him alive? After all, as a relatively free man he could still tell some of what he knew, without too greatly incriminating himself. There should, after all, be no survivors to bear witness against him. No, he thought, most of what he could tell probably would not be believed, and the rest would do little damage to the Aparat. He reached over the bedside table for cigarettes and lighter, then sat up to switch on the light. There was very little taste to tobacco in the dark.

The light called to his attention the white oblong of an envelope on his dresser. This triggered a chilling thought.

There lay his signed confession. No, it was not a confession. It was more a boast of the assassination. They would have this in their hands—that is, they could give the press anonymous tips even if police authorities did not divulge the contents. They could even send reporters to this house before the police arrived. Then, of what further use to anyone was Karl von Tetlow? None, merely an encumbrance. Why not just dump him in the Gulf of Mexico?

He needed a drink. His last night in Roger Storrow's bed held little charm. In bathrobe but barefoot he went downstairs for whiskey and ice, took the drink into the library.

The backs of the now familiar books surrounded him. The painted likeness of Marjorie Storrow starred rather blankly above his head. He sipped the drink, cool to the mouth, warming to the inside. There was another alternative, of course. He could pick up the phone right now and call the FBI or, better still, call a cab and be driven to their office. No, that would not do.

Obviously the Aparat would not completely trust him. Wouldn't they use a phone tap and keep surveillance? Somewhere, sleepless and close, he was certain the well-trained James was doing his job. Still, of the two the phone was the better risk. He could take his chances on a tap and, if there were one, hope that the law would be the first to arrive.

And then what? He had been through this scene so often in his mind. At the best he would be a self-confessed espionage agent, and without a country. He could use his Argentine identity, and take his chance on his prints not being in the Bureau files—not a very good chance, that. Could he hope for some leniency, if he told of his decision not to carry out his last orders to kill? Perhaps he could prove his story by showing the bomb. Maybe the FBI would believe him, maybe regard the story only as self-serving. A long prison term seemed the very best he could expect.

And if he left the house that night, or a strange car came to it, word would go at once to that man behind the mirror or to his stand-in, and the chances were that he would be quickly silenced; if he went out on foot seeking a cab, by knife, wire noose or suchlike; if he stayed in his house, by the pressure of a finger on some remote button. And if he tried to take the gold watch to the FBI, that way he would also be carrying his death in his own hands.

Well, that was that. There was no exit, no workable alternative. He had to rely on the doubtful promises of an unseen, unknown man. He would have another drink, perhaps then he could sleep. His fingers were just closing on the bottle when the phone behind him tore the quiet apart. He nearly dropped the whiskey. Who the devil, at this hour?

He lifted the instrument, and remembered his lines. "Storrow here. What do you want?"

"Ah, your conscience is bad. That is unfortunate." It was the voice from behind the mirror.

"What makes you think so?"

"It is very late, you answered at once, and you are wide awake."

"So?"

"So listen. I finally got through to that dragon at the hospital again. I thought you'd like to know. Jimmy is still alive, but he's under sedation and can't see or talk to anyone, not for some little while at least. I don't think they'll let you in before afternoon."

So Storrow really was alive but somehow incommunicado. Recaptured? In prison? Actually in a hospital? Apparently he had not alerted the authorities. "It's a great load off my mind. Glad to hear it. Then you don't want me to cancel tomorrow's appointment?"

"Certainly not. Jimmy wouldn't have it any other way. If there's any change for the worse, I'll let you know. Goodnight now."

It was just before two o'clock. Now he had a sense of rather grim relief. With his own decision now irrevocable, it was pleasant to know that he would probably be safe at least for the balance of the night and the morning to come. His caller had seemed quite sure Storrow would not be dangerously at large before then. This time von Tetlow was able to sleep, at least until the dismal gray of dawn.

During those lowest hours, the phone's ringing dragged him grudgingly awake. This time he had even less idea who could be calling. The voice was electronically blurred. The

206

message itself was not. It was brief and cruelly clear. "I just wanted to call you, old man, to give you Roger Storrow's very best wishes. He hopes you have a happy morning. Good-bye."

He debated calling the suite at the Bellevue, but decided against it. The Aparat must be at least as well informed as he; in any event, there again was the possibility that this was—well, certainly not a joke—but harassment on someone's part. If so, it succeeded. It was a most harried man who finally rang for James, to ask for coffee. There was not a sound from the Jamaican. And scarcely a sign of his having once been there. God knew where he was now, fled or in custody. There was nothing von Tetlow could do about it. He made the coffee himself, brewing it extra strong. It tasted vile.

Dressing carefully in one of Storrow's middle-weight suits, he placed passport and other documents in the left-hand inner pocket of the jacket. At last, with almost steady hands he placed the heavy watch in its pocket and passed the gold chain through a buttonhole of his waistcoat. He then took a long look round the living-room and library. These had been his only real refuge during these strange weeks. Certainly he would never see them again. Against all the odds, he thought, it now seemed possible that Roger Storrow would.

His gaze fell on the silver cigarette case on the desk, the one which held the miniature wire recorder. He moved to pick it up—but what was the use? It might some day provide speculation, even amusement, to the true owner of this house. He shrugged into the tweedy topcoat, picked up his briefcase and stepped into the street to await the car which would take him to his meeting with the President.

For what had seemed a very long time, Charlie Joyce had not felt that he was going to succeed in meeting anyone—at least anyone in a position to help or willing to help him effectively in Mexico.

The day had lasted much too long. He had to catch a late flight making connections with the Mexico jet, and he had not slept well aboard. He hated early mornings, he hated airports, and he detested airport breakfasts, especially in Mexico. He had only the vaguest idea where Roger Storrow might be, and only a strong working hope that he was alive.

He had to hurry, but the customs and immigration officials were still sleepy and did not care.

After the other delays normally attendant on arrival in any Latin American country, he had also encountered the sacred time of the siesta and its effect on the embassy of the United States. With the exception of a guard, a porter and a bilious duty officer, there was simply no one else about, and none of them knew where anyone else could be reached or even when.

There was nothing to do but to wait, and he elected to pass the time in the best air-conditioned bar he could find. The bar he found was more than adequate, and so were the dry and very cold rum drinks. There is something about the feel, sight and contents of a tall, frosted glass that can brighten the dullest day, and make waiting seem not so long. This is true even if you are neither a neurotic nor an alcoholic, and Charlie Joyce was neither. He just greatly admired a drink. He was a good Irishman. He had been a good, most persistent and very effective intelligence officer. He still was.

Fortified by rum and rest, he hit the normally lethargic embassy like a visit from the Inspector-General. Things moved very fast. Less than an hour found a CIA man, an assistant military attaché and Charlie Joyce climbing into the plane of the air attaché, who manned the controls. And, protocol or not, all four men were appropriately armed. Life below the border had been somewhat dull for the three pseudo-diplomats. They looked forward to action, hoped that they would find it.

The only thing which did not move rapidly, at least in a line direct to their destination, was the attaché's plane. The skies were turbulent, studded with the towering icebergs of thunderheads and lanced by doubly thick bolts of violet lightning. Colonel Tom Weaver announced that he would try to fly around the storm.

Charlie Joyce asked, "How about that damned lightning? Any danger in that?"

Weaver looked back and grinned. "Who knows? All I can say is that there have been a potful of planes knocked out of the sky without any real explanation."

"Thanks a hell of a lot."

They were not knocked out of the sky, but instead were stacked up for an agonizingly long time over Merida while other planes maneuvered to final approaches. It was, therefore, after nightfall when at last they taxied to a stop. There was very little fuel left. Charlie Joyce's instincts told him that there was cause for real worry, that there was little time left.

Roger Storrow was exceedingly uncomfortable He had been in this steaming cell too damned long. He knew that there was a great deal to worry about and that there was little time left.

His drunken neighbor had long since slid into a Mexican slump against the concrete wall, bearded chin sunk into the hollow of his chest. Even in this position he managed to snore resoundingly. Gradually Roger became accustomed to the broken rhythm and no longer fought mentally to force the man into a regular pattern: such telepathic effort was wasted.

Anyway, he had time to think. The police had arrived first. Obviously, knowledge of his presence in the city had come quickly to the ears of informers. Just as clearly, it must in the same manner come to the attention of agents of the Aparat. All occupied cells were securely locked for the night. Two men, presumably armed, and one could hope alert, guarded the institution. But this was provincial Mexico. Wives, girl friends and whores are periodically permitted to visit prisoners. Locks are not too complicated and money talks. Certainly the Aparat was not without money. Ruefully he thought: and damned near fifty thousand of it once belonged to me.

He looked about the cell again; not a single thing that could serve in any way as a weapon—nothing. In his present frame of mind it seemed much more probable that the ungodly would come for him. He had certainly better work on this assumption. All he could do was make sure that he did not fall asleep, that he maintained nerve and muscle in a state of alert. If—no, not if—when they did come, a straight charge through them, out of the cell, was his only hope.

He ached, and it was damned uncomfortable trying to stay awake. The worst part was boredom. After a while, even fear and readiness for action become inadequate companions.

Roger recited some of the same childhood rhymes he had used on the night of his homemade blast to freedom. He counted his pulse to estimate ten minutes, paced back and forth in the confining cell. He even did a few creaky knee-bends—very hard these—and quite a number of leanings over to touch the toes.

He regretted the passing of the tropic thunderstorm. It had featured spectacular lightning and near-atomic thunder. He had always loved these storms, ever since his father had dimmed all fear by asking the eight-year-old pre-Fourth of July miser to guess the possible cost of fireworks which could make the same total of explosive sound. Also there was something Wagnerian and challenging in lightning and thunder, something visceral, almost sexual, in their effect. They made him want to stand taller and shout back at the heavens. But Marjorie had wanted to shut the windows and pull blankets over her head. How lonely he was going to be without her; that is, if he lived.

He walked once more to the grilled window aperture, hating the inability to move his handcuffed arms. It was much cooler now; with the wet and the darkness, the air was less dusty, easier to breathe. Over the tilted roofs of the city hung a too large, too bright moon, blotted out from time to time by scudding, smoky clouds. What a place to be, he thought, on such a night. Why in hell hadn't Bill Walters been able to do something, even see the consul? But the man was out of town. What was more, he himself was now labelled murderer. Fresh caught murderers were not quite so easy to free as traffic violators. But still, someone by this time—how many hours had passed, seven, eight?—someone should have done something, even in Washington. What, he wondered, is my double doing now? Had the FBI . . .

Along the echoing concrete of the corridor came the clack of footsteps, the mumbling of voices, the clinking of metal—keys, perhaps. They came nearer his cell. He whirled to face the door. There stood the uniformed guard extending a hand toward the lock; beside him was another man wearing a heat-wrinkled white suit, a light-colored wide-brimmed hat. He was standing head bowed, hands clasped behind his back. The guard spoke first. "Pardon me, *señor,* at last we have come for your release. Here is the *abogado,* Señor Rodriguez, sent by your consul."

Roger had backed into the cell's corner, muscles tense for his last fight. Now he relaxed. His shoulders slumped a little as he sighed in relief. "Thank God. It certainly took you long enough."

The iron door creaked open, the two men stepped inside. He had only, just only, the time to think and say, "But the consul is out of . . ." before the suit-clad man swung from behind his back a heavy length of pipe, and raised it above his head. As the guard sought to pinion Roger's arms, struggling he heard one man say, "Too bad he fell and smashed his head on the concrete."

He saw the arm swing down, and tried desperately to dodge. Then in the same split second his senses recorded a sharp, painful shock; a deafening crash of sound, a flash of light; then he was on the floor, stunned and nearly blinded.

He began to hurt. Groggily he shook himself, discovered that in some way he was on his knees, body, head and shoulders propped weakly away from the concrete on extended arms. A voice was speaking, speaking English. What was it saying? What in hell was happening? He shook his head again, and wished he had not.

Now he could distinguish words, not quite as blurred at the edges as the face above him. "God Almighty, Roger, you look like hell. Are you all right?"

He focused on the face at last—the tough, lean face of Charlie Joyce, by all that was holy!—and in his right hand a revolver's blue-black steel. Two men stood behind the Irishman, also armed. One man lay on his back, eyes and mouth wide open, his white shirt turning dark. Face to the wall stood the treacherous guard, arms spread-eagled against it.

All Roger had strength to say was, "The US Cavalry, by God, and not one damned bugle among you."

Charlie Joyce grinned in relief. "I see you're O.K. Yes, the Cavalry came over the hill just in time, and all we can count is one dead Indian." He reached over and grasped Roger's hand to help him to his feet. "You and your hard Beacon Hill head, lucky he only caught you a glancing blow. Can

211

you stand? Yes, I guess you can. And now, Mr. Storrow, we should get the hell out of here."

"But, Charlie, I don't understand—I mean, how the devil did you . . ." He tried, and found he could walk, although unsteadily. He pointed to the man against the wall. "What about him? What about the lieutenant and the other bastards?"

Charlie Joyce slipped the revolver back into his short holster. "Oh, them. Well, you now have an escort,"—he waved a hand to the figures behind him—"of two full chicken colonels belonging to Uncle Sam, not to mention myself. We had the CIA in person, but we had to move in such a hurry we left him behind to smooth some ruffled feathers. We still have a long, long way to go. I say to hell with them."

Roger rubbed at the pain-filled side of his head, and his hand came away bloody. "And so do I, Charlie, so do I."

Joyce drove like a madman toward the airport. Between two breath-catching bounces Roger managed to ask, "Where in hell did you get this car?"

"We liberated it. Don't worry, I'll put it back where I found it."

"If there's anything left of it. How did you find out where I was?"

"I asked, naturally."

"Oh, go to hell."

They reached the nearly empty airport in record time. There was only one plane discharging passengers. There were few of them. Roger glanced casually at the small cluster of people, and stopped suddenly to stare. Joyce grabbed his arm. "Come on, Roger, times a-wasting—our plane's over this way."

He still did not move. Yes, he'd been right. A small, trim figure broke into a run toward him, shouting happily. "Roger, oh, Roger, *gracias a dios.*" She threw herself into his arms.

"Little one, what under heaven are you doing here?"

She looked up at him. "You stupid man. You said you needed help. So I came."

A solid, smiling man now stood at her side. Evita half moved away from Roger and placed a hand on the other's arm. "And this is my cousin, or second cousin, Colonel

Eduardo Mateos of the Seguridad Nacional. He can be of much help."

Roger shook the man's hand. *"Encantado,* Colonel. Yes, you surely can. Charlie?"

"Yes?"

"Do both your sidekicks know the story?"

"Practically all of it."

"Then one of them had better stay here with Colonel Mateos and explain that business at the jail."

"Well, we can't leave Weaver. He drives the plane."

"O.K., that settles it. Let's get going."

Evita still clung to his arm. "Go where, Roger? You can't go now?"

With two fingers, he gently raised her chin, looked into her eyes. "Yes, I must. There is no choice. But thank you, thank you for having faith."

"I had it from the beginning."

"Yes, I believe you did. And now I must say *adios.*"

"Not *adios,* my Roger. *Hasta la vista.* Because I shall see you again."

"You are both witch and prophetess. What do you say?"

"I think we shall meet again."

"Then, little one, how can I believe otherwise?"

She stamped a foot. "Then stop talking and kiss me."

As the plane taxied down the runway he kept in sight a gallant small figure outlined against the brightness of an open door. Her right hand was raised in a gesture of farewell. When Weaver swung the craft around, its searchlight for some seconds caught the glint of golden hair. Then she was swallowed by the night.

Charlie Joyce tapped Roger on the knee. "I think we'll take away your Myles Standish suit. You come down here to hunt old ruins or something. You get kidnapped by Communists. You blow the heads off two citizens and get clapped in a Mexican jail. And still you had time to come up with something like that. Where in the devil did you find her?"

"She's an old friend."

"That I noticed, but how . . ."

"My lips are sealed." Roger looked serious. "Charlie?"

"Yes, Casanova."

"I just thought of something. Shouldn't you have stopped to call Washington to alert the troops?"

"No need to at this hour of the night. Besides, the cloth-heads didn't believe me. This one I handle myself. And I want you with me."

Charlie Joyce, however, did make one call as they changed planes in Mexico City. It was nearly forty-eight hours since he had slept. He felt that the least he could do was murder sleep. It must be just about daybreak in Washington now. Grinning happily he placed a call to Roger's home and gave the man who answered Storrow's greetings. When he had finished he thought, that ought to help keep the fox running.

Once installed in the big jet for Washington, Charlie felt there was one more thing he should do. He unlocked his briefcase, took from it a manila envelope, and from that two 8 by 10 photos. He handed one to Storrow. "Here, Roger, is a man I'd like you to meet before you go to sleep."

Storrow studied the picture briefly. "I guess it looks like me all right. But there's something a little distorted. It doesn't quite look like the face I have to shave every morning."

"You're right. Now look at this one which the lab reversed for me."

After a second's study, Roger exclaimed, "My God, it's exactly as if I were looking into a mirror."

CHAPTER XXV

EARLIER THE WHOLE thing had been grimly spoken words, tortured thoughts, the stuff of nightmares. Now it was real. Von Tetlow sat in the same room at the same table with his prospective victims, and practically next to his heart nestled the dreadful weapon. He held his hands clasped in his lap. He knew that they were damp with sweat. He feared they would tremble too noticeably.

Earlier, when he had left the Storrow home, he had instructed the White House driver to take the roundabout way. He had wanted to arrive as nearly as possible at the last minute. To have been early, and to have to engage in idle, friendly conversation, would have been unbearable.

They had driven up M Street, along Pennsylvania Avenue and past the White House. Already, long queues of tourists were lined up for a tour, mostly youngsters, brightly dressed and chattering happily, some wearing souvenir hats, almost all carrying cameras. They next swung out around the great towering obelisk, enclosed in its bright ring of fluttering flags. Across the Potomac they turned back along its bank and by the entrance to Memorial Bridge. To his right he could see the clean marble of Lincoln's shrine, to the left the broad sweeping approach to Arlington Cemetery. He remembered a cold day, the notes of taps and a new-dug grave. Whatever happened he knew he had seen this city for the last time.

Once out of the District they rolled through the lush spring fields of Virginia, between white fence rails, past a few great houses to the appointed meeting place. Even with the delay,

215

time had passed with merciless speed. They soon arrived at a guarded driveway. With a forced calmness he did not feel, von Tetlow presented Roger Storrow's credentials for inspection. Here was the crucial test. Now he would know. The officer studied them carefully, handled them for what seemed a long time. At last he gave them back and waved the car forward. At the front door of the handsome brick house the inspection was repeated by the light of a hooded desk lamp.

This was an unusual lamp, emitting mostly ultra-violet rays. Storrow's identity card, like many others, bore a secret marking, invisible to the naked eye. Once again he passed muster. Apparently the hounds had not yet raised their heads from the scent to bay at the view of their quarry. Still, von Tetlow trembled so much that he was just barely able to tell the guard, "I'm expecting an airport cab at one o'clock. Tell him to wait."

The meeting had been going on far too long. Arthur Jackson was speaking. "To sum up, the situation in Albania is this. Hoxa and his government are out on a limb, but they have the advantage of having no common border with Russia. The people are tough, not too well educated and very independent. They are not by nature city dwellers. They dislike all foreigners, or nearly all, and still resent any form of outside domination. They are still very poor. There is a considerable faction within both the government and the military which wants out of the Comintern—and whether it be Soviet or Chinese dominated. I will not now try to assess the problems of a para-military operation. I'll leave that to Defense. Politically, I am convinced . . ."

The President had become impatient. "Oh, for heaven's sake, Arthur, stow the officialese and tell us plainly what you think."

Jackson was not annoyed. In fact he smiled. "Thank you, Mr. President. Our people there have given us the word. They have done a bang-up job of infiltration and subversion where it counts. One whale of a tonnage of arms has been smuggled in—with only one small cache discovered. We are all set to take over the radio at Tirana, and we have a

216

powerful one of our own using the same wave length. I'd say we've never had a more propitious time."

Time! Great God, what time had it become? This office, unlike most, had no wall clock in the room. Von Tetlow shot his left wrist from its cuff and glanced obliquely downward. He couldn't believe it—then, of course, he could. There was no watch. Now he remembered. In the tension and confusion of the morning he had left it on the bedside table. But he had to know what time it was. How close was it to one? It suddenly seemed that it must be dangerously near, even at the hour.

Beyond the empty chair at his left sat the Chief of Staff. He was now talking, gesticulating as he did. Impossible to focus on the dial of his watch. To the right sat the Secretary of State. This man always carried a pocket watch, never one on his wrist. Doing his utmost to move and act normally, von Tetlow undid one waistcoat button, passed the chain through it, and gingerly lifted out the gold watch to set it on the table before him. Thank God, it marked exactly 12:40—almost twenty blessed minutes to go.

"Hey, Roger!" he looked up startled. It was Jackson, and he sensed that the man was staring at him in a most peculiar way. "Why the bloody alarm clock? Afraid you're going to miss your plane?"

The words did not come out normally when he answered, "That's just about it," after too long a hesitation. "Other one at the miserable jeweler's, don't you know."

The intent gaze never wavered. "I'd have told you the time if you'd asked, Roger. I'm generous that way." He reached a hand across the table. "I've never seen that before, only the chain across your stomach. Looks like George Washington might have worn it. Let's have a look."

Von Tetlow's guts shrunk up against his heart. What now? What if the man discovered that there was something odd about it? What kind of maker's marking did it bear anyway? He'd never looked.

"Arthur, please!"

"Yes, sir, Mr. President."

"Stop admiring gadgets and listen. You've heard the

217

General's views. Could you tie things together for us now? And don't use the word evaluate, for heaven's sake. Tell us what you think."

Von Tetlow could feel the heavy, recovered thumping of his heart, could literally feel the sweat drops oozing from the pores of his forehead. He reached for his handkerchief, used it in a needless blowing of the nose, managing to mop up most of the perspiration. The watch, however, sat there accusing, deadly, almost squarely in the middle of the table. He dared not snatch it back. He scarcely dared look up at it, tried not to, then found he could not help himself. Thus for a little while its slender minute hand was, in the whole room, the one thing he could see. It crept on inexorably, as the second-hand spastically pulsed toward death. 12:47 now. He tore his eyes away.

Death. Death to these other men within a matter of minutes. He had seen before, far too often, what a bomb could do at close range. The shredded flesh, unrecognizable carrion, arms, feet, almost always shoeless, widely scattered. Heads sometimes burst like obscene exploded pumpkins, but usually with intact teeth. Once he had seen a string of purple bowels hanging, the devil's decorative festoon, on a pine tree capped with snow.

Suppose the mechanism was faulty, inaccurate? He glanced at the dial again. 12:50. It might detonate at any time, in two minutes, one minute, this very second. No, this could not be so. These people were most meticulous. If they had said one o'clock, and synchronize your own watch, one o'clock it must be.

He forced himself to turn to listen to General Thomas. "There's one thing about the bastards. They're most efficient; they try like the devil not to leave any fingerprints on the corpse. They knocked off one of the Albanian colonels we were sure was on our side—good man, had a father in Chicago as I remember. When they suspected him they used one of their agents to tamper with his plane. Thing crashed in flames. No survivors. Then do you know what they did? Nabbed their own man and had him hanged as a saboteur. At least that's what my G-2 tells . . ."

He felt the too familiar nauseous surge below his breast-

218

bone. That was it, of course. The man behind the mirror had lied to him. Certainly there'd be no car, no waiting airplane, no escape at all for Karl von Tetlow. The bomb would go off now, any second. They would kill their own agent, of course they would. They had his signed confession. There was no need for him. Much cleaner all around. Desperately he squirmed in his chair, unconsciously edging a few scant inches further away from death.

Jackson noticed it. "What's the matter, Roger, don't you like our company?"

Glancing at the watch he saw it read 12:55, only five scant minutes had passed. That is all that were left. He could force himself to wait no longer. He pushed back his chair, heard himself say, "I love it, Arthur, but when you've got to go, go!" Walking as naturally as possible from the room, it vaguely occured to him that the repartee had been unworthy of Roger Storrow.

Once in the corridor, he hurried his pace, tensing his back against the blast which must, he felt, in seconds strike him from behind. He turned the corner, heading for the stairs. The seconds to reach them seemed like hours. Then he knew he was moving too fast. Deliberately he slowed down under the questioning eyes of a uniformed guard. "Going now, Mr. Storrow? Do you want me to call you a car?"

"No, thanks, I have a taxi coming."

He looked about him, at the enormous oil portrait of somebody's ancestor in Confederate battle-dress, at the tall grandfather clock on the landing halfway down the sweeping stairs. He put a hand on the rail, felt the smoothness of the polished surface, and started down. It seemed to him that his feet on the oak steps rang much too loud, that the quivering of his muscles must be plain to see.

He reached the bottom, looked up to the fanlight above the heavy door. He took another step toward freedom. What freedom? He was certain now. There would be no car, no plane, no helping hand. He was alone. Where was there to go? Clearly, nowhere. In any direction Karl von Tetlow would be walking or running to his doom. And for what? For nothing, for nothing at all.

He did not really think these things. Certainly he no longer held a debate with himself. He made no conscious decisions. No one ever does when at long last all the chips are down. Atavism, early memories, young beliefs, things heard and seen and things at least half believed, those surely are there and play decision's part. A trumpet call long-stilled, a flag now dust under alien feet, some person loved, snow falling on a silent grave, the soar of voices to a cathedral's vault, a cult of courage turned to the services of hate, contempt for a people changed in turn to grudging respect. Self-contempt, self-pity, hatred of self, even these may lead to something else, but probably not to redemption. From certain sins how can there be redemption?

No, he did not think; there was no time—and yet, some half-known thing most surely slowed his steps, brought him to a halt near the door. His head lifted. For a fleeting second there was that in his face which recalled the younger look of his long dead father. Then the look was gone. His face contorted in a desperate effort as he turned to sprint back up the stairs.

He ran awkwardly, off balance as he was with an immobile arm. He passed the wide-eyed guard a second time. Had he been able at the moment he would have heard, "Christ, what's the matter with him? Off his rocker?"

He was driven by something beyond thought. It was, however, as one nearly mad that he burst into the conference room and awkwardly snatched up the watch with his left hand. Only Arthur Jackson understood. In a surge of violence he was on his feet, and laid hands on his President to pull him from his chair.

"What the hell, Art, damn it . . ."

"Shut up and move. It's a bomb! Goddammit, a bomb! Get under the table everybody! Quick!" The President reacted immediately. So did the General. The others sat for a moment paralyzed, faces blank in lack of comprehension. Then they, too, began to scramble.

Out in the corridor the guard now recognized that something dreadful was happening, but what? As von Tetlow careened past him to the stair-head, he raised his gun. But his finger never reached the trigger. He had heard the scream of

"Bomb! Goddammit, bomb!" but one did not just shoot an assistant to the President.

In any event it was too late. All he knew was that Roger Storrow had rounded the corner at the bottom of the stairs, was now out of sight, the desperate pounding of his feet still audible. He heard the front door crack open, then slam shut.

Von Tetlow staggered, almost blind from effort, down the front steps, out on to the lawn. Wildly he looked about. To the left was a man with a power mower, to the right there seemed to be no one. Setting his feet he drew back his left arm, and hurled the deadly watch with all his insufficient strength.

It was as though two pairs of giant hands had clapped at once, one in a terrible blow which crushed his ribs inward and drove each vestige of breath from his lungs, the other smashing against the sides of his head. Sound, sight and consciousness fled together. Blood spurted from his nose and ears. He was flung to the ground, and lay seemingly lifeless under the noontime brightness of Virginia's sun.